Lafayette's Gold

To Penn Wynne Library!
In memory of Randy Howard.
All the best,
Gene Pisasale

The Lost Brandywine Treasure

Gene Pisasale

Outskirts Press, Inc.
Denver, Colorado

Outskirts Press, Inc.
http://www.outskirtspress.com

ISBN: 978-1-4327-4590-5

Outskirts Press and the "OP" logo are trademarks belonging to Outskirts Press, Inc.

PRINTED IN THE UNITED STATES OF AMERICA

DEDICATION

To Ida and Sam- you laid the foundation and made my life possible...
to Miranda- your spirit lives on and in me...
to Phyllis- you've brought great joy into my life...
and Frankie and Francis... we'll love you forever...

Chapter 1

Jim leaned back in his chair, stunned as he observed the satchel in front of him, its contents scattered across the kitchen table. He'd waited almost a week for the papers to dry out after finding the leather case washed up on Moshup Beach while on vacation in Martha's Vineyard. Despite the uncertainty of the events on the Vineyard, the memory was soothing... Then the sharp sound of the phone ringing shook him. He glanced over and saw that Natalie was trying to decide whether to go over and see what he was startled at, or pick up the receiver before it went into voice mail.

"Honey, let me get this. I'll be right over." She put down the cooking utensils and picked up the phone on the fourth ring. "Hello?"

"Is this Natalie?"

"Yes... Who is this?" She thought the voice was vaguely familiar, but couldn't recall the face.

"It's Carla. Do you remember? Me and Eddy met you and Jim at the Beach Plum on Martha's Vineyard."

"Oh, yeah... Carla. Hi, how are you?" Natalie replied with

a hesitation in her voice, showing she had no idea why she would be getting a call from her.

"Natalie... I'm calling because... because something bad is about to happen. I can't explain now, but Eddy wants that satchel you found and he'll do anything to get it!! I think you and Jim are in danger!"

"What do you mean? What danger?" She looked over at Jim and noticed he was pointing to the table in front of him where a pile of $100 bills was spread out next to the leather case. Her eyes widened and she mouthed the words "Oh my God..." as she looked over at Jim.

"Natalie, this is serious!! You're in danger! I think Eddy is coming over to your house right now!! You need to get out of there!!"

"Should I call the police??!!"

"Just get OUT OF THERE!!" Carla hung up the phone.

Natalie looked at the receiver in shock as she heard the dial tone... and put it back in the receptacle, then walked toward the table where Jim was just starting to stand up.

"What's wrong? Who was that?" he asked, putting his hands to her shoulders as she stopped beside him.

"That was Carla. Remember – from the Beach Plum? She said we're in danger! Eddy wants that satchel and is on his way here... right now!!" She spoke with a concerned look in her eyes, as she started to piece together the same scenario Jim already understood. She saw the cash on the table and the notebook... and knew Carla was right.

"That's what I was starting to say. Look at this! It's got to be at least $50,000 in cash. I found it as I was going through the papers- and here's evidence which tells me Eddy is in the mob, with an account at Leventhal and Company. They said on the news they're under investigation. The Feds are probably all over this case right now!"

"I KNEW it was him! It was Eddy I saw in that car on the edge of our complex!! What if... he's going to... hurt us??" She almost couldn't get the last words out, her eyes wide in disbelief.

"Look hon, it's going to be OK. You were right about the car. Carla just confirmed it- and we have to take her advice. If Eddy has ties to this kind of money, he could have followed us here... or got our address from the clerk at the hotel. This is what we're going to do. First, turn off all the lights after I get the flashlights from the pantry." Jim was startled by the events, but was trying to maintain composure. "Don't worry, I'm locking the front and terrace doors. You get the side door and turn out ALL the lights." He put his hand in his pocket and felt his cell phone there. He started to calm down slightly as he turned out the kitchen lights, but his legs were feeling a bit weak going into each room.

"I'm calling the police!!" exclaimed Natalie, trembling as she walked toward the side door.

"NO – I'll get that – you just get the door locked and all the lights off!" Jim ran to the front door, turning off the foyer lights as he turned the bolt. He looked around the house and saw lights on in the dining room and office. Knowing he might only have a few minutes, he sprinted to each spot.

"You didn't believe me... and I was right!" Natalie shouted as she ran quickly back from the side door, looking up at Jim, hesitating, with tears welling in her eyes.

"Look, I said you were right and I was wrong... but who could believe Eddy would come here? Let's just go down to the basement, call 911 and wait for the police." Jim grabbed her left hand and pulled her toward the door leading down to the Rat Pack Party room.

"Wait! What about the kitties? They're still somewhere in the house! We've got to find them and bring them downstairs with us NOW!" Natalie insisted.

"No time for that – they'll have to fend for themselves."

"NO! I'm not going to risk something bad happening. Frankie!! Francis!!! Here kitties!" Natalie pulled away from Jim and ran into the conservatory – the most likely place the kitties would be snoozing.

Jim ran after her, calling out to the cats – "Frank... Francis... where are you?" As they reached the conservatory at the end of the house, they saw the cats stretching, a big yawn on their faces. They each quickly scooped up a cat and headed back toward the stairs. The kitties rested quietly in their arms, happy to get some attention. Jim looked at Frank and whispered "I love you Frankie". As Jim passed the windows, he looked up at the charcoal grey sky and hoped those wouldn't be the last words he said to her.

They walked down the tawny-yellow steps, carrying the felines with them into the storage area behind the party room. Jim looked at Natalie as they maneuvered past the empty suitcases, faded green couch and boxes of Halloween and Christmas decorations piled high along the walls and littered throughout the room. Old CD towers, workroom supplies and general junk had created a maze that Jim and Natalie had to weave around to reach the back corner of the storage area. They squatted down in the dark behind some '60s party cardboard decorations. Natalie hoped they wouldn't be seen through all the stuff piled around the room. Jim looked over at her and let the cat down from his arms so he could hold Natalie's hand and reassure her that everything would be all right.

"Call 911 – NOW!" she said in a low, anxious voice, trying to lay flat on the cold cement floor, surrounded by dark shadows of unidentifiable boxes and supplies. She wondered for a few seconds why he hadn't done so already and realized she sometimes had a sixth sense about things before Jim became aware himself. He was an expert observer, better than Natalie, but Natalie could just 'feel' things – premonitions.

"I am!!…" He pulled the cell phone from his pocket and pressed the same three numbers people chose just after the terrorist attacks of September 11, 2001. "Well… 9/11… guess no one can forget those numbers" Jim thought as the phone rang and then was answered by a dispatcher.

"911 operator– What's your emergency?"

"Hello! We need help immediately!! I think there's a guy about to break into our house…"

"You THINK? Where are you calling from, sir?" The voice of the 911 operator was lifeless, a bored person about to get off shift.

— 5 —

"This is Jim Peterson – I'm calling from 765 Wayfarer Court in Kennett Square. I believe there's someone about to break into our house!! This is for REAL!"

"Sir, I can't report on something that MIGHT happen. What's going on there?"

Just then Jim heard dull sounds from upstairs which seemed to come from the garage side of the house. He heard what sounded like taps against the outside wall… faint, yet they were sounds which couldn't be anything other than human. "We're about to be attacked!! I need a cop car out here NOW!!"

The operator sighed, thinking this was just one more of the crazies she got once a month – but then became concerned as she heard the connection go dead. "We need a police officer right now at 765 Wayfarer Court. Possible break-in. Over."

Jim and Natalie grabbed an old blanket from a plastic wash basket nearby and covered themselves as they hid in the dark behind the three foot cardboard VW Bus. He looked up at the pipes in the basement ceiling, thinking if he could just listen to the vibrations, he could figure out if someone was coming into the house and where they were walking. Then he heard what sounded like the upstairs side door opening and muffled foot-steps crossing the kitchen floor. He thought how he might use the sounds to his advantage, but couldn't gather the strength to move and follow them across the room.

Just then he heard a sound by the basement door and im-mediately the cats tore away from them and headed for the stairs. Natalie tried to get up to go after Frankie, but Jim held her still. He remembered that whenever he and Natalie would come to the top of the stairs, the cats would rush up to greet them from their basement cat condo. Jim winced, but knew he had to concentrate. Then the basement door opened and they heard footsteps coming slowly down the stairs. Natalie's hand tightened around his and he could hear her breathing hard.

"Oh NO!!" She was starting to shake and Jim put his arm around her, pulling her close to him and pressing a light kiss to her forehead. "Natalie – I promise, everything's going to be O.K."

They heard only one set of footsteps in the darkness, then a shriek pierced the silence… It was the cats… and Natalie pulled away and stood up. Jim jumped up, trying to get her down again, but then there came the thumping of someone stumbling down the stairs and hitting the floor, followed by a dull moan. It was a man's voice they heard in the darkness… and then the familiar tiny meows of Frankie and Francis. He heard the faint sound of sirens in the distance and felt a sense of relief in his chest. The sirens got louder and he felt Natalie lessen her grip on his hand.

"What's going on?" Natalie whispered as she tried to peer through the darkness to the curtain that separated the finished basement from the storage area.

"Hon… quiet! I'm going to take a quick look." Jim still heard the moans blending with the kitty's meows. He looked around the room for a weapon and spotted the Big Bertha in his golf bag, still unused since he paid big bucks for it two years ago.

"No!! Stop! He might have a gun!" Natalie insisted, trying to speak as loud as she could without revealing her location to whoever was in the house.

"I'll be ok… Don't worry." He let go of her hand, but she grabbed his right arm tightly and tried to pull him back down to the basement floor. "No… let go! I'll be fine." He felt the rush in his veins through to his heart as he started to pull away from her and head for the golf bag across the room. He maneuvered the maze of basement boxes and reached for the club. He considered the irony that the first time he finally had a chance to use the Big Bertha, it might be on someone's head instead of a golf ball.

As he walked through the gold weaved curtains and out of the storage area, he saw the glow of the fish tank and glanced to his left in the direction of the moans, then spotted Frankie, who ran up to him and brushed against his leg. Jim looked up and saw Francis pounce off the pool table landing on something at the bottom of the stairs… a deep moan emanating louder through the darkness. He adjusted his grip on the heavy club and stepped further into the room. Then he saw the body sprawled out flat on the floor.

"Ohhhh!! Help me… Oh my God! I… can't move…"

Jim glanced quickly at both cats as they ran around the edge of the room, then he looked back at the floor. There was just enough light for him to see it was a man… with a graying pony tail. He knew it was Eddy. Grabbing the golf club more firmly in both hands, he walked toward the body, listening to the meows.

The sirens were now blaring and he knew the police were out in front of the house. After a few seconds, he felt something rub up against his right leg and could see it was Francis. He looked over and saw Frankie come out in front of the fish tank.

"Ohhh… I'm dyin'. I'm in… pain. I… can't… breathe…"

"You guys did a good job. Let's see if I have to finish it." He stared down at Eddy, then at both cats around his feet. He felt the adrenalin rush into his arms, giving him the strength to crush Eddy's head if he made a move.

Eddy looked up at Jim. "Don't, man… my back… I can't… move…"

Each time Eddy spoke, his voice got weaker. The sounds were those of a dying man, about to lose his grip with life. Jim looked at his face and the glare in Eddy's eyes transforming to a concession of helplessness. Jim could just make out the gun on the floor beside Eddy's left leg and ran over to it, kicking it away before he could make a move.

"It's over… the cops will be here any second." Jim felt no remorse as he stood above Eddy writhing in pain on the floor. "You thought you had me, huh?" He looked back at Frankie and Francis. "Did you guys trip him up on the stairs? You're the heroes today!" He turned back to Eddy. "Looks like some pussycats got you this time, you piece of crap!!" Eddy let out a wince, which faded to a muffled groan.

"POLICE!! Identify yourselves! Kennett Square Police!!"

"Meeeoooowww." Frankie and Francis answered in unison before Jim was able to respond. Jim smiled and loosened his grip on the club, taking his first full breath of air since it all started 20 minutes ago. He hesitated for a second and held the club tighter in his hand. He saw the gun several feet from the body, then watched the blood dripping from Eddy's mouth and nose. "Down HERE!! We're alright! Down in the basement!!" He could hear the muffled footsteps of two officers approaching quickly, then one set stomping down the stairs.

"POLICE!! Drop your weapon!!" The officer yelled to him in the darkness, halting in front of the pool table, near where Eddy was lying.

Jim saw through the dimness that he was a tall man, late 20s, solidly built and he knew they were safe. "Yes, I'm dropping it, officer" Jim said as he let the golf club fall to the floor, hitting Eddy on the side of his cheek, resulting in another loud moan. "I live here… this guy just broke into our house. We got a tip – a phone call – that we were in danger." He looked toward the gun on the floor and the officer walked over and picked it up.

"A phone call? You got a call that somebody was about to break into your house?" The officer raised his eyebrows in disbelief as he spoke.

"Yes… well… it's a long story" Jim said as he heard footsteps coming from the back room where Natalie was still hiding. They came slowly and it occurred to him that he should turn on the lights. "Everything's O.K., Natalie… the police are here now." He walked over to the wall and flipped on the light switch, bringing the surreal scene to life. Natalie poked her head through the gold curtains, still not sure all was safe. "Its fine honey… you can come out now."

She looked toward the fish tank, then over to the stairs

where she saw the police officer standing over Eddy, picking up the gun as he holstered his own. She noticed their two cats standing about four feet away from Eddy, looking as if they were ready to pounce on him if he moved. "Hey fur heads!! You guys are OK!!" She ran over and picked them both up and held them in her arms, cuddling them up to her face.

Jim rolled his eyes and knew then with certainty that kittens were women's best friends… and he didn't try to compete with the two very cute pussycats. Natalie walked over to Jim's side, lifting her head to kiss him. He put his arm around her and stared down at Eddy. "You were right, hon. He followed us here…"

"Followed you from where?" said the officer. "I'm Lieutenant Jackson of the Kennett Police. We got a call that your house was about to be burglarized- and you say you know this guy?"

"Well… kind of. We know who he is. His name is Eddy Caniletto. We met him while on vacation on Martha's Vineyard a week or so back. It was at dinner… a place called the Beach Plum Inn… That's when we sensed something a bit strange."

Natalie put both cats on the floor and kissed Jim on the cheek again. "I saw this guy sitting in a car near our complex as we drove back from the airport after our vacation."

"Ohhhhh… help… me… I'm dying!" Eddy's voice was very faint and he couldn't open his eyes.

The officer looked down at Eddy and picked up his walkie talkie. "Down here, Jack… in the basement. Get an ambulance right away… Got everything under control."

"10-4" came the crackling voice of his partner, who was still searching the house. "There's that car outside and I heard a noise around the back. I'll call the ambulance, but still checking for other suspects nearby. Will get back with you." His partner walked from the kitchen into the foyer and realized something was moving out on the terrace. "STOP! Police!! Stop right there!!" he ordered as he saw two men reaching for the door leading into the house from the back terrace. The officer could see they both had guns and were pointing them... right towards him. "Drop your weapons now!!" The men continued to move forward and he fired four shots through the glass door in rapid succession before they could get off a single round. Glass flew everywhere as both men fell onto the flagstones.

"We have shots fired... two men down... calling for back-up NOW!!" he yelled into his phone as he walked cautiously to the shattered door. "We'll need another ambulance, too." He kept his gun pointed toward the men as he slid open the screen to the terrace, several large gashes visible through the mesh from the barrage of bullets. He could hear both men moaning in agony as he bent down to grab each of their guns. Blood was streaming from their bodies into the cracks that separated each of the stones.

"Steve... I hit two up here. They're both down now and unarmed. I called for back-up."

"Good. I'll be up in a minute... got one down here... looks like he might not make it... but everybody else is O.K." He put his walkie talkie back into his vest and said "OK folks, we're all going to the station. We have an ambulance coming

for this guy… and two others upstairs. We'll get your full statement back at headquarters. This is a crime scene now, so we're
going to tape the place off to prevent any tampering with evidence." He looked down at Eddy and said "You have the right
to remain silent", but Eddy was almost gone… his glazed eyes
rolling back in their sockets…

Chapter 2

The room was filled with tables covered in papers and folders, some held together by 2 inch binder clips, stacked on top of each other. The table next to the shredder at Levanthal and Company was piled the highest, four to five feet of folders overflowing, loose papers fluttering to the floor. The man standing near the shredder was pulling files from the table every few seconds, feeding their contents- hundreds of sheets- into the machine, the constant grinding drowning out the voices of people nearby.

"What are you doing?" Eric asked as he stepped toward Jack Cunningham, one of the senior portfolio managers who had worked with his own boss, Charles Thompson before he was killed on Martha's Vineyard. "These are all Chuck's files. I'm supposed to be support man on that team."

"Not any more. These all go... NOW! I've been doing this since 6 a.m. – you can take over."

"Why? What are we doing with all of his files?"

"Getting RID of them – all of them." He walked over to Eric, holding out a stack of folders. "When you're done with these, shred everything on those tables, too. EVERYTHING!"

"What's going on here?"

"Look! Just DO IT! This comes from the top…and if you don't get it done before lunch, you're fired! Everything… you understand??!!" He pushed the files towards Eric's chest and let go, Eric grabbing them before they dropped to the floor. "If these aren't shredded now… we're all in… deep shit!"

Eric looked down at the files sitting in his arms and read the top page. 'Gambini – FOR INTERNAL USE ONLY – not for distribution.' He put the pages in the machine, it's deafening noise ringing in his ears…

———⊚———

"So, you mean… we HAVE to testify?" Jim exclaimed, his voice rising as he tried to make sense of what the FBI Agent was saying. He stood up, glancing around the boring, grey office in downtown Philadelphia. Department store blinds partially opened and dingy from age covered the only two windows, revealing a small parking lot outside.

"Mr. Peterson… You and your wife stumbled onto some critical evidence that we believe is pertinent to our investigation of the Mafia's illegal financial activities. Your help is required if we're going to get these guys. Even though Caniletto's incapacitated, we think we have enough evidence to indict and convict several of his Mafia cronies – and in the process, bring the head of Leventhal and Company to justice – for money laundering and numerous counts of securities fraud."

Jim peaked over at Natalie and knew she wouldn't be happy about putting them in more danger by testifying against the mob. "If I testify, will you protect us?"

"Sure, absolutely... I promise." Rawlins eyed his partner at the end of the table and grinned slightly, knowing they had some important evidence. He winked, his face turned away so Jim couldn't see, then he turned back to begin the interview. "So... let's get started. Exactly how and when did you have first contact with Edward Caniletto?"

Jim hesitated for a second, making sure his memory served up the facts accurately, then focused on Rawlins. "We first saw Eddy on South Beach in Martha's Vineyard. He was in a fight with another guy arguing over kids being a bit loud. What day was that, Natalie? The third day of our trip... or was it the second?" He turned toward Natalie, hoping she remembered. "Was it September 15th?"

"I think so, hon. I didn't write it down."

"Did you have contact with him at that time?"

"No... didn't want to go near him. He pummeled the other guy and could have done some major damage if the man's wife hadn't stepped in to stop the fight."

"O.K., so you saw him fighting with another man. Did you get the man's name?"

"Oh, God... I can't remember. I think his name was... Jack? Handsome guy... tall... slender, dark brown hair... maybe around 30-35 years old. Never heard his full name. We left right after the guy's wife pulled them apart, but Eddy looked like he was ready to kill him... just for his kids being a bit rowdy."

"How did you know it was Mr. Caniletto?"

"We didn't — at the time. We saw him and his girlfriend Carla a day or two later at the Beach Plum Inn... a really nice restaurant in Menemsha. I recognized him right away from the grey pony tail and his voice. I'm on the phone a lot with clients. I always remember a voice... and a face."

"What do you mean, you remember a voice?"

"I try to be a good listener. When I hear a person's voice, it's almost as if I've seen their face and shaken their hand. At any rate, within a couple of minutes of his arrival at the Beach Plum, I knew I recognized him."

"O.K... So you have a good memory. What else?"

"Eddy and I went outside to check out the sunset. He didn't seem to be paying much attention to what I was saying, until I mentioned that we found a leather satchel washed up on Gay Head Beach. All of a sudden he focused right on me, like I'd said something extremely important."

"We know all about the leather satchel. We examined it thoroughly after you handed it over to us. It's an important part of this investigation... the money... the Leventhal accounts which were probably funded by the Mafia and fraudulently managed. Did you ever hear Mr. Caniletto mention any associates... any partners... business ties?" questioned the agent, who was showing some impatience, the pitch of his voice rising at the end.

"No... not that I recall. Only that he had some buddies who worked along the waterfront... the docks in Baltimore and Philadelphia. We... Natalie and I... met up with Eddy and his girlfriend Carla a day or two later doing some shopping in Oak Bluffs. He spooked me again when – out of the blue – he asked me about the satchel. I knew something was wrong then and there."

"So when did you find out he actually wanted the leather case?"

"Never did… until after we got home and got a phone call. It was Carla. She told us Eddy wanted it and would do anything to get it… that we were in danger. That's when we knew for sure we were in serious trouble… and within a few minutes of that phone call, he had broken into our house. We'd be dead if he hadn't stumbled over our cats on the basement steps and broken his neck."

"O.K.… she clearly knew a crime was about to be committed and likely aided Mr. Caniletto in the process. Thank God she had a grain of decency to warn you. We're investigating her now."

"Well… she did, in effect, save our lives" mentioned Natalie, hoping the questioning would be over soon.

"So… that's it? That's all you know about Mr. Caniletto and his girlfriend?" contended Rawlins, taking a cigarette from the pack of Marlboros he'd pulled from his side pocket.

"Pretty much it… aside from what we saw in the satchel, which you already know… and on T.V." said Jim.

"Well, we thank you… the FBI appreciates your assistance" he remarked, exhaling blue-grey cigarette smoke in Jim's direction. "We'll be in touch if we need anything else. You say you'd be willing to testify if we need you?"

Thinking "No" because of the smoke he was trying to avoid breathing, Jim looked him in the eye and said "Well, if... absolutely necessary. If you need me, I'll do it... with immunity and protection, of course." He glanced over at Natalie and could tell she was giving him one of her "Why did you say that?" expressions.

"I appreciate that. We may not need you at all. The satchel you gave us was a big help, so we're very grateful. In fact, because you were honest and turned over the $50,000, I may be able to get a small reward for you."

Natalie frowned again and thought "Just keep us out of this... that'll be enough reward."

"Thanks, but... I don't need a reward... and hopefully you won't need me any further. Just keep us posted on the investigation."

"We sure will."

"What if some of Eddy's associates come sniffing around here? How are we going to be protected?" Jim asked, a hint of anxiety coming through.

"We're guessing Caniletto acted alone tracing you down. We don't think there was any mob-wide effort to find the satchel."

"How do you know that? How can you be so sure?" asked Natalie.

"We don't... but it's a hunch. Like you with voices, I'm good at hunches" the agent replied with a slight smirk.

Natalie glared at the agent and then focused down at her shoes thinking "Nice... our safety and lives are based on this guy's hunches."

"Well, then... given the fact that we've been helpful to you and to the police, I want some kind of guarantee that you'll both be monitoring the situation and alert us if you suspect anyone else is trying to track us down." He peered into Rawlins' eyes, hoping for a sign of assurance.

"I can't guarantee anything, but..."

"But what??!! Our lives ARE in danger... and what do WE have? A hunch?? That's not good enough!!" snapped Natalie, her voice overpowering the agent for a few seconds.

"Calm down. I'll do my best to have you both monitored in the coming weeks... months... and make sure no one is following you because you're an important source in an ongoing Federal investigation. We'll assign an agent to watch your house and we've already alerted the police of the situation, so your names will not be released to the media – alright?"

"How can that prevent some of Eddy's friends from coming after us again when you're not around? Does your 'monitoring' cover 24 hours for Jim and me?"

"Mrs. Peterson... I realize this is disturbing. We've handled situations like this many times before and kept people like you and Jim safe through standard surveillance... we know what we're doing."

She gazed over at Jim and knew their lives had changed forever... and felt the sadness coming... a wave washing over her. She took his hand and held it very tightly in hers.

"It'll be alright, Natalie. These guys are experienced. We'll be safe" he reassured her, wrapping his left arm around her shoulders and kissing her on the cheek.

"You will be. You'll both be safe. I give you my word" asserted Rawlins, looking at Jim, then Natalie for a few seconds longer, hoping the eye contact would reassure her.

They both got up… Jim offering him a handshake as the agent stepped forward, giving his right hand a hearty grip.

Rawlins thought for a second… and decided not to try to shake her hand, simply saying "Thank you both very much."

Natalie looked him in the eye and said "I can honestly say I hope I never see you again."

The agent chuckled. "I hope so, too."

After they left the office, he closed the door and smiled. "We got what we needed, Jack. Let's move."

Chapter 3

"So what do we do now?" asked Natalie, sitting across the dinner table, her meatloaf getting cold as she'd been asking Jim questions for over 15 minutes.

"We're deep into this, I know, but we don't need to let it disrupt our daily lives. We can't let it overwhelm us" he commented, putting his fork down and taking her right hand in his. She glanced down before she spoke.

"I just want to get back to normal... no intrigue... no drama... no FBI." She started to say something else, but her voice trailed off.

"It WILL be O.K... I promise... I PROMISE." He held her hand tighter in his.

She looked up at his face and smiled... slightly. "O.K."

"Hey... we need a break. How about a canoe trip down the Brandywine this Saturday? The water's high enough after this week's rains. It should be perfect. Accuweather says sunny and around 55 degrees."

"That's a bit cool for canoeing, especially if we wind up in the river again."

"No… It's great outside and we won't tip over this time dodging shallow spots – remember, the water is higher now. Come on – it'll be fun. I'll call Northbrook Canoe Company tomorrow and make a reservation for this weekend. We can take the 2 hour trip. That'll give us plenty of time to enjoy the Brandywine and the calm, quiet solitude of the area. It'll help us relax."

"You're right. We could use a peaceful break and some fun!"

"Excellent!! I'll see if we can get the 9:30 a.m. slot this Saturday." He got up from his chair and wrapped his arms around her. "It'll be great!!"

———=»((◊))«=———

Saturday's morning sun on the maple, oak and birch trees showed them to be just past their prime… the burnt orange color radiating through before they turned brown and drifted to the forest floor, making a blanket for the chipmunks and squirrels foraging the Brandywine Valley in mid November. The display was almost over, but this time of the month was their way of saying "It's not done yet!"

The Northbrook Canoe Company had been doing business for over thirty years… taking willing, but generally inexperienced canoeists for an easy ride south down the Brandywine River, which turned officially into Brandywine Creek at Chadds Ford. This was the point where it ran under Route 1, right next to Hank's Place. 'Where friendly people meet and hungry people eat' read the sign at the edge of the parking area. Hank's had become popular as the owners spruced up the surroundings, spending thousands of dollars to provide magnificent flowerbeds fringing the restaurant, with hanging baskets of petunias, potato vines and impatiens above pumpkins and gourds below… all of which beaconed hungry drivers passing by on Route 1. Patrons included Andrew Wyeth, the late Brandywine artist… painter of the iconic "Christina's World" which had gained him national recognition and hung in the Smithsonian. Wyeth often ate at Hanks, drawing crowds due to his notoriety as the living "father" of the Brandywine School, made famous by luminaries such as Howard Pyle, Frank Schoonover and his own father, the turn-of-the-century illustrator N.C. Wyeth. The owners of Hanks loved it when Wyeth showed-up and even kept a framed photograph of him above the grille next to the counter. Locals and tourists had rewarded the owners for their good taste in horticulture and the simple American fare, which was always tasty and reasonably priced.

"Why don't we get an early breakfast at Hanks, then drive up for the canoe ride?" suggested Jim, pouring them both cups of coffee as he stood in front of the Cuisinart, set to automatically brew at 5 a.m. just before they both awoke each morning.

"Sounds good… I've always liked Hanks. They have great French Toast and Scrapple. If we wait 'til lunch, I'll be too hungry."

"… and grumpy by then."

"Hey, stop! I know I get a bit crabby when I'm hungry…

probably low blood sugar."

He smiled. "Here's your coffee." He handed her the American Coffee Company mug. The side read "Will tickle your palate… French Market… Pure Coffee… New Orleans", a keepsake from one of his trips to the Crescent City over the years. The steam rose to her face and she took a sip.

"Mmmmm… Honey… Now THAT's a great cup of coffee!!" she exclaimed.

"Hah!! Good one…" Jim snickered, remembering the movie "Witness", the line a spoof of the male-dominated advertising in coffee commercials of the 1960s. "I can be ready in twenty minutes."

"Me, too – no need to wash my hair for a canoe trip. I can be in my jeans and sweater in ten."

"I can be in them in less than that!"

"Very funny, Romeo."

The drive past Longwood Gardens towards Chadds Ford was always nicest in the Fall, even though some of the trees were already bare and the road slick with wet leaves from recent rains. The Summer fields of green, sage and gold were replaced by tawny grays and browns late in the season. They passed the Old Kennett Meeting House, circa 1710 on the left and all the antique dealers who made their livelihood from the attics of the thousands of homeowners who settled in the region over the last two centuries and wouldn't live anywhere else.

"It's early enough so there shouldn't be much of a line at Hank's. I predict we get a table within five minutes."

"I agree. We can get a good start on the day." He neared the stop light at the intersection of Route 100, which would take them along the river to their entry point. As he turned left, she knew they were in luck.

"Good move! We're early... no wait!" He put his right hand on her thigh, pulling into the lot where only five cars were parked.

"This is going to be a good day – Jim hates waiting for anything" Natalie thought. "Excellent! I'm hungry!" she declared, lifting Jim's hand and giving it a quick kiss. "At least we'll be well fed when we fall into the river."

"It is my eternal duty to shield you from danger... and soggy sweaters."

"Hah! Is that a promise?"

"Promise! I know you like tables... but do you mind if we sit at the counter today?" Jim asked.

"I don't mind eating at the counter... reminds me of my childhood days in Lenape. There was this little lunch place that had the red leather-topped counter seats in front of the soda fountain. It was great. We used to play pinball, then grab a burger. The place was torn down decades ago. A Sunoco station is there now."

"We loved the Penn Wynne Pharmacy on Manoa Road... called it Randy's because he was the soda fountain guy- and friendly with all the kids. That place also had the red stools at the counter. I actually like sitting at the counter."

They took off their coats and placed them on the back of their chairs.

"Doesn't sitting here feel like you're having lunch back in the 1950's? Makes me feel like I'm in a Norman Rockwell painting" he commented, looking around for Rockwell in the room with his easel.

"Well, it's morning and we're sitting at a breakfast counter at the moment. I don't remember much about the 1950's, since I was only six years old when they ended."

"I was only three, but my mother tells me I was precocious. I recall discussing Kierkegaard in Kindergarten."

"You were really slow. Your mother didn't want to hurt your feelings."

"I can remember back to the early 1960's, which were still, in a way, the late 1950's. Just like the early 1970's were still the '60's. I was sitting on this little air vent pipe covered by a round iron cap in my front yard. I think it was a vent from our basement. They didn't have radon tests back then, so maybe it was there to allow stale air to come up … I loved sitting on it. Also recall relaxing on the front step of our porch. My oldest sister Paula would hold me and tell me NOT to do things." He thought back to the night of the huge thunderstorm…

—————◦《◎》◦—————

"Hey!! This is fun!!" The sky was growing darker and the rain had started to pelt the edges of the chairs on their front porch, but Jim and Mary snuck out the front door as the thunder roared, hoping no one would see them climb in back of the two white Adirondack chairs. "Wowwww!! That was loud!!" he said as the thunder cracked. Then he saw lightning... and a few seconds later he heard the booming sound again. He shook as he tried to get his arms wrapped around his knees behind the white slats of the chair.

"Are you getting wet? I think I felt a few raindrops on my feet!!" Mary said, pulling her legs inward, giggling.

"It's about to come down... hard!!" Just then, another bolt of lightning cracked the sky and they shook as they sat on the cool cement surface behind the chairs. "Wooooo!!!! That was a BIG one!!!" He looked around and saw the dark clouds coming... then the rain came down in a thick curtain across the lawn.

"Wowwee!! That's a rainstorm!!! Hope mom doesn't see us out here!!" she said, putting her head down to shield her face from the splashing raindrops.

"Mary!! Jimmy!!! Where are you??!! Mary??!!!" Their mother's booming voice came through the door and they knew she'd be coming outside in a few seconds.

"Time to go in..." he said sadly, his eyes looking downward... "but it was FUN!!" They both slowly stood up from behind their fortresses, the blowing rain beginning to soak their shoes. "We're coming, mom!!..."

———◦((◦))◦———

"How the story never changes. Did your oldest sister boss you around?" Natalie's voice brought his eyes back to the counter and the coffee cup in front of him.

"No… not really, but she used to insist that I tickle her back for five minutes while we all watched T.V. on Sunday nights. That wasn't hard work. She kept me in line…watched me closely."

Jim ordered his usual omelet with fried potatoes and sausage, while Natalie tried the new stuffed French Toast topped with strawberries. Breakfast was filling and very reasonable. "I've come to be a big Hank's fan, as long as we get here early. The check's only $15.90… with tip, its just $19."

"I've always liked Hanks. This used to be a run-down hamburger shack years ago when I was a kid. The new owners have really done a great job with the menu and the outside gardens. Food's always good here. I especially like their rice pudding – one of my favorites!"

He paid at the register. "Ready to go?"

"Ready Freddy. Next stop – the Brandywine…"

They headed north on Route 100, one of Chadds Fords most picturesque and historic country roads. Paralleling the river, they saw the Sanderson Museum, where Chris Sanderson lived and chronicled the comings and goings of Chadds Ford residents from the 1920s through the 1960s. Their car passed the Chadds Ford Historical Society, started in 1968 to preserve and commemorate the historic Battle of the Brandywine - the largest and longest land battle of the American Revolution and the greatest battle on American soil until the Civil War nearly 85 years later.

"I'm looking forward to this canoe trip. It's been over a year since we've been on the water" Jim remarked as he approached the turn-off.

"Me, too. We should have some fun… finally."

They came to a stop in the gravel parking lot and he glanced over at her.

"We are in complete control of your canoe. Do not try to adjust the settings…" doing his best imitation of The Outer Limits TV show from the late 1960s.

Natalie chuckled, thinking back to her childhood as she sat mesmerized by the haunting T.V. series.

After paying the rental fee, they headed for the landing and the canoes piled nearby. The drop-in to the creek is always a bit muddy and can be cumbersome for inexperienced boaters, but they carried the 18 foot heavy-duty plastic blue canoe to the water's edge and got in easily.

"O.K… we're in… and hopefully not done for." He looked out at the water.

"Oh, stop being goofy. I'm ready for our next adventure!" she announced as she grabbed her paddle and tried to re-member which side of the canoe to start on. "Awaiting your command, captain."

"Remove your clothes immediately…"

"Only when we get at least 200 yards away from everyone else on the water- and then only if you promise to give me a back rub and foot massage tonight."

"Done deal." He put the wooden paddle deep into the cur-rent, forcing the canoe forward with both his arms, picking it up out of the pale green water and plunging it down again, splashing a few drops onto his face and shoulders. "Feels good to be back on the water" Jim called out, invigorated by the cool air and exercise.

They paddled in sync and easily made their way down the Brandywine, at least 100 yards ahead of the subsequent people who dropped into the river after them. He inspected the left bank and recalled their last canoe trip.

"Remember when we saw that beaver paddling down stream, keeping up with us?"

"Oh, yeah! He was really cute! I wish we'd had our camera, but then it would have been ruined when we tipped and fell in the water. This time I brought the camera sealed tight in a zip lock bag." Natalie made sure her oars were complementing Jim's actions at the front of the canoe.

"I don't see much wildlife" Jim observed.

"We'll see something interesting today. I can feel it."

"Well, you'll have to grab the camera. I need to keep control of this thing and can't turn around."

"Don't worry... I'll be a much better second-mate this time. I know how to paddle so we go forward instead of spinning around."

He searched the water up ahead and saw a slight bend in the creek where there were some stones placed along the bank. As they got closer, he back-paddled. "Slow down! Slow down... I see something."

"Really... what?"

"Not sure... but it appears to be an old farmhouse. Let's try to stop right up there on the left. He back-paddled harder to slow the canoe, even though the current wasn't more than 5 miles per hour in the shallow water approaching the bank.

"Looks muddy... Should we stop here?" Natalie asked as she tried to help the canoe slow down.

"We're stopping right over there" Jim indicated as he took the oar out of the water and pointed it at the stones in front of them. "We can step out on those."

The canoe came to a halt, but rotated slightly with the current despite Jim's efforts to stabilize it. He put both hands on the side and said "I'm getting out here... you wait until I've got a hold of the boat." He stood up quickly and stepped onto the stones.

"Ready? Can I get out now?" Natalie asked, not wanting to tip it over.

"O.K... I've got both sides. Get up slowly and put a hand on my shoulder. You can step on these stones, then jump to shore... no muddy shoes." He held the canoe firmly as she gingerly stepped out and hopped over. They crossed the grassy field and stood in front of the very old structure.

"Nice... you know these old stone buildings are up and down the Brandywine. For that matter, they're all over the county. Is there something special about this one?" Natalie asked.

"This one just seems interesting. Look at all the stones... well placed... still standing after maybe 200 years. It's a great example of a Colonial-era barn or farmhouse." He entered the structure, which was mostly intact except for the missing roof and kneeled down to examine the wall before him. "Look at this, hon... all these stones are perfectly placed. They've held together despite decades of flooding. They're metamorphic rock... mica-schist, which is common in this region... and lots of serpentine stacked together. Actually, it looks like mostly serpentine, which I think was the predominant building material here in the late 1700's."

"Reminds me of the house at the corner of 926 and 202... same beautiful, blue-green serpentine stone. What else do you think is here besides mice and mud?"

"Well, dear Watson, we are about to find out." He knelt closer to the wall and put his hands on some stones near a spot where a window could have been. Inspecting the mortar, he noticed something sticking out. He touched the object, which had a rough, rusty feel. "I may have to... do a bit of dissection here, doctor."

"What? Are you going to take apart the wall?" Natalie exclaimed as she walked up next to him.

"I won't disassemble it, but there is something sticking out that I need to get to. I'll put everything back when we're done. Natalie, hand me that broken stone next to your foot. I can use it to chip out the old mortar."

Natalie watched as Jim carefully pounded rock on rock, little pieces breaking away with each strike.

"This is exciting!!" He slowly picked along the edge of the wall, a small round item dropping into his hand. He pulled out two others, rubbing them around in his palm.

"Feels man made, but I'm not absolutely sure. It could just be chunks of rock, but they look different than the stones in the wall and appear quite regular, kind of circular."

Natalie peered into Jim's palm. "Nice pebbles."

"No, really, I think there's more to this one." All of the stones appeared to be typical... river-worn, roughly ½ - ¾ of an inch in diameter. The one between Jim's fingers had a raised center that had an unusual feel to it. "This could be some kind of artifact" suggested Jim.

"Wow – no kidding! If it isn't, can I have it for one of my flower pots?" she said with a grin, making a little fun of Jim's evaluation.

He let go of the other pebbles and focused on one rough-edged item in his hand. "It just has an unusual feel for a pebble." Jim spit in his palm and Natalie grimaced.

"Yuck Jim, what are you doing?"

"Just going to try and clean off some of this dirt."

He rubbed the object around in the saliva and saw some of the brown fade away, revealing an image. The object had a brassy color, though dark and weathered by many years of exposure to the elements. "This looks like, could it be, a button?"

"What? You think you found an antique button?" asked Natalie, excited at the prospect of actually discovering something worthwhile.

"Maybe a Colonial-era button from the late 1700's or early 1800's... I've seen photos of these at the Chadds Ford Historical Society in some of their reference books. This is about the right size, shape and feel." He tried to scrape off more of the rust and mold, succeeding in getting it slightly more recognizable. Then he canvassed the surface of the wall again, moving his hands under some vines that had attached themselves permanently to the stones, working to reclaim them back to nature.

"Jim, watch out for those vines – they could be poison ivy or oak."

"Don't worry, I'll be careful… and I'm not allergic like you. I think I feel something else here too, it's a bit sharp… too sharp to be a twig." Jim pulled away the vines and saw what had poked him. He pulled out a square piece of metal with a short pointed tong inside. "This is definitely not a stone or a twig. It resembles, maybe, the remains of a belt buckle?" He noticed Natalie eyeing the item in his hand.

"Can I see it?" she asked.

"Sure" Jim said, handing it to her.

"Amazing, it doesn't look like anything made in the last 100 years. It's too crude and rough" she determined as she moved the object around in her hand. "I think you've found a real antique" she declared and handed it back.

He stood up. "This edge of the wall right here might have been a window. Maybe a Revolutionary War soldier was perched here during one of the battles."

"These items could have been left behind after a skirmish" she speculated, excitement obvious in her voice. "Perhaps he died here, the body rotted away and the floods embedded the items in the mortar" she suggested.

"Gruesome, in a way… to think we're standing where someone died, but I guess that's one possible story. Anyway, these look like they could be collector's pieces. I think we should have them appraised by an expert" Jim said. He put the two items in his pocket and started to feel around the wall some more, his hands filthy and getting scratched. "I guess that's it" and he turned to walk back to the canoe.

"Hey wait! Maybe there's more here. Let me check around a bit. I don't mind getting dirty." Natalie worked her way around the whole building, pulling at weeds near the bottom of the walls and wiping away years of dirt from some of the stone surfaces. She avoided the vines. "OK, I guess you're right – nothing else here." Natalie started to brush aside strands of hair that fell over her nose and Jim tried to reach out to stop her, but it was too late. Her face was now streaked with a wide swath of reddish-brown mud.

Jim grinned and decided it looked kind of cute. He put his arm around her and they walked toward the river.

She gazed along the edge of the field, the slope rising gently as it fringed the water, when she noticed a man standing about 50 yards away, staring right at them. He had two very large dogs tightly leashed in each hand.

"Hey... it appears we have visitors. Take a look up there."

He glanced over at the edge of the hillside. "Those are big dogs... I can tell from here. I didn't see a 'NO TRESPASSING' sign, so we're fine." He turned to leave, then heard the holler.

"Go!! Go get 'em!!" The man unhooked both dogs as they strained against their leashes. Instantly they took off down the hillside, barking and growling.

"Oh, my God!! I think those dogs are after us!! Jim!!" She started to run, but slipped in the mud, falling on her knees.

The two German Shepherds were almost on top of them as Jim shouted loudly, swinging a piece of broken branch at them. "Go!! Get away!!" He picked up a large piece of serpentine and threw it at the dog on the left, hitting him squarely in the leg. "Let's get outta here!!" He grabbed Natalie's arm and sprinted down the hillside toward the canoe, pulling Natalie behind him.

She turned around as they reached the river bank. "They're HUGE!! That one's got to be well over 100 pounds. Oh, my God... he's still coming after us!!"

The dog who'd been hit by the rock ran limping after the first one, who was charging toward them as they tried to get into the canoe, spittle dripping from his snarling teeth.

"GRRRRRR....Grrrr!!!! Ruff!!!!...Grrrrr!!!!' He lunged as Jim was putting his left leg into the canoe, grabbing hold of his ankle with his strong jaws. "GRRR!!!!" He chomped down on his leg, shaking his head from side to side.

"OWWW!!! Damn it!!!" He yelled as he pulled his leg free from the dog's razor-like teeth. Jim grabbed the paddle and hit the dog broadside across his head, knocking it to the ground as Natalie got in. "Start paddling!! NOW!!" He swung the paddle again at the dog, missing it by a few inches.

"GRRR!!!! Ruff!!!! Ruff!!!!!" The shepherd lunged into the water, chasing the canoe as they floated downstream. The water rose up to the dog's neck as it splashed after them. "GRRRR!!!!" The German Shephard stopped, but continued barking and growling ferociously as they paddled away.

"My God! That was unbelievable!! Are you O.K.?"

"Hey, take over for a second, hon. My ankle is killing me!!" He pulled his jeans up slightly, rolled down his sock, expecting to see blood everywhere. Instead he just saw a deep red set of teeth marks, the skin nearly broken. "Well, it hurts like Hell, but no major damage." He grabbed the paddle and tried to look back toward the dogs. "That guy deliberately let them loose on us!! If I'd had a gun, I'd have shot the dogs AND him."

"Jim!! I don't ever want you to hurt an animal... and I HATE guns."

"Hurt an animal??!! Those were monsters!! Did you see the size of them? They were grizzly bears!! The first one almost took my leg off!!"

"Well, that man must be a psychopath. Thank goodness we're safe. Anyway, at least we discovered something interesting there."

Jim paddled quickly while Natalie glanced back at the stone building. The current caused them to go slightly sideways, pointing downstream at an angle toward the bank where a large tree had fallen.

"Hey, you're supposed to be paddling to complement my strokes" Jim reminded Natalie as she sat behind him.

"Oh, sorry, Jim. I was watching for those dogs. I want to go back sometime, but maybe the place is guarded. I love those old stone buildings and that one was very unusual."

"There are plenty of others. We may find more bounty someplace else, you never know."

"Sure, but most of the worthwhile stuff has been scooped up already" she sighed.

"Don't be so sure. Remember the news we heard on TV a couple of weeks ago about that amateur treasure hunter? He found the stash of a lifetime in some farmer's field. There's always something hiding beneath all that dirt."

They banked the canoe at the drop off point, then headed back to their car. The sky had attained the slate-colored look of a cool Fall afternoon ready for a thunderstorm. The low-hanging clouds and fog seemed to say "Don't get too comfortable outside… raindrops are on the way." Jim drove slowly, navigating the sharp curves in the road, and noticed there was a small clearing in the sky toward the horizon. "Well, maybe it won't rain after all. There's some blue sky up there."

"Unfortunately, you are looking East. The dark clouds are moving in from the West, so that means the storm is coming our way" Natalie disclosed as she looked over her shoulder and out the back of their SUV.

"You're right – I was being optimistic.

"Did you want to have someone take a look at the button and buckle you found?"

"Yes. Let's stop at one of the antique shops just south on Route 1."

Chapter 4

They walked up to the heavy oak double doors and he opened the right one, letting Natalie into the shop first. In front was a large bookshelf, over 15 feet high, stacked with hundreds of dusty old books, some cracked and badly deteriorating, others in moderately good shape. He went up and started to take one of the older-looking volumes down, it's binding falling apart.

"Don't touch that, unless you want to buy it. Very fragile... over 300 years old" came the scornful voice from about 20 feet away. "You break it, you bought it." The man, in his late 50's, balding, a big belly hanging over his belt buckle, walked quickly over to where Jim was standing and gently pushed the book back onto the shelf.

"We can't even look at them? How can you expect people to buy anything?"

"If you see something you like, you let me know first. I'll get it for you. We've had way too many accidents over the years... people picking things up, dropping and breaking them. You can look, but don't touch!!"

Jim saw his expression and knew he was serious, but couldn't believe it. He backed away from the bookcase and saw Natalie giving him the 'What a jerk' look. He noticed several bronze sculptures, stone busts and an entire table of Indian artifacts. Then his eyes caught the prize… a Civil War-era section in the corner. He strolled quickly past the man toward two long rifles standing against the wall, next to what appeared to be Union Army canteens, artillery boxes, an intact cannon and several rusty iron cannonballs.

"Are these all authentic?" Jim inquired.

"Depends on what you mean by 'authentic.' We have artifacts that we've personally documented were found in the field, at historic sites. Yes, those are authentic." His voice was irritating Jim almost as much as his attitude.

"What does he mean, depends? I can't believe this guy" Jim thought as he went up to the rifle, but stopped short by a few feet. He walked around the display to an open door, which led into another room holding dozens of items.

"Don't go in there!! That's our work area. Nobody from the public is allowed in there. It's private." He walked up beside Jim and quickly closed the door. "Can I help you with anything?"

Natalie rolled her eyes as she watched them, going up to a large chandelier hanging in the center of the room. She examined each piece of glass hanging down from the ornately carved bowl in the center, itself more than three feet across. "Is this all crystal?"

"Waterford… late 18th century. Very rare piece."

"How much is it?"

"If you have to ask, you can't afford it." He chuckled as he walked up to her, thinking she appreciated the joke, but she moved a few steps away as he approached.

She glanced over at her husband. "I see. Well, just thought I'd ask." She stepped away and stood next to Jim, who was still admiring the cannon.

"I didn't think any of the Civil War era cannons were in this good a condition. This looks… exceptional. I've never seen anything like this. It's a bit… odd."

"What are you trying to say? That it's a fake?" He strolled up to Jim quickly, putting his left hand on the barrel. "This cannon was fired by Union troops at Chattanooga. It is a genuine Civil War piece... and very expensive. Please don't touch."

"Well, we need to be going" Natalie said as she took Jim's hand and started to motion toward the door.

Jim turned away from him without responding and followed Natalie out. "What a jerk!! I wouldn't do business with that guy. He won't even verify that everything was real" he whispered to Natalie as they exited the store. He started the car and they sped away.

They turned right at the light and slowed down as the car approached Brandywine View Antiques, the parking lot partly lined with bookcases, sculptures, iron bed posts, pillars and other remnants from days gone by. "We can go in here. What do you think? We've passed by this place hundreds of times and never stopped."

"Sounds good to me. Hopefully I can do a little rummaging

around this time. Maybe find something for my chicken collection in the kitchen."

They got out of the car and meandered around the dozens of objects standing along the edge of the parking area. The grass needed to be trimmed and the flagstones leading to the back porch were a bit haphazard. Lining the path were metal plates stuck on top of poles, some with a few plastic birds glued inside. "Bird feeders?" Natalie guessed. "Sue would really like these. So would the squirrels."

Jim entered the building and saw a voluptuous woman, late 20's, wearing a thin, form fitting blouse and worn jeans.

"Hi! Welcome to Brandywine View. Can I help you find anything?" she said cheerfully while ambling toward Jim, passing an antique oak table deeply pitted, but with solid legs and a dark mahogany finish.

"Oh, well, sure. I'm Jim. That's my wife Natalie. We've passed your store many times." He took a glance around the shop. "You've got quite an eclectic collection. Is everything for sale?" Jim asked, examining a wrought iron duck weather vane which read '1823', laying alongside a porcelain bowl with the classic pin cracks of an old finish.

"At the right price! Well, almost everything. I have a few favorites I won't part with. What were you looking for in particular?"

Natalie had wandered away to investigate all the interesting odds and ends, some clearly of value, others a bit cheesy. She knew there was a chicken somewhere in the enormous collection… her eagle-eye looking for that perfect find.

"Yes, we were hoping you, or someone on the staff could take a look at these things we just found." He reached into the right side pocket of his khakis and felt the button first... then the buckle. "Do you appraise antiques, or possible relics?"

"Well, I can give you a general idea of what it is and if it appears authentic, but I don't actually give appraisals. What did you find?"

Jim felt tension in his throat before he spoke again, thinking that whatever he said and showed her would become public. He feared he was about to give away a treasure, but knew he had no choice. "Well... just these two things we found along the Brandywine. We were canoeing and came across some kind of stone structure near the bank." He pulled out the button first and put it on the table in front of her. Reaching in the pocket again, he took out the buckle and laid it next to the button. He stared at them both for a few seconds, hoping he found something historic.

"Interesting..." she said as she stepped closer to the table and viewed them intently. "I'm sorry! My name is Joni. I'm the store owner. That's my sister Anne." She nodded over toward the corner of the adjoining room where a heavy-set woman with short chestnut-brown hair sat on an antique stool. Anne nodded silently.

"Good to meet you both. Well, what do you think?" Jim asked as he glanced at both of them.

Joni examined both pieces. "I think you have an antique button and a belt buckle. Can't say for sure, but I'm guessing roughly 1800's... could be slightly earlier. They're too worn and rusted to identify any markings or tool marks without a scope, but they appear to be real."

"Any idea what they're worth?" Jim inquired with a slight hesitation, knowing that if she said a high figure, anyone within earshot would know what he was carrying around. Natalie stood next to Jim, looking intensely at Joni.

"Oh... I couldn't tell you exactly. I do know that if they're associated with a famous person or statesman, some well known historical figure, they could be worth quite a bit."

"What's 'quite a bit'?" asked Natalie with an anxious tone in her voice. She stared alternately at Joni, then the button and buckle.

"Well... don't hold me to this, but if they were... let's say... something from a high ranking Revolutionary War officer... they could each be worth several thousand dollars... maybe more. I can recommend someone who could probably tell you."

"Who's that?" asked Jim, moving closer to the table after he heard the dollar amount.

"There's a guy up the road at Red Clay Antiques who's pretty sharp. His name is Robert Smithson. His shop does appraisals."

"Are they qualified? I guess I've never asked anyone how they're trained or certified to value antiques."

"You can't get it in school" Joni said with a slight grin. "You have to learn it over time. Examining a lot of antiques over the years gives you a sense of what's real and what's bogus. There are some basic checks like type of wood, finish, construction materials, but many of these can be duplicated to make a new item look old. What you have seems real to me."

Jim felt more comfortable and stepped back slightly after she spoke. "Red Clay... I think I know that place. It's just north on Route 1 from here, right?"

"Yes, just up the road not more than a mile. It's on the right hand side. Just tell them I referred you – they know me."

"Great... thanks!!" Jim said, picking up both items and putting them back in his pocket. He noticed Joni's beaming smile... and sensed something more than just a friendly disposition.

"No problem. Can I show you anything here?" she suggested with inviting eyes, stepping closer to him, hoping he might want to explore a few of the rooms alone with her.

"Well... sure... now that we're here" Jim decided, glancing over at Natalie. Natalie smiled back and held up her find... a small, pale green antique glass container with a chicken on the top. Jim shook his head, grinned, then looked back at Joni. "Do you have anything from the Colonial period? Anything like these?" He pointed to a plate which was cracked, the insignia from 1826 and '50 Year Anniversary of the Signing of the Declaration of Independence' printed across the top.

"Let's see... we do have some antique bowls and silverware from the 1800's. They're upstairs on the second floor."

"We'll check it out. This place looks like an antique all by itself. How old is this building?" he asked, viewing the heavy wooden staircase and flooring.

"The house is over 250 years old... built around 1753. It

was partly damaged by a fire years ago. The building was here during the Battle of the Brandywine... two sisters owned it then."

Jim felt a shiver. "What a coincidence... the button and buckle... could they be a link to the history of this area?" he wondered. "Really?" he said, looking around the corners of the room, overflowing with old chairs, tables, pottery, linen, utensils, carvings and signs.

"Yes... actually the part we're in was the section added later, but that half of the house is original. Feel free to look around. I'll be here if you need help."

Jim and Natalie headed toward the old wooden stairway, making sure they didn't knock anything over. The stairs creaked loudly with each step. Jim walked into one room as soon as he saw the large glass cabinet with silverware. "This must be the spot." He looked at the three glass shelves covered with items from yesteryear while Natalie poked her head into the room just down the hall. He approached the display case, noting the huge assortment of household items, from small saucers and plates to cups, spoons, thimbles and knitting accessories... all neatly laid out, though seemingly at random. He saw a daguerreotype of a young Civil War soldier, not more than 20 years old, his rifle at his shoulder and eyes gazing earnestly into the camera. Jim drifted off...

⟿⟨⟨◊⟩⟩⟸

"Captain??!! Are your men ready for this maneuver?"

General Washington commanded loudly, staring from horse-back down to where the young man stood.

"Yes, sir!! I shall have them ready instantly." The man grabbed his musket and looked at the line of tents pitched along the edge of the Brandywine in the morning mist of late Summer. It was September and they had marched to meet the British… intent on halting their progress toward Philadelphia. The damp fog of that day… September 10, 1777… hung in front of him. He scrambled through the low underbrush to the bank of the Brandywine Creek and stood silently looking at the ripples near the water's edge. "This place… this spot… so tranquil."

———⟐———

"Honey? Where are you? Jim?" Natalie's voice came from the hallway and he broke out of his trance.

"I'm in here" Jim answered. He shook his head lightly, awakening from the dream. The faded photograph appeared to reveal a subtle grin on the soldier's face. "Well, a soldier's life is a rough one. It's been that way in centuries past and always will be. Carry on…"

"Oh, here you are! There's so much stuff, it's easy to get lost."

"They do have some great things. Look at those silver and jade earrings in the corner cabinet. Do you like them? It's your favorite color. I'd like to get them for you."

"I don't think they're antiques, but still very nice. You're so sweet!" Natalie leaned over and gave Jim a quick kiss on the cheek.

Jim reached inside the cabinet and picked up the earrings. "Well, want to move on?"

"Sounds good to me!"

They walked back to the old staircase, going down the worn and somewhat slanted steps, trying to maintain their balance as they leaned toward the wall. Jim wanted to avoid brushing up against the antique Americana hanging all around them.

"Look at that... a wooden riding horse from a carousel. It looks to be from the turn of the century" Jim exclaimed as he approached the entrance.

"It was made in 1902... carved from New England oak. Part of a carousel in Provincetown, Massachusetts for many years... the second oldest in the country" described Joni, smiling at him.

"Really... I believe the oldest one is in Oak Bluffs, on Martha's Vineyard. We saw the plaque while on vacation."

"By the way, what's through there?" Natalie asked as she pointed to a small door that was closed.

"The basement... we try not to go down there unless necessary" Anne said, glancing over at her. "The floor's dirt and the lighting is bad." This was the first time they heard Joni's sister say something. "Plus, it's haunted."

"Really??" Natalie asked, her interest piqued. "What makes you think it's haunted?"

"Let's just say that late at night there are sounds coming from down there... creepy noises you don't want to hear. We

GENE PISASALE

only go down during the daytime." Anne stared at the door, cringing a bit, then looked back at Natalie.

"Wow... can I go check it out now? It's daytime" Natalie inquired, excitement in her voice. She felt the adventurer taking charge of her usually reserved demeanor.

"Sorry... no customers allowed. The stairs are too treacherous and our insurance doesn't cover it."

"Doesn't cover what... the stairs... or ghosts?" Natalie chuckled. "Just kidding... O.K., we can go now."

"You've been a great help! We'll check out Red Clay Antiques. I'll tell them you referred us and let you know what we come up with. Who knows? Maybe we found something valuable!"

"I hope so. Come and see us again sometime, soon" replied Joni.

He paid for the earrings, then he and Natalie stepped out the front door and headed to their car.

Jim put the car in gear, revving the engine as he pulled out of the lot.

"Jim! That's a bit..."

"Frisky?!"

"Yes..." she laughed. "A bit frisky... which makes me think... we have the rest of the day to ourselves. Want to mess around?"

"Definitely, but first I want to check out Red Clay. It's just up the road. We'll stop by quickly, see what they have to say and then head for home. Maybe they can tell us more about what we just found" he commented, patting the outside of his pocket.

He picked up the speed and crested the hill. "I think that's it... up there on the right. I can read the sign from here."

"Your eyes are better than mine. I can barely see the letters."

"Good thing for Lasik surgery. It helps a lot with night vision, too... especially in the rain and on poorly lit roads. I can see so much better now." He slowed the car, turned into the parking lot and thought about the years of treacherous drives on I-95 in the snow and ice. "Too bad my near vision is worse now."

"Always a trade-off" said Natalie as he brought the car to a stop in the parking lot.

"Well, who cares if I wear reading glasses... gives me a distinguished look, I think."

"Absolutely, Lord Peterson. Distinguished it is." She opened the car door and stepped out.

The Red Clay Antiques sign, bright red lettering on a white background, stood in contrast to the backdrop of the slightly dilapidated building with a weathered roof. Two people were bringing in their antique sewing machine, about 30 feet in front of where Jim was standing.

"Well, I promise this will be brief."

"O.K... twenty minutes, max."

"Yes, ma'am. Thank 'ya ma'am!!" he said in a low Elvis voice.

She poked him with her elbow as they went through the door into the shop.

He scanned the room to see if anything immediately caught

his attention. Then he saw it... what looked like a Revolutionary War flag, yellowed and badly tattered, its corner moth-eaten and shredded, the 13 stars barely visible on the dark blue background. It was unmistakable, a piece of our nation's history from the period of inception. A gem surrounded by antique bookcases, three-legged stools, marble busts of Roman emperors and Victorian-era furniture.

"Hello. Welcome to Red Clay" came a man's voice, elderly, pleasant-sounding. The man walked over to Jim and reached out for a handshake. "I'm Robert Smithson. Can I show you around the shop?" He beamed as Jim took his hand.

Jim looked at his face. It had the wear of a 75-year old, with a furrowed brow and 'smiler's wrinkles' around the eyes. He felt immediately at ease, unlike many other times he'd gone into stores where the sales people were either aloof, uninterested... or overly pushy, trying to get a sale within the first ten seconds.

"Oh, well... yes. This is our first time here. I'm Jim. This is Natalie."

"Good to meet you both. We have a wide range of antiquities... from ancient Rome and the Middle Ages to 17th, 18th and 19th century European and Americana. We specialize in American historical artifacts from the Colonial and Civil War periods."

Jim knew he'd come to the right place and felt reassured that this would be a worthwhile stop. He'd always felt at home wandering around dusty old bookstores and curiosity shops where the shelves themselves looked like antiques and crusty old men with silvery-white mustaches hunched behind a desk giving him details on each piece throughout the room. "Looks like you have a wide variety of artifacts, collected over…many decades?"

Smithson gazed at Jim as he said the last few words. "Yes, several years of collecting." He thought back to his days in graduate school in archeology and anthropology at the University of Pennsylvania. "Many decades, going back to the early 1950's, when I was a young student."

"Oh, really? You collected in your twenties?" Natalie asked, hesitant to guess his age, stepping closer.

"Oh, yes, used to collect Indian artifacts as a kid when my parents took us to New Mexico and Arizona. We loved climbing around those cliff dwellings, looking for arrowheads, pieces of pottery. That got me started."

"We enjoy the Southwest. Spent a week in Santa Fe last year, it was amazing." She focused on his face, the wrinkles around his smile the road map of many years of exploring the world.

"I lived in Denver for eight years, then San Diego for ten. Did a lot of hiking and camping around the region." Jim examined a marble bust as he spoke, then looked up at Smithson. "I remember going to New Mexico with a study tour in college. One guy started wandering around the desert on his own. Came back with an armful of cactus needles."

"My first archeological dig was as a freshman at U. of P., did a Summer internship near Taos. My professor was an expert in many of the local Indian tribes, their culture, history and artifacts. He was such a great lecturer... persuaded me and three other guys to join him digging in the dirt in the blazing Summer heat. We'd dig... and dig... then dig some more. Next the sifting and separating began. That took hours... sometime days... but it was all fun." He grinned, then noticed Natalie mesmerized by his every word.

"Did you ever find anything special or important?"

"Sure. You've heard of the Folsom Point and Folsom Man, Indian ancestors who lived in the Southwest region over 7,000 years ago? We found several stone tools and a few arrowheads dating to that time. One may pre-date Folsom. They're all in the University of Pennsylvania collection now. I got lucky... found a nearly complete bowl from a tribe not known to have inhabited the area. Made my professor grin with joy." He looked around the shop, his eyes far away, not fixing on any of the dozens of prized pieces he collected and put on the shelves.

"Did you get any recognition for it?" Jim asked. He recalled finding a perfect crystal of blue fluorite on a field trip – better than anything his professors had ever shown him – and getting an 'Attaboy!'

"You do it because you love it. I do. Maybe we'd all be a lot happier if we pursued things we love, instead of doing a job just for the money."

"Amen" Natalie agreed.

"One small consolation... my name is listed beside his on the museum plate. That's enough for me." He glanced at Jim, then at Natalie as she walked right up to him.

"I'm envious. I'd love to find artifacts... learn about ancient cultures. What do you treasure the most?"

"Well, the most exciting time in my career was when I was doing my post-Doctoral work at the University of New Mexico. They had an exchange program with the University of Cairo that was fabulous. Every year they'd sponsor three or four senior researchers to go over to Egypt... full boat. All expenses covered."

"That sounds like a great deal!"

"One catch. You had to spend six weeks in Egypt, in July and August, working out in the desert sun. Temperatures there are regularly in the 120-125 degree range. We'd have to take 20 minute breaks to avoid heatstroke, but it was exciting!! Found some exceptional items."

"What did you find?" Natalie was standing less than two feet away, listening intently.

"You've heard of King Tut, right? In 1972, we found extensions of his tomb, dozens of artifacts from him and his family, several gold plates and coins, daggers studded with rubies. It was wonderful. Made it into the history books on that one." His voice had the excitement of a rookie college professor teaching his very first class.

"Fascinating!! It must be every archeologist's dream to be listed as the finder of some important artifacts, ancient ruins" she proclaimed as she glanced briefly over at Jim, whose attention was focused completely on Smithson.

"Never had a goal of getting into the history books, just to add to the body of knowledge in my field, to help young students coming up after me learn about the world and its many cultures. That's what I truly enjoy." He looked at Natalie and could tell she wanted to hear more. "One other find was pretty special."

"What was that?" She looked like a child, ready to open the presents left for her under the tree on Christmas morning.

"We were working in Rome in 1978. I was co-leader of a group trying to document the exact dimensions of the cata-combs, their full extent, any artifacts left there, markings, paintings and other things. We measured every inch of those tunnels. It was tedious work, but we made two critical discov-eries. First, that the catacombs were developed on a precise grid with specific ratios of length, width and depth that related directly to the ancient Roman road system. No one ever knew that before and it helped in later excavations. Second, I found a marble bust of Nero which is believed to be the very first completely intact one ever discovered of the Roman emper-or. It was considered so important that the Italian Antiquities Ministry immediately confiscated the piece, not allowing us to clean and examine it further. The bust is now on display in the Vatican. I also found several Roman coins, different from any that had previously been discovered. I got lucky. Those were wonderful times..." His eyes had the faraway gaze of a lighthouse keeper, lost in the stillness of the ocean on a foggy night. "Working hard all day, sifting through the dirt, catalog-ing each item and storing them carefully... then going into town at night with my buddies to talk about all the things we found while downing several cold beers. I loved those days... I was much younger then."

LAFAYETTE'S GOLD

"I'm impressed that you've made some great contributions not only to archeology, but also our understanding of civilizations around the world. You should be very proud." She took his hand and shook it gently, smiling as he accepted her grasp. She grinned thinking about her collection of Cracker Jack prizes from the 1960's and trinkets she found while digging in her garden or walking in parking lots… old marbles, toy army men, little rubber fish… the hobbies of an amateur archeologist. She envied his exciting past and amazing accomplishments.

"Thanks so much, you're very kind. You folks seem to be very interested in history."

"I love Americana. I focus on the Revolutionary and Civil War" Jim said, gazing around the shop. "You wouldn't happen to have any tree stumps with minie balls stuck in them, would you? They have this great Civil War tree stump standing in a case in The Little Drummer Boy in downtown Gettysburg with bullets embedded all through it- from the time of the battle."

"No, but we have a whole section over there devoted to both periods. Take a look around and feel free to ask questions." He glanced down at his watch and noticed the time. "Unfortunately, I need to leave for an appointment. I'll return in about an hour. My partner will be glad to help you. He should be out in a few minutes."

"No problem. Nice meeting you." She couldn't help noticing his eyes, intensely bright, revealing a man who was both kind and intelligent.

They wandered around the shop, picking up different

pieces and examining them.

"Look at that flag!" Jim exclaimed, pointing to the antique wooden case, the flag visible behind the glass window.

"Do you like it?" came a piercing male voice from the far corner of the room, catching Jim off guard as he tried to see who was speaking. He turned sharply to his left and saw a man, late 50's, thin, wearing faded blue jeans and a tan wool long-sleeved shirt walking quickly toward him.

"Sure." He watched the man as he came right up to him, only one foot separating them.

"Hello. I'm Martin Broom, the owner, well co-owner of the shop. I see you've noticed our great collection of antiquities... best in the Valley, if you ask me. Your name?" He thrust out his arm for a handshake. His voice was slightly irritating... and the overtly direct approach put Jim a bit on edge.

Jim took a half-step back. "Oh... I'm Jim." He turned around to see if Natalie was nearby before finally shaking the man's hand. She just stood there, her face deadpan.

"Welcome!! Can I show you the flag?"

"Well... no, although it is interesting. I was referred to you here by Joni at Brandywine View. She mentioned that you evaluate antiques, even research and assess artifacts. Do you?"

"We do, for certain periods... mostly American history, some European, a bit of Native American."

"We have some things we collected up along the creek. We thought you could take a look at them and let us know if they're worth anything." He looked Broom directly in the eye and Broom blinked several times, glancing down briefly.

"Sure, we can do that. Show me what you have."

His reluctance to maintain eye contact with Jim for more than a second bothered him. He grabbed the button and the belt buckle at the bottom of his pocket. "I'm not sure if I like this guy, but who knows?" Jim thought. "I've been wrong about people before…" He glanced at Broom again, taking the two items out of his pocket. "What do you make of these?" He placed them on the counter two feet away from where they both stood. Natalie watched silently.

Broom walked up and stooped over to inspect both pieces. "I'll need to examine these more closely." He went behind the counter and dropped to his knees, reaching into the cubby-holes below the glass-topped cabinet. He rose quickly, holding two magnifying glasses. "This'll let me take a better look at what you have." He held up the large, black-rimmed magnifying glass first. "This is a first look lens… gives me the general features." Then he held up a much smaller lens, rimed in aluminum, with a swing-out glass, ¾ inch in diameter. "This gives me detail."

Jim got closer as Broom came back to the front of the counter. He leaned over and held the button under the larger lens. "Looks like a brass button, Colonial era, probably 1800's, possibly very late 1700's. Badly weathered, but I can see some pattern there. Let me take a closer look." He grabbed the smaller lens and squinted as he looked through with his left eye. "Mmm… interesting. I can definitely see a pattern there, but to be completely confident of its age and authenticity, I'd have to get it tested. You say you found this along the Brandywine?"

"What do you mean? What kind of testing?" Natalie asked, a bit nervous, moving right next to him at the counter, ignoring the question of where they found it.

He looked at her eyes and thought of his first wife... the day they met in the little antique store in Provincetown, Massachusetts while he was a young college student at Amherst. "I was so young... didn't have much money... and she was so... gorgeous" he thought as Natalie stepped closer to him. "Why did I let her go? Well... she let me go... my screwing around... guess I deserved it." He couldn't help staring at the blueness of her eyes. "The kids never call anymore... can't blame them either... I rarely called them, especially after the second marriage. What was that worth? Nothing... wish I'd stayed with Maria. I wonder where she is right now..." He glanced at Natalie and then quickly over at Jim, trying to take his attention away from her. "We have a testing lab near D.C. We send everything there. They do it all... radiocarbon, x-ray, the works."

"Will it damage the artifact?"

"Oh no... standard testing. They take the utmost care of everything we send them. Never had a problem." He put the button down on the counter and picked up the large magnifying glass to examine the buckle. "This is a brass buckle, probably circa 1800-1825, also very badly weathered. Let's take a closer look." He took the smaller lens and squinted. "I don't see any specific markings. Very corroded. Should be tested."

"So... what do you suggest?"

"Leave them with me... I can arrange everything for you."

Jim was slightly uncomfortable with his matter-of-fact

insistence. Natalie tugged on Jim's hand. "Well, when do we get them back? Also, what guarantee do we have they won't be damaged or lost?"

"We have the highest standards. Our testing is first rate. We're well known for doing excellent work- ask any of the shops around the area… and of course, we'll give you a receipt." Broom tensed up a bit, concerned that he was about to lose a potential deal.

"O.K. So, how much will all this cost us?" Natalie asked.

Broom blinked three times and focused his gaze on the button and buckle, then her eyes. "The standard charge is $50 for testing, $75 for a brief summary including testing of the authenticity, provenance and historical significance." He felt a slight tingle in his loins as she reminded him of Maria.

"That's $75 each?" Jim repeated, still holding her hand tightly.

"Yes… $75 each. Is that a problem?"

Jim did some quick math. "Well, that's a total of $150… not that much to have a potential treasure verified. If we have to search for and then drive to one or two other places, the time alone… my time… would be worth $150" he thought. "O.K.- we'll leave these with you for testing." He felt the tug again and looked at Natalie, who was giving him the 'Let's talk about this' expression. He turned to her and said "What do you think?"

She led him from the counter, stopping about 20 feet away and leaned her head close to his as she spoke. "Are you comfortable with this guy?" She kept her voice so low he could barely hear her.

"Well… the place looks reputable. It's not a dive… and he's less of a jerk than the guy at the first shop. He said they're well known for their work and their testing lab. Plus, I really like Smithson… he seems like a great guy."

"We really don't know anything about this place."

He sensed she was right. "You have a point there, but shouldn't we give him the benefit of the doubt? I mean, Joni at Brandywine View recommended them and she seems reputable" he said, whispering low so Broom couldn't hear, although he noticed Broom watching intently, trying to eavesdrop.

Natalie hesitated, then gave him a slight nod. "O.K."

"I say we give him a chance." Jim turned around and walked back toward the counter where Broom was still standing. Natalie deliberately stayed well behind him, walking much more slowly. "We'll leave them with you… for full testing and evaluation. Can you take a check?"

Broom stood on the end of his toes, smiling. "Yes… that'll be $150. Make it out to Red Clay Antiques."

"O.K.… here you go. Of course, I need a receipt, with a full description of the items."

"Sure thing. I'll fill it out right now." Broom grabbed a small pad, writing down the total charge and a brief note on each item. "Here you go. They should be back in a few weeks."

Jim gave him the check as he took the receipt and stared at it closely. "Thanks. We'll be back in touch."

"Thank you so much for coming in!! We appreciate your business. Let us know if Robert or I can help you in any way." Broom watched them as they left the shop. Then he glanced down at the counter. He looked at what he had in front of him. "A button from the Continental Army." He took the small lens again and examined both the button and the buckle. "Looks like a senior officer's button- maybe even Washington's or one of his commanders. These two together could be worth $3,000... maybe a bit more." He picked up both pieces and walked to the back of the shop.

Chapter 5

"Well, where to hon?" Jim asked as they closed their car doors.

"You said we were done for the day... let's head home."

"I know, but now that we've found a few pieces of history... want to walk in their footsteps?"

"What do you mean?"

"How about a quick trip to Brandywine Battlefield Park? It should still be open. We can visit Washington's Headquarters."

"Oh... I don't know."

"Come on... It'll be fun! I promise I won't stay to address the troops."

Natalie relaxed a little, then smiled. "Alright General, but you have to make this a quick maneuver, not a major campaign."

"I am at your service, madam..."

"Onward... to the battlefield."

They drove up Route 1 and within a few minutes were at the park. The large blue and white battlefield sign with the three Continental Army soldiers... one standing, one bending down and one kneeling… all ready to fire their muskets… stood as a modern landmark with historical ties.

General George Washington, on September 9th, 1777, had chosen this ground to face the British under General Howe, hoping to stop their march into Philadelphia from the Chesapeake Bay. The site was selected as a possible defense on the high ground near Chad's Ford, which was one of the many fords that allowed passage across the Brandywine on the road from Baltimore to Philadelphia. Due to the recent rains, several of the nearby fords were impassable, leaving Chad's Ford the only reasonable option for General Howe and his troops. Washington's force of 11,000 was to be up against a force of British soldiers and German Hessians numbered to be around 18,000.

"This must be the place" Jim said as they made the left hand turn into the historic park. He looked over at Natalie, who nodded, signaling she was ready for the next maneuver.

"Let's check out the Visitor's Center first and see if they have any information on tours of the battlefield sites" Jim said as he got out of the car and closed the door.

"I believe they occasionally give tours of Washington's Headquarters and maybe of Lafayette's, too. I was a kid on a school trip the last time I was here. I swore Lafayette's Headquarters had a dungeon with shackles, but I could be wrong."

They walked to the front door of the Visitor Center, the rectangular tan wooden back of the building in stark contrast to the historic stone houses located around the park. There were only two people in the entire room, one of them a young man, about 19 years old, behind the counter.

"Hi! Do you have tours?" Jim inquired as he stepped right in front of the small glass and metal-rimmed counter, topped with tourist trinkets and Colonial memorabilia. The young man had a relaxed air about him.

"We do! Actually there's one starting in about 15 minutes… costs $3 dollars. This may be one of the last tours of the Ring house."

"You mean today? How late do they go?" Natalie asked, walking up to Jim.

"No – period. Looks like the park may be closing" he replied.

Jim thought for a few seconds, then asked. "Lack of funds… due to the economy?"

"You got it. Cutbacks. No one's immune. They don't have enough in the Park Service budget, what with Federal and State cutbacks. Even with reduced hours and more volunteers, they just don't have the money to keep everything open. Parks like Gettysburg can weather the storm, they bring in lots of revenue, but we're just a small park in Delaware County. It's a shame…" he said, the tone of his voice dropping into a dull monotone, revealing deep sadness.

"I thought we were in Chester County. I know they have an active group who helps to preserve the local heritage" Natalie commented.

"Don't I wish… then things might be better. We're just over the line into Delaware County. Attitudes are a bit different here" he replied.

"How long have you worked at the battlefield?" Jim asked, in an almost apologetic tone.

"This is my second year. I love it here… I'm a history major at the University of Delaware and hope to someday locate near Gettysburg to be a tour guide. Too bad this will end. It's a great job and a great honor to work at such an historic place."

"I'll never forget the first time I drove out to Gettysburg. I'd just moved back East from San Diego and was ready for a change of scenery. I sat at the bar in the Farnsworth House Tavern, Union infantry standing there, having a beer… the soundtrack to the movie 'Glory' playing. I was completely mesmerized… did some exploring of the area since then. We both enjoy American history and visiting historic sites."

The young man perked up. "Cool! I think you'll enjoy the tour. The guide is very knowledgeable. She's a local with lots of interesting stories from the past."

"Are you certain they're going to close this park? What will they do with it – turn it into a parking lot -or just let the wild life take over?" Natalie asked, half jokingly, but with a sense of disappointment.

"Well, it's not a fait accompli… I think they're giving it one last vote from the Museum Commission… asking for public input and support. There's also supposed to be some local Congressman representing the district who might do something. Perhaps there's a small chance we'll survive."

"When's the meeting?" Jim asked, leaning on the counter near the young man.

"Next Thursday at 7 p.m."

"Damn! I already have another commitment – too bad."

"Don't worry, Jim. If people are really concerned, they'll show up." Natalie put her hand on Jim's back. "Ready to check out the tour?"

"Well, I think it's great that young people like you are interested in our nation's history and show your support by working at places like this park."

"It's fun for me. I really enjoy being so close to our nation's birthplace… walking hallowed ground and feeling the souls of the soldiers who put their lives on the line for us – centuries ago. We might not be here, living as free men and women if Washington… Jefferson… Adams and all the Founding Fathers hadn't staked their fortunes to the cause of liberty."

Jim was struck by the young man's patriotism and bowed his head silently, saying a short prayer for all those who were so brave.

"The tour is just about to start. You can reach the Ring House up that road."

"Thanks very much. Keep up the good work. With people like you, I'm sure they'll find a way to keep this place alive and open for all to experience" Jim said with a quick wave as he walked out the door.

"I hope so! Enjoy the tour!"

They drove up to the stone house and saw five people in a small group standing and talking in the parking lot. There was a chill in the air… a harbinger of Winter's coming snow, but he felt warm inside. "I know it seems bad right now, but maybe some wealthy local residents will step up to the plate and help" Jim commented to Natalie as they parked and joined the group.

"O.K., folks. Gather up. We're going to walk over to Washington's Headquarters. It's that grey-brown stone building over there. Please stay on the path and don't lean on the structure." The woman leading the tour was middle-aged, her brown hair pulled back in a bun. "Washington's Headquarters was actually the home of Benjamin Ring, a local Quaker farmer and miller. Lafayette's quarters, the home of Gideon Gilpin, also a Quaker farmer, is not far away. The irony embodied by the fact that two peace-loving Quakers gave their homes to fight one of the most important wars in U.S. history is largely unknown by the general public. These were people dedicated to coexistence with all men and vehemently against war. Washington's Headquarters is visited the most and people flock to it even on the coldest days." The guide walked up to the house, gathering the group around her to gauge the size before entering.

"Everyone, let's step inside. As you can see, the room is very plain. Quakers lived simple lives. They were mostly farmers. Some surprised their associates by stepping up to support the cause of freedom. We thank Benjamin Ring for that here."

"The house is quite bare. You can see the furniture was basic, almost Spartan" Jim commented, leaning toward Natalie so she could hear his lowered voice.

"Washington was here in Ring's house the night of September 10, 1777, the eve of the Battle of Brandywine. Lafayette, the 19-year old French nobleman, actually named the Marquis de Lafayette, was up the road a ways, staying at Gilpin's house, though there has been some recent speculation that Lafayette spent most of his time here since he and Washington had become close friends." The tour guide looked at all the participants to make sure no one tried to poke at the windows or steal a chip of the structure.

"Did many Quakers actually fight in the war?" asked one older woman, with wavy, silvery hair, wearing a dark grey wool jacket.

"Surprisingly, there were several local Quakers who silently supported the cause. Some even broke ranks with their associates to join the local militia, which was anathema to most Quakers" said the guide. Her voice was upbeat and positive, the sound of helpful authority.

"There were several Quakers in the West Chester militia. Some assisted here in the battle" said a man with a British accent, a handsome gentleman with light brown hair streaked grey, pulled back in an "I'm 50, going on 20" ponytail, tucked into his collar. The woman next to him, about 45 years old holding his hand, wore skin-tight black jeans, a clingy silver top and black boots with high heels.

"Another psychedelic relic, holdover from the 1970's" Jim thought, looking at her, then him.

"Oh, are you an historian?" asked the guide.

"No, just a part-time history buff and aging rocker" he said, his accent drawing attention from most of the crowd. A few laughed.

"Well, feel free to jump in if you have anything to add. I'm not a military expert, just a local guide, with general knowledge of the area."

"There were actually two groups of Quakers in support of the war. Some did bear arms, others simply helped supply the troops with whatever foodstuffs and items were necessary for them to stay alive and fight." The man had a pleasant face and the air of intelligence.

Jim felt he'd been unfair in his calculation. How many times had he judged someone on their first appearance, without even taking the time to hear them speak their mind? Too many. He remembered when he was much younger and had long hair, wore faded jeans, even occasionally had a stubbly beard. The more he listened, the greater respect he gained for the British man.

"I believe you're right. You should talk with the man who plays General Washington. He comes here sometimes" the guide said with a chuckle.

"I met General Washington at Valley Forge" Jim said, wanting to support the Brit. "He was very tall!!" The crowd laughed and the guide turned toward him.

"Oh, do you like history, too?"

"Since I sat at my desk in Catholic school, turning the pages of my American Heritage book with the illustrations of Bunker Hill and the Liberty Bell."

"Well done!!" said the Englishman with a pleasant and relaxed demeanor about him.

"Thank you! Seems you're the local history expert." He nodded at him in recognition.

"Well, folks, Washington probably spent two days with the Ring family. The Battle of Brandywine was a failure for him. He received conflicting information and he was unsure of where to deploy his forces."

The wind picked up and Jim looked out at the sky, now showing the grey-pink of the approaching sunset. He gazed toward the West, the same direction Washington's troops faced as they waited for Howe and his army to attack...

————)(●)(————

"General, sir, I have a report from Colonel Moses Hazen that the British are marching and amassing a large force to the North, near the upper reaches of the Brandywine and may attack there."

Washington looked at Major Lewis Morris from his horse. He knew that reports from field scouts could be confusing and contradictory. "Well, sir, what does he propose?"

"General, he requests that we send at least 1,000 of our soldiers there, toward the forks of the Brandywine, near what is called Wistar's Ford, sir and a support team of another 500 men, if possible to Buffington's Ford, at the forks, General."

"I will take that under immediate review, Major." The General looked around at the late Summer foliage shrouded in dense fog along the banks of the Brandywine, grasses starting to turn a straw color from their original sage green, shrubs with leaves starting to curl up, ready to fall in the coming weeks. He felt reassured. He knew that if the British forces were split evenly between the immediate area and several miles from him at the forks, he'd have an opportunity to attack here with superior strength. He began to formulate the plan and sat atop his horse for what seemed like an hour until he heard another horse approaching. It was a courier.

"General Washington, sir, I bring you a report from Major Sullivan. It is more recent in time from the one dispatched this morning to you. He reports that he has received information from militiamen stationed near Martin's Tavern to the North, one of whom came southward to a place named Welches Tavern and noted that earlier reports of British troops near the forks to the North were incorrect, sir."

He peered down at the man's face to see if he could sense any sign of doubt, indicating either confusion or treason. "What am I to make of this report??!! It is in direct contradiction to one I received not an hour ago!!" He stared at the man, who seemed to shrink in front of Washington's large white horse.

"General Washington, my apologies for this confusion. I am obliged to give you this information, though I understand it troubles you, sir."

Washington inspected the man's hat, black three-cornered, worn by many Colonials, some of whom had helped the cause of liberty. He gazed into the fog, now lifting along the river and felt that his date with destiny... and victory... would have to be postponed...

"That hasn't been definitively corroborated" interjected the British man, his booming voice now jolting Jim awake. Jim looked around and yawned, trying to shake the vision.

"You're right, we believe he stayed with the Ring family for just a few days" said the guide, her voice trailing off slightly as she sensed that one of the attendees knew more about the local history than she did. "What we DO know definitively is that the Battle of the Brandywine was a loss for the Americans and could have been much different in outcome if Washington hadn't received the two different reports. As it was… being a cautious man… he decided the most prudent thing to do was NOT to attack. We know today that if he had attacked, early in the morning, the Battle and our nation's struggle toward freedom could have been much different."

The British man nodded approval and looked at his wife. "The Brits got that one right!!" The people around him chuckled and they walked into the next small room.

"During the early 1900's the Ring house was occupied by Chris Sanderson. He and his mother lived here for many years and often entertained N.C. Wyeth, a local well known painter. It was actually his paintings of the house that helped us rebuild after a fire ravaged it in the early 1900s. A family with small children had moved in and one of the kids stuffed a ball up the chimney. The house sat in ruins for years until the Park Service obtained ownership and rebuilt the home as it would have been when Washington was here. This is the end of the tour - are there any questions?" She searched around the room for raised hands. "Well, we thank you for coming to Brandywine

Battlefield Park and hope you'll come again. Actually, we just hope we'll stay open!!"

A few people whispered. Jim felt a sinking feeling in his stomach… the same one he had when they tore down that old warehouse in his neighborhood, a refuge for him and his buddies, site of their afternoon adventures.

"We enjoyed it" he said to the guide. "Always nice to learn something new about our local history."

"We've wanted to come here for a long time. We're just a bit sad that it could close so soon" said Natalie as she stepped up next to Jim before the door.

"Well, we'll see what develops. Miracles can happen." She said the words looking down, staring idly at the cracks in the floor. The rest of the people shuffled out. Then she looked up. "The Gilpin House is on the other side of the Visitors Center. You should stop by and see that, too!!"

Jim knew Natalie would want to at least take a look. "We'll make it quick."

They drove over to the Gilpin House where a couple of people were peering in the windows of the two-story structure, wooden trim painted red to contrast the wall of jagged grey/green stones separated by white weathered mortar.

"This is where Lafayette stayed during the Battle" Jim explained, looking up at the house against the darker grey sky.

"It's incredible that a guy who was barely a 20-year old had such an important impact on the history of our country. I think back to when I was 20… we wanted no part of war or politics, especially since Viet Nam had just ended." Natalie examined the stonework, observing the weathered trim around the windows.

"Me too, but I have to say that I agree with Churchill."

"What do you mean? What about Churchill?"

"He said 'If you're not a liberal when you're young, you have no heart – and if you're not a conservative when you're old, you have no head.'

She laughed and put her arms around his waist. "That's why I love you. You know so much about history. I've come to enjoy it, too." She kissed him lightly on the cheek. "Let's head home. I've had enough adventures for one day."

Natalie walked in and turned on the lights while Jim poured them a glass of wine. She set the IPOD to their favorite cocktail music group, pressing shuffle and stepped over to the terrace door. The white lights strung around the railing sparkled as they waived slightly in the breeze. Then the music stopped and everything got dark.

"Hey... I think we just lost power." Everything was off and Jim could barely make out the kitchen table and couch at the end of the family room in the fading afternoon light. "Time for some candles. I'll get them."

"Unbelievable... this always happens just as we are about to relax" Natalie complained as she approached Jim by the counter. "I was just about to call my sister. Well, I can still call her on the office phone... it's not cordless." She walked in the room holding a candle out in front of her and picked up the receiver. She pressed down on the base a few times. "Hey, that's strange... the phone's dead. I can't even get a dial tone." She put the receiver down and went back into the kitchen, watching Jim light more candles and place them around the room. "Jim, the phone is out too. Isn't that weird?"

"I didn't think the phone was tied to the grid. It's supposed to work regardless of any power."

She went back to the window and noticed that most of the homes in the neighborhood had their lights on. "Jim! Look... everybody else's house is fine. It's just us. What... does that... mean?" His face was barely visible in the candlelight.

"I... don't know. I can't explain it." He looked out the window and saw the lights shining from the neighbor's windows, floodlights lighting up the backyards. His pulse started to race... and he trotted to the side door, checking the lock. "Hey, check the front door... make sure it's locked."

"Why? What's going on?" The candlelight flickered off her face, fear showing in her eyes.

"Just do it!"

"Oh, my God!" She ran up to the front door, turning the lock, then came back to the kitchen. "Do you think it's... Eddy's thugs doing this?" She started to shake and ran up to him, grabbing his arm. "Jim- are we going to be O.K.?"

"Look- don't panic. I... don't know. I just want to be safe." His voice trembled as he took her hands, wrapping them around his waist. "We'll be O.K... don't worry."

"I think you should call the police on your cell phone!! All the other houses have their lights on!! Why is this happening to us??" Tears came down both her cheeks.

"Natalie... don't cry. We're going to be fine!! I... can call the cops… if you want me to…" He wiped each tear away, then gave her a long hug.

"I'm so scared!! Eddy tried to kill us! Now his buddies are going to finish the job!!" The tears kept coming down across her face. "Oh… my God!!"

He walked her in his arms over to the table where four candles shone light all around them, illuminating their faces and the flowers in the vase. "See? Aren't they pretty? Let's calm down for a minute…We're going to be fine… I promise."

The music came on, picking up the jazz piano right where it left off as the sparkling white lights lit up around them on the terrace. He let out a deep breath and kissed her lips. "We're safe. Just a temporary short somewhere…"

Chapter 6

"Louie?" The man with a thick head of very dark brown hair, almost black and piercing blue eyes looked around the parking lot as he held the cell phone close to his ear.

"Yeah. Who's this?"

"It's Vinny. They got Eddy. Mike and Tony are dead... shot by those FBI guys." He started walking around the parking lot to keep warm.

"Is Eddy O.K.?" he said in a low voice as he looked over at his wife sitting on the couch 15 feet away, watching T.V..

"Well, not exactly. Carla called me. He's in the hospital. They think he's paralyzed from the neck down. He fell going down the stairs at Peterson's house... broke his neck. He can talk, though."

"What'll we do now?"

"Yeah... what WILL we do...?" he thought as he looked at the phone in his hand. He remembered when he was six, his father holding him and his brother in his arms as they stood near the dinner table, the embrace making him feel so... safe. Then he recalled how thin and fragile his dad was, spending all his time at the hospital, taking care of patients, never exercising... and he'd been determined to be different, to get tough and strong, like his buddies at Presentation B.V.M... Them trying to show they were tough in all the fights with the public school kids up the street at Penn Wynne... He knew he'd lost respect for him because he'd let his mother boss him around... he wasn't a man in his eyes. Doctor Palamo wanted him to study hard in school and become a professional- a respected man- doctor, lawyer. Vinny wanted none of it... He started lifting weights to get tough like Joey, the biggest kid in the class... who was always in fights... and always won. Getting into Joey's gang was necessary to gain respect among his friends... but then it became much more. "Wow... Has it been that long? I got into the family when I was... 22? Seems like a lifetime ago... yet it's only been six years. I haven't spoken to dad or mom for... over ten..." He wondered what his dad would think of him now, but didn't want to ponder the question. "I'll probably never see him again..." he speculated as he tried to get back and maintain the conversation. He looked over at the delivery truck pulling up to the loading dock and spoke quickly. "The Feds have the $50,000, the notebooks from Thompson with all the stuff on our payments to Leventhal, so they're onto the whole deal by now. We have to LAY LOW... and hope somehow... it doesn't get back to us."

"What about Peterson? He saw all the dope on us, the money..."

"I'll take care of it. He won't be a problem after my next

call. Look, this could get real hot!! The Feds are probably all over Leventhal's offices by now... and they're lookin' for a target. We have to limit the damage and stay under the radar for a while. I'll call you soon." He hung up and quickly dialed again, watching to see if anyone was nearby.

"Hey, Joe... Vinny. I have a job for you." He eyed the parking lot as he spoke, then clicked off the phone and walked back into the meat-packing warehouse...

———⫸⟨⬤⟩⫷———

Jim looked at the Christmas ornaments set up all around the family room, the three embroidered stockings hanging in front of the fireplace, flames burning a yellow curtain below, a fluttering backdrop in the early morning darkness. Walking into the foyer, he saw the white lights above the Conservatory mantle providing a delicate glow to the silvery tree ornaments and reindeer all along its edge. Sadness came over him as he realized it would all be gone soon, replaced by Winter's stark cold. "It all comes and goes so fast" he thought as the firelight cast alternating shadows and light around the room. Then he saw the angel standing in front of the wall, her head delicately laced with flowers amidst a sea of ribbons and lights and he paused, staring at her for several seconds.

"Did she move? No way" he thought, focusing on her face and outstretched arms. Then he sensed it again, the slightest movement of her face in the lights, almost nodding at him as she stood there. As he got lost in her shadowy smile, he saw some movement. He knew it happened. He stepped back to the olive green couch and took in the whole scene. Stillness. Nothing. Looking at the fireplace, he felt the calm wrap its arms around him and he got past the recent drama, looking forward to the days ahead. Walking toward the French doors at the front of the room, he glanced back. Her face was looking right at him and he turned to go into the kitchen.

"Early one today. What time did you get up?" Natalie asked as she took the last step down the staircase.

"Around 5. Couldn't sleep. Just enjoying all the Christmas decorations. Want some coffee?" He walked slowly to the counter, the small window allowing the morning light to high-light the edges of the granite island at the center of the room.

"Sure. I was thinking. We don't have any plans today. This might be a good time to do that historic tour of some of the local inns we always talked about. There are several here in Chester County, some of the oldest in the U.S., within a 30-40 minute drive."

"A superb idea! I've always wanted to check them out."

"Great! I'll bring the camera. We have that book I bought years ago at the Book Barn, 'Inns, Tales and Taverns of Chester County'. Let me get it." She went into her office and grabbed the book from under the window table, adjusting the others to stand upright next to a piece of petrified wood and a carved bull.

Jim opened the book. "Based on this map, we can start at the Red Rose and work our way back. By lunchtime, we should be up around Exton" he determined, looking at the layout of old Inns along Routes 1 and 30.

"Good plan. Red Rose is the launching point, then up to the Barns-Brinton House and the dearly departed Chadds Ford Inn. We can do a reconnaissance of the Ship Tavern for lunch, stop by the General Warren Inn and finish at the Dilworthtown Inn on the way back" she suggested. "Do you think Washington slept there?"

"No, but his troops had martinis nearby after the Battle of Paoli. Had to celebrate something."

She grinned. "Let's get dressed."

Going South from Kennett Square on Route 1, it's easy to understand why farmers in the 1700's and 1800's chose the area to make their living. The countryside is filled with lush grasses in the Spring and fields rising to gently rolling hills without any major obstacles to travel. The soil of the Red Clay Creek watershed is fertile and at times in the Summer there's a strong musty odor, proof that the area has become the mushroom capital of the world.

"General Howe selected this route for several reasons. If he could take the area between the Chesapeake and the Brandywine Valley, he could cut the colonies in half. Also, this region was rich in supplies for the American cause… food, cloth for uniforms, livestock, wagons… even paper for the Continental Currency. What do you think Washington was contemplating before the Battle of the Brandywine?" Jim inquired as he neared the intersection of Route 796 at Jennersville.

"I better win, or else we're up the creek!!"

"He knew that a good portion of the British army was after him, but he couldn't do anything too aggressive, or else he'd lose his shirt- and the war." He turned left and came up to the stoplight at the intersection with Old Baltimore Pike, then turned right into the Red Rose.

She read from the book as the car pulled into the gravel lot. "Says here that the deed of the property dates to 1731 and the payment was 'one red rose on the 24th day of June yearly.' This deed is believed to be the only one of its kind in the country. The practice dated back to feudal times, when lords demanded a pledge in the form of a rose symbolizing both service and freedom from the farmers working the soil." She looked up and saw the back of the solid red brick building. "The structure matches the color of a rose." She closed the book and unbuckled her seat belt as Jim started to get out. They both walked to the front of the building facing the few cars going up and down Old Baltimore Pike as the early morning sun shone down on the property.

"This building is on the highest point of land between the Delaware and Susquehanna Rivers. At one time it was a well travelled dirt trail for both the Lenni-Lenape Indians and the settlers driving their teams of horses as they brought their goods to Philadelphia." He looked at the Red Rose Inn sign, its dark maroon letters on sharp white background in contrast to the earthy, rustic structure all around it. The front door opened quickly.

A man in his early 50's, with dusty brown hair, long over his ears and a thick mustache and goatee walked out onto the stone porch. "Hi there. We're not even close to open. Tavern and restaurant serve at 11:00 a.m. Can I help you?" he asked, giving the half-smile of a store owner wary for thieves, but welcoming visitors.

"We're just checking out the local historical sites. This place was around during the Revolutionary War, wasn't it?" Jim asked, walking toward the porch.

"Sure was… built around 1740… popular trade route. Lot of British sympathizers in the area, supposedly a major reason why Howe chose to attack Philadelphia from the southwest, right through here. The original land grant was paid with a rose and the memorial tradition still continues. Town of Jennersville here got its name because a local doctor who lived next door to the Red Rose was so impressed when Dr. Edward Jenner invented the smallpox vaccine, he called a town meeting and they voted to change the town's name."

"Interesting. The book says the Inn is haunted. Have you heard about any ghosts?" asked Natalie, walking up closer to him, hoping he hadn't tired of questions about sightings over the years.

He stepped down from the porch toward where they were standing. "That's what they say… story's well known. Back in the 1700's, a young girl, the innkeeper's daughter, was murdered and the local residents were enraged. They had only one clue. Some of them had seen her with an Indian earlier that day. They found him and hanged him. Only later did they find the real culprit, a young man drunk in the woods behind the inn. Legend has it the townsfolk were so embarrassed by what they did, they took the Indian's body and buried it in the walls of the tavern's cellar so they wouldn't have to look at it. To this day, people regularly report seeing strange things happening down there, shadows moving, a stale smell, sometimes the smell of perfume, which is what the girl wore before she died."

"Fascinating. I'd love to come back when we can get a look inside." She nudged Jim hoping he'd be open to the idea of looking for the ghosts. He ignored it, watching the Red Rose sign move slightly in the breeze.

"You folks should come back for dinner sometime. We have red roses at every table. Good for Valentine's Day."

Jim looked up. "Not a bad idea. Take care." They walked to the car and she got in, but just before he did, Jim took one last glance at the building. "Doesn't look haunted, but I'll take his word for it." He got in and the car sped back toward Route 1.

"Where to next?" She looked over at him and after a few seconds noticed he seemed preoccupied with something, not responding right away. "Everything O.K.?"

"Not sure. Thought I saw a face in the shadows looking down at us from the third floor window. I heard the upstairs has been closed for years." He looked at her with a blank stare.

"You're serious? What, you think it was a ghost? That Indian?"

"No. Couldn't have been. He didn't have any cigars."

"Hah!! Cute... always making fun of me. What's our next stop?"

"Barns-Brinton House. Check it out in the book. Actually older than the Red Rose, I believe." The SUV sped up the road, nearing the western edge of Kennett Square in less than the usual 16 minutes.

"I found it. Initially a tavern, at the time of the battle, it was the Brinton family residence. Did you know Route 1 used to be on the other side of the building? That's why we see the back of the house when we drive by today."

"Really? New freeways have a way of changing the landscape. It's up the road, no more than a mile on the right. I'll point it out. A very simple brick building. I like brick; you don't see it used much anymore in new homes."

"Guess it's too expensive now. Everything's either prefab or plastic." She looked out the side window. "I wonder which lasts longer... brick or plastic?"

"My money's on brick... but plastic mortar would help" Jim said. Natalie rolled her eyes. "We have to go past the building to get in the parking lot." He drove around the corner and parked. "Unfortunately, we can't go in, it's closed most of the time. Only open for special occasions, like the Tavernkeepers events I worked with the Historical Society. Those were really fun. People in period garb, serving beer, making fresh bread in the oven, demonstrating Colonial-style knitting. It was great." They both got out and walked to the front of the structure. "Pretty simple, right?"

"Very simple. People liked simple things back then. Life was simple. You worked hard. You got married and had a family, went to church and raised chickens, or became a merchant. Though simple didn't necessarily mean less stressful" she commented.

"I like chicken, sautéed with scallions and a bit of white wine."

"Sometimes I think the things we have to make life simpler

just make it more complicated – like computers, cell phones and Blackberrys. We can't live without them, yet they have a way of controlling us, adding more stress. I try to avoid stress whenever I can." She gazed up at the old oak door, its brown wood rimmed with dark scarlet bricks, a symbol of strength to her. "Look at that. It's basic, but beautiful."

"I agree. To me it's a symbol of American strength. You know, the Hessian troops under General Knyphausen, who were supporting Howe in the battle against Washington, marched right by here that day. They tried to destroy everything in their path so the Colonials wouldn't have anything left... but the house stood. Pretty good for a 250-year-old tavern... and the tavern survives. Beer's a little stale by now."

"Funny!" She continued to view the front of the building as cars roared by.

"The structure was immortalized in a painting by a local artist, Rubincam, 'Hessians Marching by the Barns-Brinton House.' He focused on the door and felt its simplicity as he put his hand along the frame. "Ready?"

"Yes. Want to stop by the Chadds Ford Inn? They give it a great write-up in the book." She started walking with him back to the car.

"That ship has sailed. The owners of the place either didn't like the rustic appearance, or couldn't afford the upkeep. It's too bad. The atmosphere is what I and everyone else loved about the place." He started the car and pulled back out onto the highway. "Remember the first night we met? I was waiting for you there, standing outside on the porch as the fog rolled in, it was a stormy day."

"I remember you were a complete gentleman. We had a glass of wine by candlelight and some hors d'oeurves, the fireplace going. It was a lovely way to meet. You took me upstairs to see the ghosts - you said. Later I found out it really was to see if you could sneak a kiss" she recalled, smiling.

"Well it's definitely haunted. I think they had a PBS crew there with parapsychologists. The stone fireplaces... candlelight in the tavern... the place was wonderful. Why did they have to mess with a good thing?" He kept driving up the road.

"When restaurants change hands, the new owners often do something completely different. Remember the 'fern bars' in the 1970's? For a while, it seemed like you couldn't go into a bar without there being a bunch of ferns hanging all around" she recalled.

"I liked Fernwood 2 Night and Mary Hartman Mary Hartman. Remember the Gong Show and the Unknown Comedian? The guy who used to wear the brown paper bag over his head and another over his hand, like he was a ventriloquist? That was hilarious."

"I guess, in a strange sort of way. Not sure those shows would fly today."

They pulled into the parking lot at Brandywine Prime. The wooden porch was rimmed with gaslamps, all unlit at that time of day. Walking to the front, he glanced around the porch. "They got rid of the 13-star Colonial flag. I loved that flag. Used to have big bales of hay, pumpkins and the flag flying around Halloween and Thanksgiving. It's all gone now. Want to go inside?"

"We don't have to. It's not the same, anyway. I'll just keep the memory alive in my head" she decided. "Book says the Inn bears the name of one of the first residents in the area, John Chadsey, who settled here around 1702. His son started and operated the only known ferry in this region crossing the Brandywine, which remained in service for nearly 100 years. Chadsey shortened his name to Chad and opened a tavern. The spot was so popular with travelers, the name of the town eventually changed from Birmingham to Chadd's Ford, due to people telling other travelers about the tavern at "Chad's ford-ing place, people later adding the extra 'd'.""

"If I were driving a team of horses all day long, I'd stop for a grog. Nice area." He examined the outside of the structure, largely unchanged from the night they met. "At least that's left."

"Another sad story, though. The proprietor of the tavern, in the days leading up to the battle, hosted Colonial troops here and they all toasted to victory. Many of those same men lay dying in the dirt out front at day's end on September 11, 1777. The British plundered local farms and slaughtered over 200 cattle on the grounds all around here, then ravaged the Inn, taking everything. Tavernkeeper apparently had the largest loss of anyone in Chester County after the melee." She examined the building for a moment. "I hear they kept some of the Wyeth paintings anyway. Want to go?"

"Let's." They walked back toward the car without saying a word, but just as they were getting in a man came out the tavern side door facing the parking lot and stood there on the porch.

"You folks looking for something?"

"We were just talking about the history of the area – visiting some of the old Inns."

"Well, did you know that this parking area, right around there, was where George Washington held council with his top advisors to discuss their troop positions just before the Battle of Brandywine?"

"No, though I did know he stayed down the road at the Ring House."

"Right there, where you two are standing. Washington chose Chad's ford because it was the closest place for Howe's troops to cross the Brandywine. Most of the nearby fords were impassible due to heavy rains, making the Brandywine a perfect place to counter Howe's march towards Philadelphia. Unfortunately, Washington didn't consider that Howe would be willing to split his force in half. He had a smaller group stay at Chad's Ford, engaging in mock attacks to distract Washington, while the larger force traveled six miles north and three miles east, crossing the Brandywine twice… at Trimble Ford and Jeffries Ford, led by a local Tory. The maneuver allowed Howe's army to flank Washington." He motioned around the lot, a couple of cars parked at the end. "Come in for a martini sometime. We're thinking about adding some hanging ferns in the Spring, too!" He turned and went back inside.

Natalie turned to Jim, a look of disbelief in her eyes.

"I'm sure he's just kidding. Well, I did learn something new about this place. If he's the owner, at least he seems to know some history." They left, pulling out onto Route 100 going

North. He thought for several minutes as the car wound past
the woods in back of Hanks, then up past John Chad's House
with the small sign out in front. "I have an idea." He looked
up to the right and saw the old stone house on the hillside, its
façade sharp against the late morning sky. "I'd like to start an
historic driving tour of the Inns in this area. We could do five
or six of them in an afternoon, under three hours. Start at the
Red Rose, come up to the Barns-Brinton House and Chadds
Ford Inn. I still have to use the old name. Next, head to the
others off Lancaster Avenue. Make it a late afternoon wine and
cheese tour with a van or small bus. We could do it through
the Historical Society! We're members and I've volunteered for
things before. They know me." He waited for a reaction.

"Sounds feasible. How much would you charge?"

"We'd have to cover the cost of the van, printing flyers and
any materials we hand out- and the wine and cheese at each
location. Make it six stops, with a place set aside by each Inn to
have the event. We could have the speaker do a summary discussing the history of the Inn and the role it played during the
Revolution. To keep costs down, we'd limit the group to maybe
ten people, who could easily fit in one of those oversized vans.
Cost maybe $45, with a ticket stub giving everyone one drink at
each location, plus some light snacks. If anyone wanted more
drinks, they could buy them separately. We might even get the
Society to donate use of a van, or a speaker for the tour." He
glanced over at her to see whether she looked interested.

"Why would they do that?"

"Because, my dear, the trip would end at the Chadds Ford

Historical Society, where they'd be given a short tour and asked if they want to shop in the store… perhaps become members. It's a win-win."

"I like it, but someone would have to drive me home after six drinks. Don't we turn up there on Route 30?" She looked out the window and saw the Inn, cars slowing to turn at the light.

"We do, indeed." He saw the sign out front as they approached the Inn. "Nice ship. I'd like to take a cruise on that."

Walking into the Ship Inn, they sensed that the owners wanted to preserve its history. The side entrance took them past the oak and brass bar located in the original room from the 1700's, with the huge stone fireplace in the corner. Inside the fireplace stood the original carved tablet reading '25M to P' indicating it was a 25 mile journey to Philadelphia, the capital of the Colonies at the time. They sat down at the bar and Jim noticed the side room to the left, wallpapered in ornamental Colonial-period style, with a ship in each square and a wooden masthead perched on the wall overlooking the scene.

"Can I get you folks some drinks?" The bartender was a man in his early 40's, very short dark brown hair, wearing black pants and a white shirt. His voice was sharp, but pleasant.

"You bet, drinks and lunch. Two menus, please. We'll each have a glass of cabernet… help warm us up."

"Sure thing." He brought back the wine and the menus. "Here you go."

"This place is lovely. I bet they've put a lot into restoration"

Natalie commented before she took her first sip.

Jim looked around the bar, pausing to peer at the oversized fireplace, a heavy copper kettle hanging down in the center. The bartender returned and waited for their order. "We'll have something simple – the calamari, soup of the day and salad for each of us."

"Very good. Coming right up, sir."

"Want to do a little exploring? We can walk around while they get our food." He got up from his seat and headed toward the side dining room, past the reception stand where a waitress stood.

"Feel free to walk around. We have fireplaces going in all the rooms."

"I'm coming." Natalie caught up with Jim down the hall. "Look at that... what a beautiful fireplace. This is a romantic room. The book says these were the original rooms used by travelers who spent the night back in the 1800's."

"There's another fireplace blazing in that room. It's what you'd expect a rustic country inn to look like. We'll have to come back for dinner sometime." They circled back to the bar where their food was already sitting on the counter. "Great. That was quick."

He took another sip of cabernet and asked the bartender. "Do you know much of the history of this place?"

"Well, I know it's been here since the late 1700's. This is the original building."

"Does it have a scary basement?" Natalie interjected.

"What do you mean? Scary- how?"

"You know, dark and dank with an old dirt floor, lots of cobwebs… maybe a ghost or two, buried skeletons. Things like that."

"I don't think so. The floor's cement, plenty of light. It's cool, so we store the wine along with general supplies down there. I do remember one of the waitresses a year or so ago swore she not only saw a shadow rush by her, but claims something bumped into her. She was the only one in the cellar at the time. I've never seen or heard anything." The bartender was pouring a beer from the tap for another customer.

"I don't believe in ghosts. It's not scientific" Jim scoffed, finishing his wine and pushing the glass forward, hoping the bartender would notice it was empty.

"I do. I believe there are spirits in us, all around us. Once you come into being, your spirit never dies. You've got scientific training - remember what Einstein said? 'Matter can neither be created nor destroyed.' Once that energy is here, in someone's soul, it's here forever, in some form." She took a small sip while waiting for his reaction.

"Sounds fair. Not sure if I want them pouncing on me at Happy Hour."

"I believe ghosts, even other life forms, are possible." Natalie turned to the bartender. "Can I have a look downstairs?"

"Well, I guess. It's not busy here yet. Just a quick one. Let's go, follow me." He sauntered around the bar and headed for the back hallway.

"I'll just stay up here and hold down the fort" Jim said, lifting his glass to them. "Good hunting! Let me know if I should call Ghostbusters" he added, chuckling to himself.

The bartender unlocked a splintered old door and walked down the stairs, flipping on the light.

When they reached the bottom, Natalie looked around, disappointed. The walls were freshly painted white, the floors cleanly swept cement... not a spider or creepy shadow in sight. The large room, about 40 feet x 40 feet, was nothing more than a well kept storage area.

"See, I told you. Nothing spooky here. Ready to head back up?" he said.

"I guess you're right, but I'd still like to look around" Natalie remarked, scanning the neatly stacked boxes of supplies along the walls lined with metal and plywood shelving.

"Whatever. I'll wait here, but you need to be quick."

"Oh, I will... don't worry!" Natalie wandered towards the middle of the room to get a better perspective. Glancing around, she noticed everything was spotless and neatly stacked. "Unlikely I'll find any ghosts here" she thought. She read some of the boxes... Brawny Paper Towels, Maxwell's Colonial Candles, Pepperidge Farm Breadcrumbs and Quaker Corn Meal.

The bartender picked his teeth and looked down at his watch. Natalie headed toward the back wall which opened to another room. Looking in the smaller area, maybe 10 feet wide and 12 feet long, all she saw were more shelves filled with boxes. The space was darker, relying on the light from the main room. The walls had yellowed over time and the boxes were covered with a light coating of dust. "Probably holds the junk they don't use very often" she decided. She entered the room and examined the items on the shelves, not sure what she was looking for. "Well, nothing reads 'Witches Brew... Store in a cool, dark area'." She strolled around, then shrugged, turning to leave. The main room's light spread across the shelving and broke through a gap in the boxes, illuminating a small section of the back wall. Natalie stopped.

Leaning against the railing, half asleep, the bartender jolted upright at the first loud thud, then heard two more. He sprinted toward the back, panicked that something had come toppling down on Natalie as she bumped into it. "What was I thinking, letting a customer down here? If she's injured, we could get sued. Probably lose my job, too" he grimaced as he rounded the corner and halted.

"Don't just stand there! Help me get these boxes off the shelf" Natalie instructed as she dropped another one on the floor.

"What are you doing? I thought a box fell on you. You can't move those!"

"See the wall? There might be a door behind this shelf. Help me get these boxes down so I can get a better look."

"What?! No... stop, now!" he ordered.

She peered over at him, then approached within a foot of his face. "Come on... don't be such a wuss! This could be important! Maybe your waitress was onto something after all."

The bartender just stared as she turned around and continued setting the boxes down. Natalie then grabbed the empty metal shelf and struggled to pull it away from the wall.

"Hold on... let me help before you knock everything over."

He easily slid the shelf out of the way.

They both stared at the imprint in the wall, at most five feet high and two feet wide. Natalie scraped along the edges, trying to get her nails into the crack, but was stopped by the bartender. "I think I can get it. There's a long screwdriver over on the utility table where we came in."

He went back into the light, thinking "What the hell am I doing?" Returning to the wall, he put the screwdriver into the cracks, trying to clear out some of the built-up paint. He then shoved it into the right edge and pulled with both hands, but it didn't budge.

"Try again… I'm sure you're strong enough" she asserted, a bit sarcastically.

He shrugged and pulled again. The door creaked, but held firm.

"Push against it first before pulling. That should break the paint seal."

"Alright, one last time… here goes." He kicked the door, then pulled again with the screwdriver. The door opened slowly, screeching as the rusty hinges moved.

Natalie leaned forward, trying to see around the bartender and into the area behind the door. "What do you see?"

"Nothing, it's pitch black in there. Looks like a small hallway or storage area."

"Let's go in, check it out! Maybe there's a few skeletons hanging from shackles on the walls" she said, grinning.

He looked back at Natalie, frowning, but she was already pushing past him and ducking into the dark passage. "Hey, wait! You can't go in there! Damn… women" he muttered to himself. He opened the door all the way to let in as much light as possible and headed in after her. "Wait up!"

Within a few steps the light faded to complete darkness. Stooping to avoid the low ceiling, he put his arms out in front of him as he slowly took each step. "I can't see anything in here!"

Natalie stopped, feeling along the walls, waiting for her eyes to adjust. "You wouldn't happen to have a lighter or flashlight, would you?"

"No… and don't go any further."

"I won't, we need more light, but there is definitely something down there. I can't really make it out." Natalie looked down and noticed that her feet were covered in dust from the dirt floor. "This place hasn't been disturbed for decades" she thought, trying to see what was on the ceiling above them. She felt her hair and sensed something odd. "What… is this?" She put her hand in front of her face, but could barely see what was on it. "This feels… very strange… kind of sticky."

"O.K., let's get out of here, now" he said firmly.

"Only if you promise we can come right back with a flashlight."

"Fine" he said, knowing full well he had no intention of letting her back down there again.

Natalie felt an icy breeze blow past her face. The door shrieked shut, instantly enveloping them in pitch black. Natalie's heart jumped and they both ran back to the door, stumbling.

"Fuck!" shouted the bartender as he hit his head on the

low ceiling. He pushed against the door, but it didn't budge. He pushed again.

"Push harder!" Natalie yelled as she came up behind him, putting her hands on his back.

"I am! It's not moving. HELP!!! SOMEONE... WE'RE TRAPPED!!" He waited, then called out again. Several minutes passed as he caught his breath, hoping someone from the bar would hear him.

"Hey! Cut that out! What are you trying to do?!" Natalie shouted.

"What are you talking about? We need help getting out" he said angrily.

"You just put your hand on my ass! Cut it out!"

"You're crazy, lady! How can I do that when you're standing behind me?"

"Look... keep your hands off!"

"It's not me! We have to get this door open... now!" He stepped back, then started to run toward the door, putting the full weight of his body against it, shoulder first. The door opened easily and he went sprawling across the floor.

Natalie ran past him into the light, then stopped to look back. "What was that?"

"What?!" He got up from the floor, rubbing his left shoulder. "Owww!"

"I just saw something dark cross that wall – over there!" She pointed to the far corner.

"Probably one of our shadows... lets get going."

"No, there's not enough light in here to make a shadow,

plus it didn't look like a shadow. It looked… darker, more defined."

He saw her face, knowing she was serious. "Come on! Let's get outta' here."

They sprinted up the stairs and into the bar. Natalie turned to see him locking the basement door behind them.

"Hey wait, let's go back down with a flashlight!"

"Not on my watch, lady!" He brushed the dirt off his arms and wiped his hair back into place.

"See anything interesting?" Jim asked.

"I'll tell you later" she replied, shimmying onto the stool and grabbing her glass of cabernet.

"Alright… must have been pretty uneventful, I guess."

Natalie looked at the bartender, but he busied himself pouring drinks, refusing to acknowledge her glances. Gaining his composure, he gazed over at her once, then went back to the far edge of the bar.

"Do you know the story of the old sign?" Jim asked as the bartender poured a glass of cabernet in front of him.

He topped off Jim and Natalie's glass, avoiding eye contact with her. "Not exactly. Original sign disappeared a long time ago."

"Story goes that Thomas Park, the owner of the Inn in the 1700s, was an avid supporter of the British Crown. Hated the Colonial revolutionaries, called them traitors, criminals. Well, a few days after the Battle of the Brandywine, a group of Colonial soldiers stopped by the Inn for some refreshment. Park turned them away, saying he refused to serve rabble rousers. The troops protested as they were thrown out of the Inn. After leaving, the men shot 13 holes into the wooden sign, signifying the young Colonies in their fight for independence. In the months after the incident, business at the Inn dropped off considerably, forcing Park to close. It was called 'the patriot's curse' - his allegiance to a cause which later proved to be on the wrong side. Park went out of business, but a few years later a new owner friendly to the Colonials bought the name, including the sign and built a new tavern here." Jim took a long sip from the glass.

"Didn't know that. You folks enjoy your day" he said as he handed Jim the bill, hoping they would leave soon. His tone had changed from pleasant to terse. He watched as they put on their coats to leave a few minutes later.

Heading east on Route 30, locally known as Lancaster Avenue, Natalie finally said something to break the silence. She watched him for several seconds before speaking. "It really happened."

"What happened?"

"The basement IS haunted. We found an old door that was painted over and managed to pry it open. We went inside this narrow space and then the door slammed shut – all by itself- I swear!! It was completely dark… we couldn't see anything. Then I felt something… or someone… touch me. We pushed and tried to get through, but the door wouldn't budge. He finally forced it open and we got out… but then I saw something dark move across the wall. Maybe just a shadow… but it looked so… strange. I know it was a ghost… "

"Sounds pretty scary. Glad I didn't go down with you." He

looked at the road, then extended his right arm to bring her close to him, kissing her. The car slowed down as they approached the parking lot of the General Warren Inn, stopping 20 feet from the painted white stone building. He turned off the ignition. "Ghost Riders innnnn... the sky!!!"

She squinted, then shrugged. "I'm telling you it HAPPENED! Someday you'll believe me." Picking up the book, she flipped to the section on the General Warren Inn, putting their conversation behind her.

"I seem to remember there's some interesting history about this place, too" Jim commented.

"There is." She looked at the pages under the dashboard light. "On the night of September 20th, 1777, Howe's troops under Majors Grey and Andre marched through here in the darkness. They met up with a local blacksmith, wearing a blue patriot coat, who secretly guided them to General Wayne's encampment. Less than an hour later, the British butchered some 200 of the Colonial soldiers in what became known as the Paoli Massacre."

She stopped to look up at the Inn, then focused again on the book in her hands. "Rumors circulated as to how General Wayne escaped. One said that in the early morning hours, as there was more light for the British troops to identify those fleeing, Wayne turned his jacket inside out, showing the red interior so as not to attract attention. Thus was born the term 'turncoat'." They got out and walked around the structure, Natalie taking a couple of photographs.

"Ready to head for the Dilworthtown Inn?"

"Sure... Let's move on."

He drove back down Route 30, taking Route 202 South, finding the road much more crowded with traffic. "I've never been on 202 when there wasn't a long line of cars in front of me." He turned onto the side road and parked by the inn. "Right there is the Dilworthtown Country Store, said to be one of the oldest continuously operating general stores in the U.S."

"Why do they call them general stores? Where did that come from?" She looked through the side window before they got out.

"Served Generals. General Wayne, General Washington, Howe."

"Well that explains it!"

"Explains what?" He glanced at her face to see if she was serious.

"That's where the term 'generality' came from. I try to avoid making them."

"Seriously, they sold a wide variety of items, not generally available on the farm or even at nearby road stands. Thus, the term 'general store'.

"Book says the place has been here since 1758, over 250 years, as a general store and saddlery. British took it from the owner, Charles Dilworth. After using it temporarily as a prison for Colonial troops, the Brits wrecked the place, causing over 820 British pounds worth of damage in sterling, equivalent to over $2,000. Doesn't sound like much to us, but that was an enormous amount in those days. Later accounts state that Dilworth sustained among the worst damages to property, livestock, dry goods and building structure... in the entire region." She looked at the edge of the property and saw a huge oak tree, its branches bare in the brisk wintry breeze. "That tree over there was a hanging tree. The Colonials hung James Fitzpatrick – Fitz - for allowing the British to attack General Wayne and kill all those soldiers at Paoli."

He looked at the tree, then at the historic buildings up and down the street. He stared up at the sky, now a deep, dark charcoal blue, the last rays fading toward the horizon, the late afternoon light blanketing the scene in a warm glow. "Do you ever feel this is not an accident?"

"What do you mean?"

"That all this happened for a reason? A special purpose? The people in the fledgling government back then, flawed as they were, did something that the world had never seen before. They established a country and a government for the people. Not just for those in power - and not just for a lucky few. For all the people. I know, the argument goes that these were all rich men who owned slaves, who didn't give a damn about anyone unless they had property or owned a business. Well, maybe at first glance that was true, but look at what they did. They put in place a system which has become the envy of the world. Not bad for a bunch of rich landowners."

"Yes, but many of them did own slaves. I just can't reconcile that with what we know is fair and reasonable today. It seems so hypocritical."

"I know, some of them owned slaves. Washington owned slaves- so did Jefferson. Yet, they both felt it was something that had to end. It was legal back then, but thank God some enlightened minds knew that it was a practice against the very grain of our souls. Jefferson wanted to put a clause in the Declaration that would have freed the slaves, but the wealthy landowners in the Southern states wouldn't agree to it. They stripped it from the final document." He observed the scenery and thought how different the world would have been if they'd been able to get that one line included.

"So Jefferson was on the record as being for the abolition of slavery, he was just overruled?"

"Exactly. He was way ahead of the rest of the country on that one. Did you know Washington actually had all his slaves freed after he died?"

"No, but I'm glad he did" she said, looking up at the sky.

"E Pluribus unum- 'from many, one'. From their notions, a new nation. They were honorable men. Many were strongly against slavery. Like Thomas Garrett, who lived right nearby in Upper Darby. He helped thousands of black men and women to their freedom via the Underground Railroad in Chester County. This place... this country... our nation, despite its many flaws... was truly blessed... by Divine Providence. God was guiding them." They walked back to the parking lot and started to get into the car. Jim stopped as Natalie closed her door. He stared at the old oak tree, still strong, its base more than three feet wide, the many branches extending out over the edge of the property. The late afternoon light was bathing the tree in a warm yellow glow. He knew there would be many buds in the Spring.

Chapter 7

Rawlins stared at the 'Most Wanted' posters, the weekly updates on the corkboard across the room and then picked up the phone, pressing in the numbers he was reading from the case file in front of him. On the third ring the voice came through.

"This is Jim." He looked out past the terrace and saw the same red fox nibbling the extra nuts he'd scattered at the base of the bird feeder, a welcome treat in the early Winter.

"Mr. Peterson, this is Agent Rawlins."

"Hi. What's the latest on the investigation?" Natalie heard him as he spoke and approached his side.

"Well, mostly good. Some, well, not so good. We've analyzed everything in the satchel you gave us from Gay Head Beach. Edward Caniletto is alive, barely, but we believe still very much involved with mob connections in New York and Philadelphia. He's been in the hospital and will probably never walk again... paralyzed from the neck down. Maybe that'll hamper his activities a bit. The papers we examined, all the account statements, along with the notebook detailing the payoffs to

Leventhal, led us to some very interesting connections."

"What connections?"

"We'd been monitoring three different Pennsylvania Congressmen with suspected ties to the mob- Bartlesby, Konigsson and Youngblood. The latest financial and anti-terrorism tools allow us to trace cash flows of $10,000 or more to and from any financial institution worldwide, along with monitoring unusual patterns of transactions between various parties. These three seem to have been on the mob payroll for at least the last year, perhaps much longer. We won't know until we analyze more records. Appears these same Congressmen also have close friends or family members who own antique shops in the tri-state area which have been suspected of dealing with the mob. The Mafia is getting pretty mainstream these days, trying every legitimate type of business to launder money and hide their activities. I mentioned the names of the Congressmen because one, you may see them in the news soon and two, it's possible that somehow through their mob network, you may become intertwined." He took a cigarette out of the pack and lit it as he put it to his lips.

Jim grimaced as he heard the last words and tried not to look up at Natalie. "What about the investment accounts? Any news there?"

"Oh, yes. A lot. A very close friend of Jack Leventhal himself is U.S. Senator John Harding of Delaware, who happens to be on the RICO Committee investigating Mafia activities. We suspect he's not only gotten kickbacks from Leventhal for keeping his mouth shut, but has actually approached two other

U.S. Senators on that committee- Senator Gilchrist from New York and Senator Cogway from Maryland, offering cash if they pull back on the investigation."

"Now that's pretty shocking. Who would've guessed a satchel on the beach containing some cash would lead all the way up to the United States Senate?"

"It goes a bit further. Senator Gilchrist is also on the Financial Regulatory Committee investigating potential corrupt practices on Wall Street! No wonder Harding offered him a payoff. Gilchrist was Finance Director for the Committee to Elect the President and was also a major beneficiary of donations and volunteer support at OAKTREE, a grassroots organization with offices nationwide. They're about to be indicted for illegal lobbying and money laundering activities in six states." He took a long drag off the cigarette. "This thing could have legs that have walked all around Washington- and may still be walking."

"Sounds like a pretty big circle. What about all the papers I found in the satchel?" Jim gazed up at Natalie and shook his head.

"Even more interesting. Turns out the bond traders at Leventhal are under investigation by another unit on the team for deliberately giving bogus bids to create excess volatility in the markets. One of their equity portfolio managers has already been arrested on several counts of securities fraud for posting fictitious values to client statements. We expect to arrest most of the other ones there pretty soon... eight in all." Rawlins finished the cigarette, grinding it into the stone ashtray

LAFAYETTE'S GOLD

— 109 —

he'd gotten as a souvenir many years back in Santa Fe.

"Where does that leave Natalie and me? Are Eddy's buddies on the prowl? Are we safe?" Natalie put her hand on Jim's shoulder, leaning closer to see if she could hear Rawlins reply.

"We have a guy watching your neighborhood on a regular basis and we're monitoring all of Caniletto's friends. We're on it."

"Well, that makes me feel a bit better. Just watch our home, don't let your guard down." He finally looked up at her. Natalie's expression was deadpan, as if someone had just told her they were repossessing the house.

"One last bit of news... this one good. You were so helpful with the information you gave us, we don't think we'll need you to testify. We may have an agent stop over with a few more questions, though... maybe in the next day or two."

"Fine with me... and great news. We really don't have to testify?"

"Nope, you're done... but we'll be in touch."

"Thanks very much!!" He put his left arm around her waist and gave her a long hug.

"Thank you, Jim." He hung up the phone and closed the folder on his desk.

"Good news, babe... we don't have to testify."

"That's great!!"

"They're also watching the neighborhood closely, so none of Eddy's guys get near us. Eddy won't ever again... he's paralyzed." He stood and wrapped his arms around her. "These guys are on top of it, they've got it under control. For the first time since that night, I feel safe with Rawlins and his team watching over us. There's nothing to worry about." He kissed her gently and rubbed his nose against hers.

"I feel much better." She kissed him and looked at the pale blue sky through the window. "How about a treat today? Let's go to one of your favorite places" Natalie suggested.

"O.K... Where's that?"

"Let's take a drive over to the Book Barn. You can pick out a book on local history and I'll buy."

"Hey... that sounds great! Let's do it!"

They drove up Route 52, past Natalie's old neighborhood where she grew up as a child and continued towards West Chester. Halfway there they pulled off the winding country road onto the gravel parking lot of the old building. Baldwin's Book Barn is located in a 200 year old converted farmhouse set in the rolling hills of Chester County. Its four floors contain rows of dusty shelves filled with used books stacked floor to ceiling, often three deep in some corners, giving you the feeling that the owners had so many books, they lost track of them all.

"I'll pick out one book... a history book... but I may get something else, if I see a Hemingway I don't own.

"You get whatever you want. This is on me." They entered the front door and a small bell rang.

"Hello! Welcome to the Book Barn. Let me know if I can help with anything" came the greeting from behind the counter. The silver-haired man with dark horn-rim glasses was pleasant, a friendly voice from someone who'd served thousands of book lovers over the years.

"Yes, actually you can. Where's your Revolutionary War section?" asked Jim as he stepped toward the small, black wood-burning stove near the back of the room.

"That'll be up on the second floor in the far corner."

"Great." He and Natalie walked past the shelves overflowing with books toward the narrow wooden stairway which had a low, overhanging beam. On it was a sign reading 'Duck or grouse'.

"Look at all these books! I could live here" Jim exclaimed as he put his hands on the side of the staircase, the floorboards creaking slightly with each step.

"I really enjoy books. Let's hope they don't completely disappear with E-books and the Internet."

Jim stopped at the next floor and looked around the room, old books everywhere. He thought about how much his life had been enriched by the great stories he'd read over the years. "It's unthinkable. Let's make sure it never happens – just keep buying me books."

She chuckled. "O.K. Shakespeare – where's the American history section?"

"Right over there." They passed the several bookshelves, many just old wooden fruit crates stacked to the ceiling, filled with more books. "I think it's… right… here." He leaned over and saw several familiar titles. "Now if I could just find something on the Battle of the Brandywine."

"I'm going to wander around. Let me know if you find anything good." She walked to the other corner and ducked behind a short wall separating the stacked books from a small storage area that appeared abandoned and encased in dust. Workmen's tools were scattered on the shelves next to old, damaged books covered in cobwebs. She glanced at the shelf in front of her. "Now that's interesting. An old key… rusted badly. What's it doing here with all these old books?" she thought. She picked it up and then grabbed one of the leather-bound volumes. "Hmmm… this looks very old." As she opened the book slowly, its corners frayed, dust fell from the page as she read the title sheet. 'The Printer Boy, Or How Ben Franklin Made His Mark' by William M. Thayer, Boston, J.E. Tilton and Company, 1861. She picked up another book and opened it. "What is this?" She held the title page with her right hand as she pulled a thin grey-white sheet away. "Hey, I found something! Come over here."

Jim slowly rose to his feet and felt the tingle in his legs, signs that the circulation had resumed after squatting in front of the bookshelf for a few minutes. "I'm coming."

She held the opened book in her hands as he stepped in front of her. "Look… this one's from the 1850's… 'An Inquiry into the Formation of Washington's Farewell Address'. I can't see the author, but the preface is by Horace Binney, Philadelphia, August 9, 1859. All of these books look to be about 150 years old."

Jim took the book carefully in his hands and examined it after pulling out his reading glasses. He focused on the wafer-thin sheet. "A tissue guard… you only find these in really old books… looks like there's faint writing on it, too. It's pretty faded, but you can tell it's not recent because it was written in script- and with a fountain pen. People rarely use them anymore." He held the sheet delicately in his left hand and looked at it closely. "I see several lines, though I can barely read them." He brought the book closer and stared at it intently. "Signed Joshua Pyle."

"Could be valuable" Natalie suggested as she leaned over and squinted, trying to read Pyle's words on the fragile paper.

"Don't know… could be. Let's buy this one. We wanted a book about Washington anyway." He held the dark brown leather-bound volume in his hands and noted the binding was badly cracked. The book's edges were scraped, showing the interior of the cover material, now weathered, stained a rust-color and frayed. "Looks like there's several more old ones right over there." He pointed to the dusty bookshelf and walked up to it, putting the book down on an old black iron anvil sitting on the desk. "Perhaps we should pick up one of these books, too. Maybe they'll give us a deal if we buy a few."

"Always looking for a discount- a treasure at Wal-Mart prices."

"Why not? We can bargain with them. Store owners know people look for good deals. Look at all these books! There's got to be over 100,000 volumes in this place. How can they keep all this inventory?!"

"They're book lovers… like us. Thank God for books. The keepers of knowledge… and good friends on a rainy day."

He kissed her cheek, knowing she was his best find ever. "Let's check out at a few more of these… and if there's anything else worth buying, we'll get them, too."

"I agree. Look at this one... 'The Poems of Allan Ramsay', 1813 and these... 'Irving's Life of Washington', 1857 and 'Society in America' by Hamlet, 1837."

Hearing Washington, he drifted off…

———◦((◦))◦———

Small fires were burning in the near distance, their glow difficult to detect, as soldiers sauntered out of their tents…

"Gentlemen… at attention!!" The major yelled from atop the brown speckled muscular horse as he gazed at the line of canvas tents pitched in between the oak and beech trees scattered along the river. The fog showed signs of slowly lifting, the mist dissipating as the morning light bathed the landscape. Soldiers quickly left the confines of their tents and saluted, lining up in front of him.

"The British under Howe are estimated to be in a force of over 10,000, perhaps as many as 18,000 nearby. We will NOT let them have the field today. Is that clear??!!"

"Yes, sir!!" echoed the shouts from the hundreds of men standing at attention.

"Very well, then. Keep an eye out for the enemy. They may be within a mile of where we now stand." The mist rose around his horse as it stood motionless, eyes pointed toward the small grasses at its feet…

———◦((◦))◦———

"Ready to go, honey?"

The lovely voice that had greeted him for the last several

years brought him back. "Oh, yes. We can go. I was somewhere else... I was there..."

"Well, sounds interesting. Want to take these downstairs? We have enough books for today."

"These three should hold me for the evening. Let's pay and head home."

Chapter 8

"Well, our trip to the Book Barn certainly added some interesting items to our collection. I have one other book that's about this old. Years ago, must have been in the early 1970's, the Penn Wynne Library near where I grew up had a book sale. They had hundreds of volumes stacked on tables in front of the building. I looked through them, but didn't find anything I wanted- until I saw this golden brown, embossed leather volume, with the edges very weathered and torn. The cover had no title, just an elaborately imprinted design, which they don't do anymore. The book was clearly well over 100 years old. I opened it and there was no price listed, so they gave it to me for free. The title is 'Quits', a novel by the Baroness Tautphoeus, author of 'The Initials'. It's identified as being published in Philadelphia by J.B. Lippincott & Company, 1863. A name I can only partly decipher... 'Herman P. Kohan' is scrawled in black fountain pen across the title page. On the back inside cover, the name Sir John X. Byer is written, also in fountain pen. That was the first time in my life I had held something so old in my hands."

"Did you ever find out if the book is worth anything?" asked Natalie as they sat at the glass table, the first heavy frost of the season coating the terrace around them in silver.

"No... never did. Intend to. I'll do a search. Anyone with 'Sir' in front of their name was either a nobleman or a wealthy merchant back then." Then he thought of the book they'd just bought at the Book Barn- even older than the one he prized in his collection- and he sensed he had something special. "I'm going to examine that tissue guard a bit closer."

"What? You mean in the book we just got?"

"Yes. I could barely make out the words, but I have a good magnifying glass there in the drawer. Let me get it." He walked over to the small pale green and rust colored wooden desk on the side of the kitchen and got the glass, then took the bag from the Book Barn and came back to the table. "The best adventures are in your mind..."

He opened the copy of 'Washington's Farewell Address' and saw the delicate tissue guard with the handwriting on it. With the magnifying glass focused on the page, he spoke slowly. "I can just barely make this out. It's difficult to read... 'On my dying father, loyal to the King, a note I find.' Not too bad for a first try. I'm surprised I could even read that much. 'Hid while the waters lapped nearby.' The rest of this line is tough. It says 'House where the rainbow ends' and next is 'Out of place at the steps to nowhere.'" He looked up at Natalie with a confused expression and saw she had been leaning very close to see the words. "Sounds like a cryptic message. Clues to something hidden?"

"Maybe. Why don't we do an Internet search on the name Joshua Pyle and the author of the book? There may not be any relation, but who knows?"

"Good idea, but I also want to go back to our source. The guy at the Book Barn must know where they got the book, perhaps an estate sale. There could be some clues there. I'm going to call him." He went over to the counter and dialed the cordless phone.

"Baldwin's Book Barn. How can I help you?"

"Hi. This is Jim Peterson. My wife and I were just in your shop. We bought a few old books. One of them is 'Washington's Farewell Address' by Horace Binney, dated 1859."

"Oh, yes... I recall the book. We picked up a couple of boxes filled with books about a month ago at an estate sale in Radnor. I believe many of them were from the 1830's to the 1880's."

"Right. Well, this one has a tissue guard signed by Joshua Pyle. Know anything about him?"

"No, I don't, but I do know the estate name, Matthew Pyle, who used to own the Red Rose Inn way back when. Think they've changed hands quite a few times. That's a really old place, from back before the Revolution."

"So this book was owned by the estate of Matthew Pyle?"

"Yes, sir, as it was represented to us. I can't verify that legally, only that it was included in the boxes of books we bought from the estate. We often buy hundreds of books at a time. We don't go through every one, page by page. We just take a quick look and make an offer."

"Understand. Thank you!!" He hung up the phone. "Want

to get a snack and a beer at the Red Rose Inn in Jennersville?"

"Absolutely! I wanted to go inside when we did that tour of the Inns."

The drive down Route 1 parallels the path where General Howe marched his troops from the Chesapeake Bay to Chadds Ford. Taverns at the time were more than places to drink- they were spots where people received messages from travelers coming from faraway places, exchanged thoughts about the political and religious trends of the time and discussed business. Taverns were a critical part of the dissemination of information back during the Revolution. The introduction of the railroad in the mid-1800s saw the demise of many taverns in the Chester County area. Only a few, such as the Red Rose and General Warren, still function as active inns. Others, like the White Horse Tavern and Blue Ball Inn are now private homes. He gazed at the surroundings as he pulled into the lot.

Jim and Natalie strolled in and sat at the long wooden bar, waiting for the bartender, who was pouring a beer from the tap near the middle of the counter.

"What can I get you folks?"

"Well, we'd both like menus for lunch."

"Sure thing... be right back."

"Should I ask him now or wait until after lunch?" Jim said in a low voice, leaning close to Natalie's ear as he spoke.

"Why wait?"

The bartender came back, stretching out his muscular arms with the white shirt sleeves rolled up to his elbows. "Here you go. Can I get you anything to drink to start?"

"Yes, what do you have on tap?"

"We have several selections – Flying Fish, Dogfish Ale, Samuel Adams, Anchor Steam, Sierra Nevada."

"Hmmm… two Sierra Nevadas, pints please."

"I'll have the regular size. Don't need the extra calories" she stated and glanced at the menu.

"Will do… be right back with your beers."

"They do have a nice menu… lots of appetizers and sandwiches."

"I'm going to have the chicken quesadilla. How about you?" Natalie asked Jim.

"Sounds good, but I want something more robust. I'm getting the chili and a burger."

"Here you go. Two Sierra Nevadas. Pint for you, sir. Know what you want to order?"

"Sure, she'll have the chicken quesadilla and I'll have the chili and a cheeseburger. Do you have any grey poupon mustard?"

"I'll check with the kitchen. Is that all?"

"Actually I have a question. Did this place recently change owners?"

"Well, a few months back – yes. Spent a lot of years in the Pyle family. First Conrad Pyle and his Star Roses Company and then the Pyle sisters in the 1950s. Matthew Pyle owned it for many years and now its run by the Busseys."

Jim nudged Natalie, sensing they were in the right place. "Was Pyle related to a guy named Joshua Pyle? This goes way back, well over 150 years." He stared at the bartender's face intently, hoping for some clues to the mystery.

"Uh, well, I know the Pyle family has been in the area for a very long time, so possibly. I can't say for sure. Actually... you know what? I do think I've heard that name – Joshua Pyle... probably a great, great grandfather. Several of the Pyle family lived here, some in Gettysburg. I believe his grandfather's side of the family was in Gettysburg. One of them fought in the Civil War... could have been Joshua."

Gettysburg... the name rings with history. An epic battle, a turning point for the country. A place filled with the names of hundreds of famous war heroes, monuments, memorials and statues depicting Generals on their horses, cavalrymen in their charge, infantrymen on their way across the battlefield, most to their death for a cause which each side believed in so fervently. Jim thought back to the cemetery there where he walked among all the fallen heroes. "Thanks very much. You've been quite helpful." He peered over at Natalie and raised his eyebrows.

"Very interesting! Maybe we should check it out?"

"I say we hit the new visitor center in Gettysburg. We can drive up tomorrow morning, tour the area, check on the Pyle family history, have lunch, then head back and be here in time for dinner."

"Sounds like a plan." She took his hand and held it in both of hers, kissing it gently. "Another adventure with my personal tour guide."

"Here you go – chicken quesadilla for the lady and burger with chili for the gentleman."

They ate silently as each of them tried to piece together the story that was slowly evolving. He thought about the hundreds of families who lived in the area during the Revolution, unsure of what was happening around them... wary of the rabble-rousers who called for independence. They distrusted the Crown, while also distrusting local hotheads, in their opinion, who were willing to risk war with the most powerful country on Earth. Times were strange back then, as the citizen-farmers weighed the consequences of the insurrection, yet continued moving forward on a path of their own.

"On cold days like this, do you miss San Diego... the sunshine, the beaches...the rollerblade babes?" She chuckled a little.

"No. I love California... but I don't miss it at all. It's a beautiful state- with horrible problems. Over-regulation, sky-high taxes and real estate prices, rampant illegal immigration- pick your topic. San Diego was a great place to live... wonderful weather, gorgeous scenery... and I'm not talking about the girls... but I've always loved the East Coast. It's my home- plus I found you here, so it always will be." He glanced at her eyes as they both finished their meals and got up to leave...

———◦((◦))◦———

They both heard the morning FM radio alarm, set for an early rise the night before. She got up first, then he left the comfort of the bed and they both went downstairs, drank a quick cup of coffee and headed out. The drive to Gettysburg can be done two ways from Kennett Square. You can take the quicker way along the Pennsylvania Turnpike, or you can take the back roads directly west through the scenic Chester County countryside and Lancaster's Amish farmlands. The latter takes you on narrow winding roads past turn of the century town halls, old stone churches, bucolic scenes of barns rimmed with Holsteins, barnyard dogs and roosters roaming about looking for stray seeds. It's the preferred route for those not in any particular hurry to get to their final destination, not watching the clock, enjoying the fresh air and sunshine. The crisp air of early Winter rejuvenates you as your car winds past farmland held for generations, across the Susquehanna and onto sacred Civil War soil.

"I hear the new Visitor Center is really wonderful... a major step up from the old one" she said, not noticing their car was approaching the building. He glanced around and spied two empty spots near the middle of the tarmac. As they walked up the recently built cement ramp with the switchbacks leading to the new structure, he remembered the many winding trails he'd climbed in Colorado toward Grey's and Torres Peaks- "switchback country"- then looked up and examined the gleaming edifice, a modern version of a rustic Pennsylvania barn.

"We'll soon see. The last time we were here, it was finished, but not open to the public yet. I've been eager to see how well they restored the Cyclorama."

Cycloramas were 360-degree paintings done to portray famous scenes from history, giving the viewer a unique 'circular surrounding' glimpse of the area. Popular in traveling exhibitions in the late 1800's, artists in America tried to depict important events in the nation's history. Paul Phillopoteaux painted one of the famous "Pickett's Charge' at Gettysburg, now on display at the Visitors Center. They walked there first, anxious to see the difference from when they last saw it just a day before the old exhibition closed several years ago. He gazed around the circular room. The perfectly restored painting hung about 20 feet up from the floor, set in a landscape of rocks, fences, trees and valley grasses, completing the diorama. As the lights were dimmed, stars in the skies sparkled and smoke billowed from the cannons as the action moved across the painting, flashes of gunfire and grimacing injured men lying bleeding in the fields. His eyes wandered all around the circular room as Natalie peered up at the painting.

"Unbelievable! They did an exceptional job… well worth the wait" Jim exclaimed. "Now, let's get to what we came here for. We can ask at the front desk if they have a records section where you can check the database of soldiers. I believe they have everything on the computer now… personnel, guns, ammunition, wagons, horses. I'll ask and see what they come up with." They walked slowly behind the dozens of people going back down the ramp toward the front desk.

"Welcome to Gettysburg. How can I help you?" said the middle-aged man with a 1950's-style crew-cut, standing erect behind the counter.

"We were wondering if you had a records section. Is there any way to check on whether a person fought here at Gettysburg?"

"Sure. All our records from the surrounding areas are

now on computers… open to the public. It took thousands of hours to enter, but it's done and a great way to do research. Covers everything from the 1700's up to the present."

Jim felt Natalie's hand giving his a 'good squeeze'. "Great! Where do we go?"

"Over there to the far corner. Do you see that area with the terminals? You can log in there… you don't need a Password or Username. Just put in the names of the people you're looking for and it will give you whatever we have."

"Appreciate your help!" He kept Natalie's right hand in his as they walked to the corner of the large room, past the museum store and glass cases filled with rifles, soldier's caps and uniforms. As he sat down, he noticed the screensaver was the Cyclorama rendition of Pickett's Charge and felt a shiver run through him. He looked at the battle scene and for a few seconds, felt the heat of the sun shining down amidst the dust of the infantry charge, the waves of men running towards him as he knelt at the copse of trees, waiting to fire.

"Well, here goes." He clicked 'Soldiers and Residents' and typed Joshua Pyle into the Name Search dialogue box. Up came a list of seven persons and he read down after clicking on the first one. 'Joshua Pyle, born August 17, 1922, died November 3rd, 1994, resident of Coatesville, PA, moved to Mechanicsburg in 1982, where he lived until his death. No military service.' "Well, it's just the first Joshua… keep going" he thought as he reviewed the screen. He clicked on the second and third names, finding nothing of interest that could be linked to the cryptic note they'd found in the book. Then he clicked on the

4th name, read the first three sentences and sat up straight in the chair as he leaned close to the screen to make sure what he saw was really in front of his eyes.

Jim read out loud in a low voice. "Joshua Pyle, known also as Joshua Lewis, born March 17th, 1770 in Turks Head, Pa., father Curtis Lewis, a Quaker, Tory sympathizer and supporter of King George III during the Revolutionary War. Father known to have fought and been killed at the Battle of the Brandywine, Chadds Ford, Pa., Sept. 11th, 1777; son Joshua was a flag bearer and participated in the battle. Evidence father, Curtis Lewis, led British troops to the site of the battle, but was mortally wounded crossing the Brandywine. Family (led by mother) returned to London, England in 1783 after Colonials won independence. Joshua became involved in local British politics and was an ardent critic of the Colonials due to the loss of his father at the hands of Washington's troops. He joined the British Navy and sailed back to America to fight against the U.S. in the War of 1812 on the British frigate 'Surprise', where he met Francis Scott Key, who was held prisoner there during the battle and they became close friends; Lewis is suspected of having gone AWOL soon after the bombing of Fort McHenry in Baltimore Harbor."

"Sources indicate Joshua Lewis traveled up the Chesapeake Bay and settled in the Brandywine Valley area around 1814-1815. He changed his name from Lewis to Pyle, which was his mother's maiden name and he became active in the community, working at a local tavern. It was during this time that some say his allegiance changed and he became a strong supporter of the young nation in its rise toward Democracy. He left the area around 1852 and settled in Gettysburg, where he owned a farm less than a mile from the present Eisenhower estate. Pyle, despite his significant age, fought with Union forces as an unenlisted man at the Battle of Gettysburg, taking a bullet in the leg during the final assault of Pickett's Charge on July 3rd, 1863. Died Sept. 12, 1865 at age 95, one of less than 50 people known to have fought in all three wars from early American history – the Revolutionary War, the War of 1812 and the Civil War, though the first two were as an enemy of the Republic."

He couldn't believe what he just read and took a deep breath. He glanced up toward his left shoulder where Natalie was standing, leaning slightly on his chair. "Do you believe this? It's incredible! This guy fought in all three wars… but more importantly, he started out against the U.S., then eventually became a major supporter of our nation."

"He must have been about seven years old at the Battle of the Brandywine, where he lost his father. That must have made him really hate the Colonials, which is why he took revenge and fought against us in the War of 1812. The most interesting thing is his change of heart – why? What made him change sides – and go AWOL?"

He thought for a few seconds and recalled when they'd visited Fort McHenry on a trip to Baltimore, reading the descriptions and backgrounds of the soldiers involved in the battle, where Key wrote the Star Spangled Banner. "Wow!!… This is even more intriguing… As I recall, the U.S. commander of the fort during the British bombing was a Major

George Armistead. Pyle was a British sailor who participated in the British bombing of Fort McHenry during the War of 1812... Major George Armistead was the uncle of Major Lewis Armistead- who nearly 50 years later charged against the Union soldiers on Cemetery Hill at Gettysburg. Amongst them was Pyle himself- a civilian and a very old man- who was fighting George Armistead's own nephew!! Major Lewis Armistead was mortally wounded as he led the Confederates to the copse of trees during Pickett's Charge- up to the stone wall where Pyle was firing against him with the Union troops!!"

She stared at him, then back at the screen in disbelief, thinking they'd somehow read the material incorrectly. Then she remembered Key's name from the visit to Baltimore. She could picture cannonballs bursting overhead, men yelling, horses trying to pull themselves free from their posts inside the fort... *'And the rocket's red glare, the bombs bursting in air, Gave proof through the night that our flag was still there. Oh, say does that star-spangled banner yet wave?... O'er the land of the free... and the home of the brave'.*

"Truth is stranger than fiction... What a wild twist of fate... Time for more detective work." He looked up at her at her and felt it- the tension building, just as he did when he touched Lincoln's sculpture the first time in Evergreen Cemetery before walking the length of Cemetery Ridge.

"That is fascinating!! Can you get a printout of this?"

He saw the summary on the screen and adrenalin raced through his veins. "Yes – PRINT!" He clicked and heard the grey Hewlett Packard printer about 10 feet away churning out the two pages he'd just read.

"Wait! What's that at the very bottom? A footnote?"

"I think it is… in very small print." He put his right hand in his jacket and took out his reading glasses. "Looks like 'Pyle became well respected in the Gettysburg area as a strong supporter of the Union, although he had been against independence and fought with the British. In his later years, he was known to have collected many books on the Founding Fathers and had even come to admire George Washington.' He stood up from his chair and stared at Natalie. "Does it get much better?"

She smiled at him. "Let's talk over lunch at the Farnsworth House. We can have a beer and some Game Pie. You might even see a soldier or two at the bar."

He thought about the Tavern, where he fell in love with Gettysburg ten years before, the soundtrack to the movie "Glory" playing as he gazed up at the Civil War artifacts along the walls, the long oak and brass bar- and the bookstore across the terrace with row upon row of volumes highlighting the conflict amidst bronze busts of Grant, Lee, Chamberlain and Stonewall Jackson. "I'm ready! Now that we have this, we might be able to decipher that note. It said 'On my dying Father, loyal to the King, a note I find.' That must have been something he got at the Battle of the Brandywine!" He walked quickly over to the printer and grabbed the pages, folding them in thirds to stuff in his jacket. "What was… the next line?"

"Slow down, Inspector. Let's do lunch at your favorite Civil War tavern."

"The Farnsworth House, it is…"

Chapter 9

The antique shop was empty. He unlocked the front door and put out the "OPEN" sign, then looked over at the Civil War table. He noticed that a few of the buckles had an unusual luster, sensing it even from five feet away. Smithson picked up one of the buckles, the oval brass plate with "U.S." embossed inside appearing different from the one he remembered placing there just a few weeks ago. He examined another buckle next to it and suspected the same thing. "Too new looking and too good a condition for being almost 150 years old" he thought. He put both down on the table as Broom came into the room.

"Martin, I was looking at a few of these buckles. They don't appear to be the ones I put here two weeks ago and I know we didn't sell any." He watched as Broom walked toward him at the table.

Broom picked them both up. "They look fine to me. Your eyes aren't as good as they used to be, old man."

"Wait a minute. My eyes are fine and I say those two pieces look… fake to me. I know my Civil War artifacts and those look like reproductions."

"What are you saying, I switched them? What the hell kind of operation are you runnin' here? I came here a little over a year ago and saved your ass!! You needed cash... big time... and I supplied it... saving your precious shop from bankruptcy! Cut the bogus artifact shit and leave me alone to run the business the way it needs to be run." He glared at Smithson who stood less than a foot away.

Robert was visibly shaken and didn't say a word, moving slowly away from the table. "I won't be threatened in my own shop!!" He turned his back and headed toward the check-out counter.

Broom ran up behind him, grabbed his left shoulder and spun Smithson around to face him. "Listen, I run this place... O.K.??!! Without my money, this place would be closed. So shut up!! I don't need this shit!!" He pushed him toward the counter and walked back to the storeroom...

⸻ ((◍)) ⸻

The soft light of early morning came through the windows surrounding the breakfast room as the parakeets made their first chirps of the day. Jim looked at what he was holding delicately in both of his hands. "This book is so fragile. I wonder if I should try to take the tissue guard out so we can examine it more closely" he said as he held the book, glancing briefly out at the snow, the soft white powder blanketing the yard and nearby forest.

"I wouldn't. First, it's delicate, you could tear the sheet and make it worse. Second, it's part of an historical document... an antique. Why separate it from the book?"

"Right. I'll leave it in. I just wish I could read the page a bit easier. The writing's hard to decipher while it's attached to the binding, even with the magnifying glass." He let the book sit flat on the table and turned the page slightly to see the faded inscription. 'Hid while the waters lapped nearby, see what warms the old Blacky' O.K... what does that mean?" He looked at her standing in his favorite clingy, light blue top and black hip-hugger pants at the end of the table.

"Well, O.K... waters lapped nearby... obviously a body of water, an ocean, a lake..."

"The Brandywine!!"

"Could be... it's logical. I don't know if the water in a creek 'laps' against the banks, but who knows?"

"Now who's Blacky? A black man? A slave?"

"Either one could work, don't know."

"Blacky. Black man. Black... blacksmith? There were a lot of blacksmiths around here back then."

"I thought they called them 'smithy's', like in the poem, 'where the village smithy stands.'"

"Don't know, could be a black man, could be a blacksmith. Could be anything. The words they used back then were so different from the way we speak today."

"It's the foundation of our language." She remembered her many searches of American history on the web, fueled in part by her growing interest in their heritage, largely kindled by him.

"Right. Let's just get this figured out. Next line. 'House where the rainbow ends.' What is this guy doing, chasing leprechauns?"

"Hah!!" She pulled the wrought iron chair closer to read the inscription. "Well, O.K... rainbow ends. You know what's there, right?"

"A pot of gold. I know. You're always after me Lucky Charms!!"

She laughed so hard, she was nearly out of breath. "Who knows? It's not out of the question that there could be some kind of treasure buried around here. It's happened many times before. Remember the story we saw on T.V.? That British guy found a huge cache of coins, pottery and collectibles worth millions. Spent his free time canvassing farms with his metal detector."

"We should be so lucky. I'd be pleased to find another belt buckle" he said, looking at the book.

"Let's figure this out... 'House where the rainbow ends.' What house? It's got to be some house around here, maybe right here in this immediate area. There are several houses nearby that existed at the time of the Revolution."

"Exactly. There's John Chad's House. The Barns-Brinton House. There's that interesting house, though probably newer, turned into a museum in Chadds Ford on Route 100- the Sanderson House."

"I read about that. Wasn't he a major collector? Lived in the Ring House for a while, same house that Washington stayed in during the Battle of the Brandywine?"

"Believe so. Sanderson apparently loved the area. He even gave tours of the battlefield. His house is supposed to be filled with Americana from the region, old news clippings, photographs and a lot of interesting stuff. We should check it out sometime."

"Why not today? We don't have anything planned. We could have breakfast at the Longwood Family Restaurant, then hit the Sanderson Museum and see if there's anything about the Battle."

"Oh, I'm sure there is. Sounds good, but first one more clue. It reads 'Out of place at the steps to nowhere'. What in the gawd dang hayell does that mean?" he said in a Texas drawl.

"Steps to nowhere. Who would say that? I have no idea, which is as insightful as I'm going to get on an empty stomach. I'm really hungry."

"Right, me too. Let's head out to eat before the morning crush hour." They went back into the garage and got into the Mercedes SUV. Jim sped up the highway, hoping to get to the parking area before many cars pulled in. "In luck again." He opened the wooden door and expected a long line- but kept walking right up to an open table.

They ate quickly without talking and Jim looked up, not surprised as he noticed the restaurant was eight deep at the front door. "Ready to go? I can't finish all of mine."

"Sure, lets get to the Sanderson Museum and see what's there." He took the last bite of scrapple. "Why does anything that's fried crispy taste so good? We must have survived eating things scorched to a crisp as Neanderthals."

"I like fried food, bit it doesn't like me. I can't eat it very often. Seems like when I was in my teens, I could eat anything... burgers, fries, chips... and nothing happened. Now I feel like a car drove over me the day after I eat that stuff."

"A car did drive over you. I saw it and filed a report with the State Police."

"Very funny. Let's go."

"Next stop, Sandersons!"

They drove up Route 100 and saw that the tiny parking lot in front was full, holding only four cars. Jim continued on and pulled into the gravelly, grass-fringed lot of the Chadds Ford Historical Society.

"Isn't there any place else to park? We have to walk across the road and back along the shoulder to get to the museum. I don't like all the traffic coming down Route 100." She looked at the road, cars flying by doing 40 miles per hour, some much faster.

"I don't either, but it's the closest place to park. The museum's not that far, just up the road around the bend. Just remember to jump in the gully if an 18-wheeler whizzes by."

"Great. Any other sagely advice?"

They jogged across the road, then went single file along the narrow shoulder. Reaching the front yard of the museum safely, they walked hand in hand up the steps to the entrance, with its white-painted front porch and old screen door, a scene out of the 1940's.

"Welcome to the Sanderson Museum." The older woman

wore a red Christmas sweater with reindeer and had a slightly wrinkled, yet smiling, friendly face.

"Thank you. I've actually been here before, many years ago. It's her first time."

"Oh, we love first time visitors! Where are you from?"

"Right down the road, in Kennett Square."

"Wonderful. Will that be two for admission?"

"Yes, do you take AAA?" Natalie rolled her eyes and turned to face the display of old postcards.

"Sorry, we don't. We're a small, private museum."

"No problem... Never know when you can save 10%. Two adults, please."

They walked around the first floor, which had bookshelves filled with Americana from the 18th through 20th century. Revolutionary War cannonballs, helmets from WWI, Civil War artifacts... all intermixed in a kaleidoscope of memorabilia.

"This place is neat! I feel like I'm traveling through history, but I'm not sure what decade I'm in."

"Look at this. Sanderson made a map of all the military movements and encounters during the Battle of the Brandywine and- guess what? There's a blacksmith shop right there." She pointed to the edge of the hand-drawn map.

"That there is. Blacksmith. Blacky. One and the same...?" He focused on her face and knew she was thinking the same thing.

"Possibly. We should wander over there sometime."

"O.K., but we need to go upstairs first. There's a lot of stuff in this old house."

They made their way up the white painted creaky stairs, the balustrade rimmed with old newspaper clippings from World War II and oil paintings of the Brandywine Valley.

"A great painting of this area. Looks like an antique. Maybe from the 1920's or 1930's."

"Look at the bottom corner. That's where the artist usually signs and dates it."

"Right. It's hard to see… Says 'Mitchell, 1928.' An antique… nice."

They walked past dozens of newspapers encased in wood and glass, local ragsheets, play invitations, public announcements from the 1920's through the 1950's… and he stopped. "Hey, an N.C. Wyeth print, signed by Wyeth, entitled 'The Spring House'. Looks interesting."

"There are a lot of paintings here, most originals, but all unknown artists. Maybe they're worth something just because they're so old."

"Let's never get old… If I ever say I want an exciting game of checkers with my buddies, lock me in my room." He looked at the signs, advertisements from the 1930's and noticed there were many play invitations, a few re-enacting the Battle of the Brandywine. "Hey!! I should have been born around 1900. I could have been in that play!!"

She laughed as they walked slowly down the stairs to the front desk, itself an antique, with several coats of paint covering decades of dents and scratches.

"See anything you like?" asked the friendly older woman who had greeted them earlier.

"That's the problem, I like it all!! Sanderson must have been a packrat… Looks like he saved everything. I would like to have met him. Do you have any books on this place, or on him?"

"Yes, we have his biography... It's called 'Chris'."

"Great. I'll take that- and these Colonial dice. Soldiers needed some diversion aside from whiskey."

She chuckled and looked over at Natalie, who was grinning. "Here you go." She took the cash and handed him a receipt. Natalie's eyes signaled she was pleased.

"Glad you came. Please tell your friends about this place. We need more visitors!!"

"Absolutely. We'll be back." He took the bag holding the book and the dice and went out the door. They crossed Route 100 and noticed the traffic was lighter.

"Not bad. We got to walk through Sanderson's attic, see America from the 1770's through the 1950's and we only spent 28 bucks. Extra bonus- we didn't become two-dimensional crossing the street."

"I'll alert the media. Want to check out the next clue?"

"What do you mean?"

"The blacksmith's shop. It's right up the road, maybe a 10 minute drive off of Route 926, near Dilworthtown. In fact, I think it's in Dilworthtown." She stared up at his eyes, waiting for a response.

"Perfect. We'll scout around and then maybe go there later for dinner."

"I'm not ready to plan dinner yet. Let's just head out and see what we find. It's getting cold."

As the Battle of the Brandywine shifted from the South in Chadds Ford to the North near the Birmingham Meeting House in the late afternoon of September 11, 1777, fighting raged in several locations, with skirmishes throughout the area. Hessian soldiers began a cannonade and assault around 5:00 p.m.. Colonials under General Nathaniel Greene rushed to the East near Sandy Hollow, where Lafayette was wounded in the leg, trying to rally the troops against an overwhelming onslaught. Washington knew late in the day that he had succumbed to a larger force with a superior strategy and retreated with his troops around 8:00 p.m., clearing the path for the British to capture their prize. On the morning of September 26th, 1777, British troops under Lord Cornwallis rode into Philadelphia along with Hessian grenadiers to settle in for a nine month occupation of the Colonial capital.

"That place up there definitely needs some work" Natalie said pointing to a dilapidated wood and stone structure as they drove up Dilworthtown Road. "It could have been an old home...or maybe even a tavern?"

"Or a blacksmith's shop."

"We're about to find out. Hope you brought your hammer."

"Well, it looks like it could have been here during the Revolution. You can tell from the rough cut stonework and the irregular wooden beams along the walls. Notice all that rot. The place looks like it could collapse any minute." He drove up alongside the building, slowing the car.

"Oh, I doubt it. Let's go in!!" she insisted as he stopped to park. She got out, quickly walking around the back, looking for an entry point. "Maybe there's an open door around here" she yelled before he even got completely out and locked the car.

"Wait a minute. Are you sure you want to go inside??" he exclaimed, but she was already behind the structure. Normally the adventurer, he was hesitant this time as he examined the cracked walls. He'd heard too many stories about people going into abandoned buildings and getting seriously injured from falling debris and collapsing floors.

"Absolutely!! Come on!!" Her voice trailed off from the back of the building. She strode through a roughly-hewn door held open by half-split, severely weathered beams, into a darkened room filled with debris.

"Hey, wait!!" he shouted, but she was already out of earshot.

The inside floors were unmatched wooden boards which showed open cracks to the cellar. Stepping cautiously, she saw a brick fireplace, dilapidated, but with signs of human use. Splinters and fragments of charred wood covered the floor in front of it and each step brought a creak, a give-way enough to stop even a daredevil explorer.

"Are you sure you want to walk around in here?" he said as he entered the back doorway, maneuvering slowly around the debris.

"Yes!! Look over there, it's a fireplace. Looks a few hundred years old. There's another one over in that far corner, too. Let's explore a little!" She approached the mantle above the fireplace, which was partially rotted and burned. "What is this?"

"I can barely see in here. Did you bring the flashlight?"

"Oh, yeah. I did. Here it is." She took the miniature flashlight out of her coat and shined the narrow beam onto the mantle. "Looks like a carving or drawing of... a river, maybe?"

"Let me get a bit closer, assuming I can walk through this mine field without falling to the dungeon below." He stepped carefully over to the fireplace, dodging the empty beer bottles, engine parts and old newspapers. "Yes, looks like a crude drawing of a river... or a stream leading to some kind of simple structure... maybe a house. That over there could be a small anvil." He pointed to a spot about ten feet away, where a blackened, rusty object was sitting under a pile of rubble, its edge partly exposed.

"Oh, let's check it out!!" She went over quickly over and knelt down. "It does look kind of like an anvil."

"Remember what we read? 'See what warms the old Blacky'... a blacksmith. This place could have been an old blacksmith's forge. Then, the other clue... 'House where the rainbow ends'. Could this be the house?"

"Not unless there's a rainbow over in that corner. I have... no idea. All I know is this place is neat and I want to get a few artifacts to take home." She stepped around all the pieces of broken boards, piles of leaves and dirt and felt the floor give again.

"Just don't take a floorboard or a piece of the wall, the whole place will come down."

"Shush!! I don't like it when you say those kinds of things. It's unlucky."

"Unlucky… lucky… lucky leprechaun… pot of gold? That's it, we're finding the pot of gold here within the next 20 minutes or else… "

"Or else what?"

"Or else I'm not pouring you a martini at Happy Hour."

"Who cares about Happy Hour? I want to see if I can find anything interesting and- who knows? Maybe some clues to the mystery." She headed for the edge of the room and knelt down again on one knee. "Here's one…" She held up a small weathered brass plate containing a scene of someone hammering on an anvil. "Well I guess this kind of confirms it- the place probably was a blacksmith shop." She rummaged around and picked up a piece made of iron which appeared to be a crude measuring device. "What is this?"

"Looks like something from a carpenter's toolbox… and very old. The craftsmen back then had many skills- woodworker, blacksmith, barrel maker. We could use all of them at our house. Take it and let's get outta' here."

"Oh, you're no fun! Why can't we stay for a while? There's got to be more. It's fascinating!!"

"It'll be less fascinating if you fall through the floor. Look at how they give almost an inch with each step." He put his left foot in front of him and tried slowly to move forward. "See? This place is a disaster area. I'm out of here." He walked a bit more quickly, but gently toward the door and turned around just before he left the room. "Coming?"

"Yes, but just give me a minute. I want to poke around a bit before we go."

GENE PISASALE

"I'll be back at the car. If you're not back in five minutes, I'm calling the Mounted Police."

"Make sure they get my best profile along with their horses- for the photo in the Post Office."

"Seriously, if you don't come to the car in the next five minutes, I'm honking the horn to alert all the blacksmiths around here. Then you'll really be in trouble." He walked outside, hoping she would be right behind him, but she disappeared into the darkness of the room.

Natalie shined the flashlight around and immediately noticed the stairs. Holding the light in her hand, she climbed toward the rafters. Dust filled her nostrils and she sneezed several times, almost falling off the ladder. Cursing, she continued up. Reaching the top rung, she panned the flashlight around the floor at face level... and beamed. It was an attic filled with broken furniture, boxes and other debris. Lifting herself onto the edge of the floor and standing, she took a couple of test steps. "Seems secure enough" she decided and continued in. Sifting through two decaying boxes, she quickly pushed them aside. "Just some old magazines and books... nothing interesting." The flashlight pinpointed several shelves containing electrical supplies and a few crude sculptures of masks and vases. Spotting a clay hippo, she grinned, grabbed it gingerly and headed back down.

Entering the next room, she noticed another set of stairs in the back corner. The ceiling was bowed at least a foot in the center, paint chipping everywhere. Holding the hippo in one hand and the flashlight in the other, she carefully made her way over to the stairs. Looking up, she decided not to risk it and shined the flashlight on the floor again to leave. Next to her foot, only a few inches away, was an open shaft. She grimaced at the close call, then peered down following the beam of the flashlight as it landed dimly on the dirt floor below. She leaned over further, but couldn't see anything... just a shaft surrounded by four walls... going nowhere. Putting down the hippo, she kneeled on the floor, adjusting the angle of the light and put one hand on the wall so she could peer in closer. There, right below the room, was what appeared to be the entrance to a side tunnel. "Wow... very creepy..." she thought. "An adventure for another day." She picked up the hippo and headed out.

Sitting in the driver's seat, he stared at his watch, knowing it had been over ten minutes. Raising his arm, he reached for the car horn, but stopped when he heard her voice outside.

"Look what I got!!" She ran up to the door holding the hippo and got in next to him, putting it on her lap and the flashlight in the glove box. "That was exciting!! I found this clay hippo. Also saw an old plaster face... a face mask, maybe... along with some other fascinating things."

"Congratulations. If anyone owns the property and they were watching, the State Police should be waiting for us up the road."

"Oh, calm down!! The place is deserted, probably abandoned decades ago. Guess what? I discovered an abandoned shaft leading to a tunnel going under the floor... very creepy. Let's come back tomorrow with a ladder."

"No way!" He started the engine and pulled away.

Natalie sighed. "I'll just drag my brother out here later in the week" she thought to herself as the car pulled away from the curb...

⸺◆⸺

Twenty-eight miles to the East as the crow flies, Rawlins was sitting at his desk, examining the file on Edward Caniletto, along with three other documents linking him to the largest Mafia families in New York City. He started to take another Marlboro out of his jacket as the phone rang.

"Rawlins here."

"Frank- Director Cunningham."

"Oh- hello sir!! How are you?" He put the cigarette pack back into his inner pocket and grabbed his pen as he sat up straighter at his desk. "What can I help you with, sir?"

"A lot. Our agents in New York have been in touch with reps from the SEC and the Treasury Department. They've actually met several times over the last few months. The mob investigation you're working on, with links to Levanthal and Company, has legs. Long ones."

"I knew there was some pretty big money involved..."

"We're talking more than money, Frank. A lot of the volatility we saw in the market collapse last year- the wild swings in mortgage and derivatives that severely depressed the stock market- appear to have been caused at least in part by coordinated efforts of questionable parties in other countries. We think traders in Russia, Mexico and the Middle East – with direct ties to international mob syndicates – deliberately manipulated bids to cause wild swings in prices – from which they later profited."

"You think mob families in other countries did this?"

"I don't just think… I know. We've been analyzing trends of bids from international wirehouses and there's a clear pattern that we can see of extreme bids at the high and low end from these traders. When large amounts of money… tens of billions… are involved, it can sway the markets in a big way."

"So – what are you saying? Do we have a paper trail on these players to move forward on an indictment – or are we just fishing?" Rawlins asked.

"Right now, we just threw the line into the pond… but my sources tell me they'll be able to gather enough evidence to nab some big players soon."

"How extensive is the data?"

"Pretty convincing. I'm not sure if you're following me Frank. What I'm saying is these bogus bids, coordinated by several entities, caused the mortgage market to fluctuate more wildly than it ever conceivably would have… causing equity markets around the world to crash…"

"It sounds… pretty incredible. So, Caniletto and his mob ties to Levanthal are fairly important."

"That's the biggest understatement I've heard in the last 40 years. This is huge!! If people were to find out that their mutual funds, their 401k's, their investment account statements were showing manipulated results – we'd have a revolt on our hands. We're talking hundreds of millions of people in the U.S. and around the world finding out that their accounts were showing illegitimate, or at least unreasonable values. It's... nearly incomprehensible. So now you know that your little investigation of Caniletto and his mob ties could have immense importance. This needs to be kept completely confidential. You are not to share this information with anyone... do you understand?"

Frank stared at the ashtray in front of him as the words came through the phone. "Yes... of course, sir. I will keep this to myself." His mouth hung open as he thought about what he'd just heard. "Will you keep me updated?"

"Can't promise that on a daily basis. This is an enormous investigation, encompassing three major Federal agencies and potentially dozens of other entities here and abroad. All I can say is this is the largest investigation I've seen in my time at the Bureau... going back to J. Edgar Hoover himself... and if any of this conversation gets leaked, I'll know who to come looking for."

"No – sir!! It will remain completely confidential!"

"Good – keep it that way!" He hung up the phone and put his head down on the desk. "God be on our side on this one...

Chapter 10

"Maybe we can do some more research... cruise around the area..." Jim suggested.

"Let's drive over to John Chad's House, then we can stop in the Brandywine River Museum on the way home."

"Sounds good. Don't know if Chad's House is open, but we can drive up to it. It's only a few minutes from here."

They cruised down the back roads of Routes 52 and 926, "deer country" known for its many white-tailed friends which always seemed to want to cross the road only after your car had exceeded 45 miles per hour and was less than 20 feet away. "We continue straight onto Route 100 and it takes us right there." Fallen birch trees and flattened tawny-colored grasses fringed the blacktop. As they approached the house on the hill over-looking the floodplain, he looked up at the small sign. "Our luck, they're closed."

"Well, I'm making note of the structure. Looks like a typical Colonial frontier house. They must have done a lot of main-tenance to keep it in such good shape." She took photographs of the front and side.

"I'm glad. At least something from our local heritage around here has been saved. Let's hit the museum."

They drove to the intersection at Route 1 and Hank's parking lot was packed, the strands of holiday decorations beginning to glow in the fading afternoon light. The car turned south and went less than a quarter mile before turning left into the parking area. He noticed the well-worn stone flywheel as they made there way up the path to the entrance.

"Welcome. Two adults?" The woman at the front counter sounded if that was the 800th time she'd said that since opening for the day.

"Yes, we're members. Here's my card. Which floor has all the N.C. Wyeths?"

"Second. You can take the stairs or the elevator over there."

They walked up the cement stairway and entered the gallery. He focused instantly on the huge painting in front of him. "This is it. This is my favorite N.C. Wyeth! Look at it, isn't it spectacular?" He stood right in front of the 12 foot by 8 foot work and gazed slowly at it from left to right across the canvas. His eyes were fixed on the General, leaning down off his white stallion, pointing toward the battle.

"Beautiful. That's George Washington?"

"You are correct, madam!! The title is 'In a Dream, I Meet General Washington.' It's a masterpiece. I think the grandfather was the most talented of the bunch. I also like a lot of Andrew's paintings." She stood alongside him as he looked up at the work, noticing the Colonial and British soldiers marching through the fields. "Jamie did a good one that's hanging in Brandywine Prime. It's of a young man, blonde hair slicked back, with dark sunglasses on, wearing a leather jacket. Kind of a countercultural hero type piece. It generated some controversy when it first came out and earned him a well deserved reputation for being a solid painter." As he stared at Washington leaning down to talk with Wyeth, he imagined the British troops marching nearby... the soldiers hit by gunshots, lying on the ground, cannons exploding overhead.

"Want to move on? You've been standing there for almost 10 minutes."

"Yes. Let's walk around a bit first. There are some nice illustrations by him, although I would call them great works of art."

After a quick stroll through the gallery, they went back down the stairs and into the shop, past dozens of holiday visitors examining the elaborately decorated Christmas trees with the handmade ornaments. All-natural materials- pine cones, twigs, bark, seeds, gourds and fragments of fruits and vegetables formed the bodies of each animal. The trees were themselves works of art in their yuletide splendor.

"Hey, look at this! It's a really great print of 'The Spring House'. Isn't it nice?" He held it up and examined the details.

"It is a good painting. Springhouses... near small creeks or underground springs... that mantle, the drawing of the creek and this... 'The Spring House'. You think there could be a link to one of our clues?"

"We know they were all around here then. Must have been

dozens along the river."

"That spring house in the print looks small. All spring-houses were pretty small, right? Perfect size for a leprechaun."

"Maybe. Want to pick up a canoe for a quick ride down the river? If we see a springhouse there, you'll get a chance to examine it up close. If I see a leprechaun, I have some rope. I get the pot of gold."

She laughed, giving his arm a friendly shove as they left the shop. "We have to make this quick. It's pretty cold outside. Do they rent canoes when it's this cold?" They drove back up to Route 100 and turned north.

"Look… the gates up… must be open. We'll probably be the only ones there. We'll get it for an hour." He stopped the car in the muddy lot and they went into the small brown wood-en building.

"Can I get a canoe for an hour?"

"You can get it for as little or as long as you want, no-body came in today. You're it" said the man, about 35, thinning auburn hair and a thick mustache hovering above the 3-day stubble on his face.

"Great. How much is it?"

"Well, twenty bucks an hour. If you're done in less than an hour, I'll give you half off. Just leave the canoes past the bridge. Call and we'll come pick you up."

"Will do. Can we put in right here?" He turned around to look out the window facing the creek.

"Sure can, see the bank? You drop in right there."

"Great." They both picked up the canoe, brought it to the

water's edge and she slowly got in while he held the canoe to stabilize it. Then he got in at the front and sat down.

"O.K., just paddle on the side opposite from where I'm paddling to keep the boat stable and going straight. If I say slow down, back paddle slightly in the same way, opposite me. Got it?"

"Yes, sir. Will this be a three-hour tour?"

"Could be longer… rough seas ahead. I trust you brought sufficient supplies."

"Now I'm scared. I only brought one pair of nylons."

He laughed. "I hope they're white."

"Don't get too ahead of yourself. Just steer this thing so we don't end up as tree ornaments."

They paddled at about three miles an hour with the current, the water high after the recent snow melt. "I'm looking for the key…"

"Key to what?"

"The cryptic message. 'Hid while the waters lapped nearby… House where the rainbow ends.' There's got to be some more interesting old structures along here… maybe related to our clues."

"Let's get this moving faster and then see what we can find." She looked up ahead to make sure there were no rapids nearby.

They scanned both sides, the banks in most places covered with dying Winter brush, piles of brown leaves washed up on mounds of mud. Then he looked at the left bank and saw them. "Looks like remnants of some stone buildings, coming right up. Let's steer towards that stump. They're right on the edge of the water." He stopped the canoe. "You get out first."

She stepped onto the bank and the mud engulfed her shoes. "Glad I wore these beat-up old Topsiders." She was already at the structure as Jim secured the canoe. "Looks like a pile of rocks." She pulled a few stones away from what had once been a wall. "Just a big pile of leaves and mud – let's go up to the next one." She went back to the canoe and got in, then leaned forward as they approached the next building. "I'll get out – you stay here. " She strolled up and saw the same thing. "Not much – we can go. Just a pile of stones. Maybe most of those things aren't still standing."

They paddled and then he saw a larger structure down river. "There's one, except we can't easily reach it from here. It's up well off the bank, plus it's too muddy and steep to climb."

"Are you sure? I'm willing."

"Not unless you want to look like the Mudmen of Indonesia. Anyway, your thigh highs will get dirty and I need them for later- on you."

She laughed. "Well, if we don't try to get there from the water, let's just drop off the canoe and drive back there. I want to check that place out."

"O.K. The drop-off point is right up ahead. We'll leave the canoes, take their shuttle van, come back in the car and see what we can find." He steered to the right bank and saw the canoe storage spot. After getting through on the cell phone, they both sat and waited for the van.

Driving up the road, he kept his eyes on the riverbank

area while watching for any place nearby to park. "That looks like the approximate area where we saw it. This intersection is Brinton's Bridge Road." He stopped the car and looked around as they got out. "Great. Nobody here. Did you remember the metal detector?"

"It's in the back with the shovel."

"I'll get them. You start walking up into the brush. It's over there near the edge of the river. It can't be more than 50 yards from here." He opened the trunk and grabbed the device with both hands, lifting it and the shovel, then closed the door. Walking quickly across the road and into the floodplain amidst the grasses and river plants, he felt the mud sink beneath his feet. Then he looked up and could barely see it, behind a small grove of birch trees along the river. "That's it, right up there!!"

Natalie turned back to look at him pointing, then gazed ahead and saw it herself. "Good one!!" They both walked more quickly through the marshy scrub-covered zone to the edge of the house. "Which way in?"

"Usually toward the water." He went around the corner of the small stone structure and turned the detector on. "Here it is, we can get in. Hold the shovel for me." He stepped slowly along the scattered rocks at the small entryway and ducked beneath the weathered, cracked oak beam to get inside, putting the front of the detector along the ground. "Maybe we'll get lucky."

"Let's hope so."

He proceeded slowly, crouching down, the only light

coming from the three-foot wide doorway behind him. The detector began to click, slowly at first, then a steady round of equally-timed ticks.

"There's something nearby. It's getting louder. Oww!!" He ducked down after hitting a small wooden beam ajar in the ceiling.

"Are you O.K.?"

"I'm all right... don't feel any blood." The detector got louder and the ticks more closely spaced. Then they erupted in a cacophony. "There's something right at my feet. Let me kick around to see if I can locate anything. This thing is going nuts!!" He leaned down and used his hands to dig into the mud. Pebbles. Leaves. Twigs. Two worms. "Hand me the shovel." He started digging, then heard the shovel hit something metal. Setting it down, he felt around in the mud again. "Wait, I feel something in my hand. Not sure what it is because I can barely see it."

"Let me help you. I'm right here." She knelt down beside him and dug into the muddy hole. "I feel one... two... actually three things right here. I have them."

"I've got a few more here. I'm still digging a bit. Nothing... nothing... just a bunch of twigs... a skeleton... a chicken... Just kidding! I have three things which feel pretty round. Wish I could see them better. I'm putting them in my pocket."

"I've got these in my pocket, too. Want to do a check around the corners?"

"Will do." He got up slowly to avoid another bump on the head and pointed the detector toward what he could sense were the edges of the floor of the structure. "Looks like a small platform here... stones piled up. Don't feel or see anything interesting. Nothing over here on the ground either and the detector is quiet. I've checked all around. Want to go?"

"O.K. It's getting so dark, I can barely see how we got in here. Should have brought the flashlight, but I didn't think the sun would go down so fast." They went back to the entrance, ducking out into the Chester County twilight.

"I'm turning this thing off now. We're done for the day." They walked to the car, put the detector and shovel in the back and got in as a car came up with its high beams on. "Don't people know they should turn off their brights when they're approaching people walking?" The car rushed toward them, slowing slightly as it got within 20 feet of their car and then cruised up the road. "Other people canoeing. That guy had one on top of his SUV, but he didn't have to swerve so close to us!!" He rolled his eyes and got into the car. "So... what do we have here?" He pulled the items from his pocket and held them in his hands on top of the dashboard under the light.

"Looks like... coins? They're definitely not buttons." Natalie leaned next to him and put her face close to his right hand.

"No way they're buttons. I think these are coins. Let me scrape off some of the mud." He wiped the mud onto the sides of his jeans and then stared for a few seconds. "These are definitely coins. I can see... a face? Some guy with long curly hair. Maybe Roman numerals? Yes, looks like Roman numerals. X. V. I can't make out the rest. Other side has... is it a crown?"

"Yes, that's a crown and I thought I saw numbers on the other side, at the bottom. Flip it back over. See? That looks like... seventeen... forty-four?"

"Yes, right. What do you have?"

She took each piece out of her pocket and held them under the small dome light. Another car approached with its high beams on and the driver honked for about three seconds. "Jerk!! We're not blocking anything. We're well off the road."

He looked in the rear view mirror. "That might have been the same car as last time. Hard to believe...dark colored SUV with a canoe. Driver definitely gets an 'A-plus' for being a bonehead."

She wiped the mud off the first item in her hand. "This looks very similar. I can see a face...and some numbers. Seventeen fifty-six?"

"That's what I make out. Look at these other two. That's the same kind of coin. Dates are very worn, but it looks like 1763... and 1745."

"These... look like the same thing. Can't make out the dates, but they appear similar. That makes six... six coins of the realm!!" She bounced in her seat, then kissed him on the cheek.

"I hope so. If these are authentic, they could be worth some money. How much, I don't know, but they might be important. I'm ready to head home, but we should go back in there sometime soon and dig some more."

"Definitely! Homeward, Throckmorton. Will you have my Royal Bath prepared before supper?"

"I certainly will, madam. Especially if you have a glass of champagne waiting for me..."

Chapter 11

A heavy mist hung in the air as the first few longshore-men made it down the ramp to the loading dock along the Delaware River. Darkness enveloped them as they stepped onto the cement platform, barely able to see each other, a dim light coming from the one lamppost 40 yards away. The first ship had docked and the heavy iron door was being slowly lowered to the ground.

"Hey, Jack!! Over here."

Jack saw Dominic as he stepped toward him near the edge of the water. "Hey – Dom! How'z it goin'?"

"Good – well… maybe not so good… We got three big crates comin' in right now. Vinny says these have to get through… with no eyes on 'em. You see that guy down at the end of the platform?"

"Yeah… so?"

"He's undercover Customs… I know… I've seen him before. He took one of Vinny's shipments couple months ago… Vinny wanted to strangle the guy. We can't let it happen again. Vinny says this is important merchandise… so nobody takes a look... O.K.??!!"

"Sure, Dom... but what am I gonna do if he stops us from takin' the box?"

"You let me handle that. There's nobody else here yet except our guys... Sal, Tony and Patrick. Had everyone show up early..." Dominic peered through the fog toward the other man. "Well... looks like trouble. Here he comes... right when Sal's takin' the forklift to get that crate."

"Good morning, gentlemen! Hope you're doing well today." The Customs agent took out his badge and flashed it in front of Dominic. "I'm going to need to take a look at that crate your guy is loading over there." He smiled slightly as he started to turn to walk toward the forklift.

"Hey, what do ya' need to do that for? There's nothin' wrong with this shipment! Here's the manifest. We're not smugglin' endangered species... or drugs from Tijuana."

"Doesn't matter – still need to check it out." He took three steps toward the oversized crate as it sat on the tongs of the forklift.

Two muffled pops came from the back of the platform as Dominic held the gun with the long metal silencer. He watched as the agent fell forward, hitting the ground.

"Dom!! You killed him!! What the fuck!! You tryin' to throw us all in jail?!!" Jack yelled as he grabbed Dominic's arm.

"Let go of me!! It's BUSINESS!! Vinny's orders!! Nobody sees this crate..."

"Yeah, but Dom... this place has surveillance cameras... they could've seen us."

"Think I'm stupid?… I had Sal take care of them last night." He strode up to the body, the agent's legs twitching as he moaned. "Sal, Patrick… take him outta' here!!"

"Where to, boss?"

Dominic looked around and saw another smaller crate sitting open at the rear of the platform. "Put him in there – and get him onto the truck. NOW!!"

The two men picked up the body and struggled as they carried him slowly toward the open box…

———⟫⟪⟨⟩⟫⟪———

"What do you want for breakfast?" she asked as she turned on the rim lighting in the kitchen, then started the coffee grinder after filling it with the dark roasted Rwandan coffee beans.

"Keep it simple. Eggs Benedict, smoked Norwegian salmon. Fresh-baked butter croissants and a fruit mix of blueberries, strawberries and raspberries from Nantucket."

"Dream on."

"Bagel and cranberry juice. I want to get these things appraised. Maybe we should go back to Red Clay and see what they have to say about them."

"They still haven't gotten back to us on the button and belt buckle. Not even a phone call."

"I know, that guy wasn't exactly Mr. Congeniality, but Smithson seems reputable."

"Your call. Coffee?"

"Yes, please. Let's have a look at these again." He pulled the chair up and examined the pieces, holding all six coins in his hand. He then moved the magnifying glass over them slowly, one at a time. "This is interesting. Did you notice that the face looks like royalty? Maybe a King?"

"No, but I didn't look that closely. Let me see." She stood next to him and peered through the lens. "I see a profile and it looks vaguely patrician. Perhaps a nobleman."

"Don't know. A weak area in my experience, but we can find out."

He buttered the bagel and thought about what was in front of him as he took a small bite. "You know, these are great!!"

"The coins?"

"No, the bagels. Costco at Christiana has a bakery on site. They make the best bagels I've ever had."

"Very funny… Let's finish and head out. When we go to Red Clay, I'll stay in the background. If it's Broom, you get to deal with the guy."

The drive up Route 1 after a recent snow brings obstacles and treasures. The melting snowpiles on the side of the road cause huge puddles, not immediately apparent traveling at 55 miles per hour on the blacktop, shaded in spots by overhanging trees. The treasures come in the form of vibrant wildlife near the edge of the highway, exuberant as the snow melts away and they can see food lying on the ground. Cardinals, robins, bluejays, morning doves and red-topped woodpeckers amongst deer, silver fox and groundhogs all feasting on newly found seeds, insects and berries, a Noah's Ark of friends eager to share in the Winter treats.

"Are you sure they're open right now?"

"Its 10:00 a.m. Every sensible storeowner is open by now unless they want to turn away business. If they're not, we'll go somewhere up the road. There are plenty of antique dealers in the area." He turned right into the lot and stopped before the white-painted building.

"Hi. We were in here before. Is Robert here?" Jim asked as he partly unzipped the heavy black leather jacket he'd bought in San Diego 15 years ago, one of his prize cold-weather possessions from his sunny California days.

"Robert's not in. I can help you. Did we meet? I'm Martin. Martin Broom."

The cold steely voice bothered Jim just as much as it did the first time and he felt a chill, despite the warm jacket. "Yes, we did meet. Will Robert be coming back shortly? We can wait."

"No. He won't. As I said, I can help you. What do you need?" Broom squinted a bit as he peered into Jim's face.

"I gave you a belt buckle and a button a while back. You said you'd have it evaluated. We never heard from you. Do you have a status on them?"

"Of course, I remember! You're... Jim?"

"Yes, Jim Peterson."

"Glad you stopped by. We don't have the results as of now, I've been a little short on help, but we should get the report in the next few days. I'll call you as soon as it arrives."

"Just curious, where is Robert?" Natalie asked, coming up to the counter, standing next to Jim, staring Broom straight in the eye.

GENE PISASALE

"Oh… ummm… Robert is out of town on business. He'll be away for the next few weeks. Standard stuff, reviewing potential acquisitions, giving advice on antiques, meeting with new clients."

Jim remembered how comfortable he felt talking with Smithson and hesitated. "Well, we have some other things we may want you to evaluate." He thought for several seconds before feeling them in his pocket, then slowly took them out with his right hand. "Here are some things we found in an old building." He laid the six coins on the counter and watched Broom's eyes.

He glanced up at Jim briefly, restraining his excitement. He'd seen many gold coins from the 18th century before and could tell they were genuine without using a magnifying glass. "Well, it's not clear exactly what these are. I'll need a closer look." He went to the back of the counter and took out the two lenses. "First- this appears to be a Colonial era coin, highly weathered, date is legible, imprint still visible. Appears European, perhaps French or English. Both countries minted gold coins at the time." He examined each of the other five.

Jim and Natalie watched his every move, hoping for a sign indicating the value of their artifacts. None came.

"What do you think? Are they very valuable?" Jim stated as he moved right up against the counter.

"Well, they're worth something. I can't tell you exactly how much right now." He sensed that what he had in front of him was worth a significant amount. "I'll have to send them to the lab, as always."

"What do you mean? You can't give us a rough appraisal? Haven't you seen things like this over the years?" Natalie's tone showed her irritation as she moved closer to Broom holding the coins under the magnifying glass.

"Well, ma'am, I can, but it might not be accurate. Yes, I have seen these, or ones like these before. I can tell you that, if they're authentic, they could be worth some money."

"What do you mean? How much? Is it $500 per coin? Maybe a $1,000 per coin? Give me an idea." Jim was also getting impatient, despite the fact that he had chosen to come back.

"Jim, I'm sorry. I didn't mean to treat you like someone I've never met before. These, if authentic, could be worth a few thousand dollars, perhaps." He felt comfortable with the conservative estimate and his clients' lack of knowledge. "We definitely need to send them to the lab for appraisal, though... to be sure."

"The same lab that hasn't gotten back to us yet on the first things we gave you?" Natalie grabbed Jim's left hand and squeezed it very firmly.

"I apologize... uh, Natalie. Normally they're quite prompt and get back to me in just under a week. I will call the lab and check. I'm really sorry for the delay and for any inconvenience. I promise I will get back with you tomorrow."

Jim was in that place he'd been so many times before. He knew to trust his instincts, but occasionally they were wrong due to impatience and homegrown biases. He knew the way he felt... and that was slightly uncomfortable. Then he did the scenario analysis again in his head. "If we have to drive to 2-3 other places, it could take twice as long and cost just as much, if not more money. These guys are nearby..." he considered as he stared at the coins on the counter in front of him. "O.K., if we leave these with you, we get a receipt with a detailed description and can expect to hear back from you, when? I want an exact date."

Broom tried to smile, looking straight at Jim. "We appreciate your business. My job is to provide you with the best service possible and I sense that you're not quite satisfied right now. I promise to have these six items back to you within the next week. You have my word." Broom stood up on his toes and leaned toward him, then back, on the edge of the counter.

"O.K., here you go. I'll expect a call by next week." He felt a sharp kick on the back of his left shoe.

"Very good. Thank you- and we'll get back to you promptly, both on your first order and this one, Jim." Broom started to gather the six coins into his hands.

Jim looked at Natalie and sensed she was steaming. "What do you think? Is that O.K. with you?"

"Maybe we should just give him one and keep the rest? They're all basically the same." She stood upright, not moving.

"Actually yes, that's a good idea. We'll keep these five."

Broom frowned. "Well, sir, if you like. I must remind you that evaluations can vary considerably between items based on wear... depth of markings... metallurgy. You might not get a reliable appraisal with just one."

"You know, hon, he has a point. If we really want to know their true worth, he has to take all of the coins." Jim put the five coins back on the counter.

"Excellent decision... I can see you're a reasonable man" Broom said, reaching for the coins.

Natalie pushed by Jim and grabbed a coin. "Let's hold onto this one. It shouldn't really impact the evaluation. If your lab's as good as you say they are, five should be more than enough to get a good idea of what all are worth."

"Very well. That will be $75 for each evaluation... but I'll give you a discount, make it $300 total. We'll have these five evaluated shortly. Anything else I can help you with?" Broom inquired, watching Natalie closely.

"Thanks... No, we're done. Looking forward to your prompt evaluation." He handed Broom the check, then turned around and left the shop. Approaching the car, he sensed her annoyance. "Anything wrong?" He knew before the words came out that there probably was.

"Well, yes!! We find these very old coins, six of them, which could be worth a lot of money and you were ready to just hand them all over to this guy, who I still don't like. He was borderline rude to you when we first went in."

"He is a bit distant, I agree. I actually thought he warmed up some after I told him we were still waiting for the other evaluation."

She stared at him. "He knew he'd lose the sale, that's why! He did get a bit more cordial as you talked, but that doesn't mean anything. Do you trust him?"

"Sure… well… I think so. That's why I only gave him five out of the six."

"I said to give him just one out of the six. At least if something happened, we'd have five left."

He thought back to all the discussions he'd had over the years with people far more intelligent than him. He knew she was right. He just hoped it was the right choice. "We'll hear back soon. Don't worry. At least we know where he lives… or at least where he works."

"O.K. Your call. We'll see what happens."

"Let's go over to the Chadds Ford Historical Society. Maybe they can comment on all these cryptic messages and give us a few clues."

"Clues to the quality of this establishment we just turned our treasures over to?"

"Not necessarily. I was just hoping for some insights on that note." Driving through the gated entrance, they parked near the back along the edge of the grass fringing the lot.

"Let's just see what they say. These people know the area and its history pretty well." She didn't respond, just took his left hand in hers and walked around to the front entrance, watching three SUV's cruise by at well over the posted speed limit.

"Hello. Can I help you with something?" The man speaking to him was dressed in jeans, loafers and a plaid red and green shirt appropriate for the holiday season. He gazed directly into Jim's eyes before glancing briefly at Natalie.

"Sure. I'm Jim… Jim Peterson. This is Natalie. We're

members of the Society and I had some questions about the history of this area I was hoping someone could help me with."

"Perhaps I can help. What is it you had a question about?"

He felt the tight squeeze and decided not to show the coin. "We were doing some exploring in the area, actually canoed the Brandywine a couple of times and we've seen a few spring-houses, some on the river, others a distance away. Were most of them near the water?"

"Many were. There were dozens of active springhouses in this immediate area from the late 1700's all the way up to the 1850's. Why do you ask?" He focused on Jim's eyes with a piercing gaze and Jim almost took a step back.

"Well, just curious." Her grip lessened and he could feel the circulation in his fingers again. "We've seen them scattered around and were wondering if there was any particular pattern or planning for their locations."

The man frowned and then laughed slightly while glancing at him. "Springhouses were dug and built in areas where there were either cool streams or underground springs close by to keep dairy products and other food fresh. Some were on the banks of rivers, others much farther away. No special significance."

"Oh… O.K., thanks." Jim paused, then asked loudly as the man turned to walk away. "Did any of them ever hold treasure from the period? Gold? Silver?"

The man turned around and stopped, staring at both Jim

and Natalie for several seconds before responding. "You're treasure hunters?!! We had a few of them back in the late 1960's and '70's. I thought they gave up."

"Gave up on what?" Natalie asked firmly, taking a step closer while letting go of Jim's hand. She returned the stare.

"Oh, nothing, really, I'm sure. Many years ago, back well before the turn of the century, there was a rumor that there was gold hidden around this area."

"You mean right here in Chadds Ford?" Jim said as he walked up and stood in front of him, studying his face as he spoke.

"Yes, right around here. The story goes that during the Battle of the Brandywine, Lafayette stayed at the Gilpin House up the road and he was so grateful to Mr. Gilpin for the hospitality, he left a large sum of gold coins as appreciation. No one's ever found any gold, but a lot of people have looked. One guy back in the mid-'70's even rented a backhoe and started tearing up the riverbank, thinking he'd found the treasure. Nothing."

"Lafayette was a nobleman, quite wealthy."

"That he was- and thank God for it. Without his money, Washington may not have been successful. He and his troops were close to starving several times, with few provisions and nearly unable to fight. Lafayette came just in time and spread his wealth around. Of course, he got a command in return, which is what he really wanted."

"I know, he fought bravely and was wounded at Sandy Hollow. Lafayette was revered as a hero by his French countrymen back home." Jim waited for any signs of there being more to his story.

"He was and was rumored to have put a pile of gold coins... hundreds of them... in some kind of spice box in the back cupboard in Gilpin's pantry. This was done on the morning he left the area, knowing Gilpin wouldn't find it until after he was gone... and as a modest Quaker, Gilpin wouldn't have accepted them directly."

"So what happened?"

"Well, story goes that when the British captured the area after Washington retreated, they commandeered the Gilpin and Ring houses, ransacking both of them. The British were known to have trouble with soldiers plundering everything before the commanders could step in. A soldier apparently found the gold coins in the spice box. Later, he hid the treasure nearby, knowing he couldn't bring the gold into camp for fear of others finding out. He couldn't hide the spice box on himself and had planned to come back and retrieve it later, but apparently never did."

"What came of the spice box and the gold?" Jim was focusing on his expression for any signs of truth... or fantasy.

"Nobody knows, but the rest of the story goes that he was killed later that day in one of the last skirmishes in the area, not far from the Birmingham Meeting House, but he'd written a note describing where the treasure was hidden."

Jim pressed his fingers between Natalie's and held them there. He glanced at her and then caught himself, turning quickly to look back at him.

"Why, do you know something about the treasure?' the man asked harshly.

"Oh, nothing. I didn't even know there was a treasure. So the guy died without giving anyone the clues?"

"Not exactly. Rumor has it that as he lay dying, he gave the note to a Tory supporter, who fought along with the British and also was later killed in a skirmish nearby. Some guy named… Lewis, I believe… Not sure. At any rate, this guy supposedly died with the note in his pocket, but nobody's ever been able to verify the story, or find the treasure."

Jim stared at him for several seconds as his heart pounded in his chest. "That's interesting. It would explain the treasure seekers over the years." Natalie put her arm on his shoulder, the 'We should be leaving soon' signal.

"Yes, it would. There's never been any proof of this, although I believe a few people have found some gold in the area. Just ask the local antique dealers up and down Baltimore Pike."

"So the CFHS doesn't have any written documents about this? No one's ever done a report?"

"Report of what? There's nothing to report. It's a fable and like most fables, its baloney. Nothing to it. Look, is it possible there's some treasure, some gold coins hidden around here somewhere? Sure, it's possible… Bigfoot's possible."

Natalie laughed and started pulling Jim's arm. "Well, we appreciate your time and your comments." She started to walk away, but Jim held firm and stood there.

"What do you know about any of these local antique

dealers? Are they all reputable?"

"Oh, yes, they're generally high quality people. Never had any problems. Of course, there are crooks in every profession." His brow furrowed. "What I do know is, if I found some treasure, I'd keep it for myself." He walked away and said "Good day, folks" as he entered the office area.

Jim looked at Natalie and thought for a few seconds. "We're onto it! The cryptic note in the book... the 18th century coins in that springhouse." He turned to look around as he said the words to make sure there was no one nearby.

"How do you link the note to the coins? That guy was talking about a whole spice box filled with gold coins... maybe hundreds of them. We just found a few and even if they are related, where are we going to find books about a story that is 200 years old? They're either in the private libraries of wealthy people or the Library of Congress."

"Or Macaluso's Rare Books. It's right in downtown Kennett. We've driven by it dozens of times. I've always wanted to stop in there."

"Next stop?"

"Right. I promise we won't max out your VISA card."

"MY VISA card? You mean YOUR VISA card."

He laughed as they turned to go out the door, stepping onto the newly built brick path done through the efforts of a local Boy Scout and back to their car. "I hope he also takes AMEX."

They drove up State Street and turned right at the Old Kennett Inn, passing the police station before turning left to get into the municipal parking garage. "Not too crowded, there are spots right up front."

"We have to get lucky sometime. I just hope the wind isn't blowing too hard. It's three blocks to get there." She buttoned up her coat.

"Two really. It's just off the main drag, down on the right near the stop light. Looks like someone's old house." They exited the parking garage and felt the strong breeze on their faces. Jim zipped up his leather jacket, adjusting the flaps up around his neck. He could feel Natalie shivering and put his arm around her shoulder. "Here, button this up. If you use the top buttons near the collar, it keeps your face much warmer."

"Thank you." She put both hands in her pockets. "Too cold!!"

They proceeded to the old grey house with the small front porch where two tables stood holding dozens of dusty books. The sign posted on the outside of the window said '50%- 70% OFF!!' and he almost stopped to browse through them, but Natalie pulled his hand to go inside.

"Hi. We've driven by your shop many times. I've always wanted to come in." He stood speaking to a short man, in his mid 70's, balding, with white hair pulled back in a ponytail. He wore suspenders over a white pullover and slate-green pleated pants.

"Well, hello. Welcome. Anything I can help you with in particular?"

"Yes, we're looking for books on Chester County history, specifically the Chadds Ford area."

"Well, there's a few over in that corner, illustrated. There are also some up on the second floor in the History section, narratives."

Jim immediately went to the corner where he'd pointed while Natalie flipped through a few of the dozens of old books scattered on the glass counter and adjacent tables. "Hey, hon, look at this, a map of Chester County from 1853."

She walked over to him and glanced at the map. "It'd be nice to find a good description of the history of Chadds Ford, with comments on the battle, the local inhabitants..."

"There are a few of those upstairs." His voice cut her off before she could finish, but the sound was gentle, grandfatherly.

"Let's head up." They climbed up the narrow wooden steps to a room which was probably a bedroom 50 years before. "There's the history sign." He walked over to the stack and knelt before it. "Here's one... 'West Chester to 1865- That Elegant and Notorious Place' by Douglas R. Harper. It looks to be well over 400 pages. There's got to be something in here about Chadds Ford." He paged back to the Index and went to the "B's". Battle of the Brandywine- pages 183, 187, 207, 224. He flipped to the first listing, a general description of the battle, then to the later pages. Then he saw it. 'Tory sympathizers were common in Chester County and the Chadds Ford area in particular, many wanting to stay true to their religious convictions and prevent a major conflict. Ironically, to do this, several of them took up arms against their countrymen, fighting in the battle. Known local Tory supporters who fought in the Battle of the Brandywine on September 11, 1777 included

Amos Hess, Anthony Burgleston, Jonathan Townsend, Peter Boyle, Curtis Lewis… He stared at the sentence and read it again. "Hey, Natalie, come over here. I found it!"

"Found what?" She was browsing in the far corner of the room, but put the book down and walked over.

"Curtis Lewis! The guy at the Chadds Ford Historical Society said some guy named Lewis was involved in the battle and the rumors about the treasure." He flipped to the later referenced pages, but didn't see the name mentioned again.

"Oh yes, I remember he said the last name, but how do you know it's this guy? There could have been dozens of men named Lewis in the area. Anyway, what would that prove?"

"Lewis! The guy was a Tory supporter who fought with the British and was killed on the battlefield. Remember what we read at Gettysburg? His son could have been Joshua Lewis, later Joshua Pyle!!" He looked at her for a few seconds. "Let's buy this book and head home." They moved toward the staircase and Natalie stopped.

"Did you see these? Several Hemingways."

He turned to his right and went over to the smaller bookcase up against the tan painted wall, a few chips missing near some vertical cracks. "Mmmm… no I didn't." He opened one. "This is a first edition Book of the Month Club printing of 'The Old Man and the Sea'. One hundred fifty dollars. A little above my price range." He paged through the book, with the original cover of the tan wooden shacks all along the edge of the beach, fishing boats ready for their masters to commandeer them out into the Gulf Stream to catch the biggest of the big fish, or at the very least, dinner. "Hey, look at this one. 'Men At War'... edited with an introduction by Ernest Hemingway. This is a first edition. I don't have this one. Supposed to be the best war stories of all time. It's only $45. Hell, I'd buy it just for the introduction by Hemingway." He held both books in his right hand, the Chester County book in his left. "Let's go." They walked down the stairway, Jim noticing the cracks in the ceiling, the chipping paint- all signs of the tough times for independent booksellers.

"We found a few good ones. This one on Chester County looks interesting. I also saw your Hemingway section. 'The Old Man and the Sea' and 'Men At War'. If I buy all three, can you make me a deal?"

The store owner took the books in his hands and opened them to the title pages where the prices were penciled in. "Well, let's see. These total $225. I can do... $200." He looked at Jim with his big eyes above the age-furrowed smile, the lines along the sides of his mouth formed years ago, speaking and smiling and reading late into the night.

Jim felt comfortable with him. His face was friendly, honest. His gaze never wavered. He thought of all the vendors he'd met over the years who couldn't look him straight in the eye. He trusted him and wanted to make a friend. "Are you the owner?"

"I am."

"I'm sorry, I don't know your name."

"Tom." He smiled as he put out his right hand to shake Jim's.

"Jim and Natalie Peterson. Very good to meet you. We love your bookstore. Reminds me of Wahrenbrock's in downtown San Diego." He thought back to all the times he strolled through that store, stopping by the old oak front desk covered with books, talking with the proprietor who always knew the answer to his questions. The store was filled floor to ceiling with books, old books, new books, oversized picture books, cracking, aged first editions, books almost falling apart sitting in the corners, three floors stacked with row upon row of books... his old friends. He looked up at Tom. "How long have you been here?"

At this location, almost 20 years. Before that, I was a professor of English, which I taught for over 30 years."

Jim did the math quickly. "This guy must have gotten his Ph. D. when he was in his mid-late 20's. Pretty good." Then he thought back to his own stint in graduate school, when he'd considered going for a doctorate himself- and decided against it. A Master's degree was more than enough work. "We'll take all three." He took the AMEX card out of his wallet. "Do you take these?"

"We take everything." He ran the card through the machine, giving Jim the receipt. "Here you go. Enjoy the books."

"Are you into history?" Jim asked, not wanting to leave.

"Yes, a bit. I enjoy reading. You can't teach English for 30 years without picking up a good book now and then." He looked at Jim and his brown eyes were wide open, deep wrinkles at their corners.

"My two oldest sisters are teachers. Got their degrees back

when teaching was still a popular thing to do. Then it was called West Chester State College. Years afterwards it became a University."

"Have many friends who went there. Good local school." He stepped in back of the counter and started to gather several of the dusty volumes lying in disarray on the glass.

"Do you know much about the Chadds Ford area, the Battle of the Brandywine?" Jim asked as he looked at his ponytail, a snow tail on his sloping shoulders.

"Had a wonderful book I took in, oh 20 years ago. Very old, dated around 1850, maybe 1855. On the battle. Lafayette. Washington. Too bad I sold it. A good read."

Jim stepped up to the counter. "Anything of particular interest?"

"Just a very well written book. Told the story of how Lafayette wanted to support the cause of independence in revenge for his father's death fighting against the British in the Seven Years War. The loss of considerable territory to the Brits in America that the French previously held."

"The French and the Brits were at each other's throats for centuries." Jim was hoping for more details.

"Still don't like each other. Lafayette was a rich young man, inherited his mother's fortune when he was just 14, then later married into another wealthy family... lucky guy. Wanted to come to the Colonies to support the cause when his wife was pregnant, but the French King was strongly against anyone going to America getting involved in the struggle, stirring up trouble with the Brits. He didn't need another war on his hands. Lafayette bought his own ship and left in the dark of night, taking the trip the hard way, sailing straight from France non-stop, landing in Carolina after a two-month voyage. Major seasickness."

Jim was amazed at how much he knew. He kept watching his face.

"Took him another month to get through the backwoods to Philadelphia, then the capital. When he rode into town, he wasn't exactly greeted with open arms."

"What do you mean?" Natalie came up to the counter, caught up in the story. His voice rose in pitch with enthusiasm.

"The Founding Fathers, especially those who were helping to organize the military, didn't have good experiences with foreign volunteers, especially a lot of the Frenchmen... either spoiled prissies or drunks. So Lafayette, who spoke almost no English, was suspect in their eyes."

"But he had money" she said.

"A fortune... and they needed it! End of story... almost. Lafayette went to Independence Hall to meet with Robert Morris, a signer of the Declaration of Independence. His namesake the Robert Morris Inn served the best crab cakes in the Chesapeake Bay region for many years, according to James Michener. John Hancock had introduced Lafayette to Morris. Lafayette was an inexperienced young man, although he did have some military training and the Colonials in Philadelphia thought 'No way'. He was rebuffed, but he appealed to the Continental Congress. As we know, Congress always wants money. Lafayette agreed to take a position with no pay and

LAFAYETTE'S GOLD

no immediate command, so he got his wish and joined the Continental Army. In return for his monetary help, Lafayette was given a military rank of Major General, second only to Washington himself... really just a title. As you can imagine, this didn't sit well with some of the other commanders."

"How did he meet Washington?" Natalie was now leaning close to him on the counter and couldn't take her eyes off his face.

"Lafayette got his position. So, he wanted to celebrate. Where do you go to eat when you have money? The best place in town... the Old City Tavern. He went there for dinner. Lafayette attracted attention wherever he travelled, especially around Old Town Philadelphia because he was kind of tall and quite thin. When he sat down to eat, who walked in? Another very tall man, several inches taller than Lafayette. General George Washington. Lafayette noticed him immediately and went up to him to pay his respects. Somehow they exchanged enough words to communicate. Young Lafayette had no living father... and Washington, in his mid 40's, never had a son. They bonded instantly, probably over a pint of ale."

"Was Washington much of a drinker?"

"Don't think so. He had bad teeth. In fact, almost no teeth. Never see a painting of him smiling, ever notice that?"

"Actually, you're right" Natalie realized.

"Washington asked Lafayette to sit at his table and there began the friendship. Lafayette supported the troops with his gold, fought at the Battle of Brandywine, became a hero

— 181 —

because he held his ground while others were retreating."
He put two books onto the pile he'd already formed on the
counter.

"You said Lafayette supported Washington with his gold.
Did he bring money into camp?"

"Very wealthy man. Multi-millionaire by today's standards. So yes, a lot of golden Louis D'Or's."

Jim and Natalie turned towards each other, raising their
eyebrows.

"Came just at the right time. The continental Army was
facing major desertions daily." He glanced briefly at Natalie
and gave her a little wink.

"Yes, but apparently most of the men held Washington in
awe. Kind of like MacArthur. There must have been an aura
about him."

"Too bad it didn't help at the Battle of Brandywine" Jim
exclaimed.

"Information is one of the most precious commodities we
have. He got bad intelligence, conflicting reports and it cost
him the battle. Yet he survived, regrouped and came back with
victories in just the next few months." The man scratched his
chin, shifting his stance.

"Was that it for Lafayette?" She grinned after thinking
about his wink, enjoying the conversation.

"No. He halted the retreat and held firm near the Birmingham
Meeting House, taking a bullet in the leg. Eventually they lost
the position, but Lafayette rallied the fleeing troops and waited
for Washington to arrive at a nearby bridge. He was later taken

to Bethlehem, Pennsylvania, the nearest decent hospital, to heal. He recovered and joined Washington three months later at Valley Forge. Now that was a disaster waiting to happen."

"I didn't realize Lafayette went to Valley Forge. Why didn't he just put himself up in a fancy chateau and sit out the war?" Jim asked, expecting a long, well researched answer.

"Guts. The man had character. What foreigner would travel halfway across the known world, risking his life, then give a good part of his fortune to a cause which looked hopeless? An honest man with deep convictions. A true American patriot. He even insisted on taking dirt from Bunker Hill outside Boston with him back to France. He was buried near Paris, with the soil of two republics. A remarkable man."

Jim felt the intensity of his words as he spoke. "Yes, he was. You have a strong understanding of U.S. history. It's refreshing to hear. Most people don't pay attention to history books anymore...We've got a whole generation of kids who don't know the difference between the Liberty Bell and Taco Bell. Your insights are appreciated."

"My pleasure. Looks like you enjoy books as much as I do."

"Yes. Reading is my favorite hobby."

"Well, take care... and come back soon."

"We will. Thank you." He nodded his head out of respect to the older gentleman. "We'll be back."

Tom went back to the counter, arranging the rest of the fragile books into a small pile. "Oh, books... so many books... and never enough time to read..."

———((○))———

The large grey truck with no markings on either side pulled up to the loading dock in back of the Red Clay building. The driver maneuvered the rear end toward the edge of the platform, then turned off the ignition, got out and rapped on the heavy metal door with his keys. The corrugated door slowly rolled up, exposing a pile of boxes and Martin Broom. "Next delivery, courtesy of Vinny and the team. Remember, we get 60% of the take and we want receipts for everything you do."

"Jimmy, good to see you. How's Vinny?" Broom extended his hand, but he didn't take it.

"Where's the money from last month's sales?"

Broom put his right hand into his jacket and took out a bulging manila envelope, along with some papers stapled together. "Here you go, that's $30,000... including the receipts. It's all there." He held them out in front of his face.

Jimmy opened the envelope and counted the cash. "Only $30,000 this month? You wouldn't be holdin' back on us, would 'ya?" He scanned the papers showing each transaction.

"No, Jimmy... no way!! Look, sales are down. This market's lousy! Even the rich folks aren't buying as much. I wouldn't cheat you guys." He watched as Jimmy put the envelope in his coat.

Jimmy stepped towards Broom, towering over him. He pushed Broom against the cement wall at the side of the platform, his leather jacket's zipper scraping along Broom's chin as he held him tightly. "Yeah? I'm not so sure. Maybe I need to provide a little incentive… knock some sense into that smug face of yours!!" He slammed his head firmly against the wall. "Look… hand over ALL the cash! We expect our full cut! I don't want to go back to Vinny and explain why sales are down."

"Jimmy, you got EVERYTHING! Honest… I swear!!" His face was red and he could hardly breathe. He put his left hand on the back of his head, rubbing the rising bump.

Jimmy backed off and walked over to the open truck, taking five boxes out, one at a time, dropping them onto the floor of the back room. "Here's the shipment. I'll see you next month." He turned to walk down the steps. "Don't forget… I'm watchin' ya'." Jimmy jumped in the truck and sped away.

Chapter 12

He got up, went down the stairs and could already smell the coffee brewing as he glanced out onto the terrace. "Good, no raccoons, no red fox, just the Christmas lights and the snow" he thought. The sky was charcoal grey, too early to tell if it would be a clear, sunny day. The first glimmers of sunlight were beginning to give the naked birch and maple trees a warming Winter glow.

He walked up to the plate glass sliding doors leading to the terrace and searched for the ducks. "There they are. The wind last night didn't blow them away." The collection of small rubber ducks with various designs had become one of their favorite diversions on the terrace over the last few years, picking up a few new ones during their travels. The pirate duck. The aviator duck. The surfing duck. They were all sitting on the flagstone, braving the cold air. He stepped outside and observed the dozens of trees in the forest, then walked up to the wrought iron railing, admiring their leafless skeletons silhouetted against the morning sky.

"Hi Mandy. I hope you're well." He remembered all the

Sundays he would get to church early, so he could kneel in the pew at St. Patrick's and pray for her. He was lost in the memory… the light pink walls of the church highlighting the altar and large crucifix of Christ hanging in the background… the low lights bathing the room in His grace. How many times had he prayed? He knelt in the pew, only two other people in the church, 20 minutes early for the 8:00 a.m. Mass and looked up at the statue of the Virgin Mary, then over to the crucifix. "Our Father…" The plaques marking the Stations of the Cross stood in relief at the end of each aisle. Then a few weeks later, the phone call came…

"You're planning the day?"

"Kind of. I'll get us each some coffee and we can sit in the Conservatory." He thought again about the cats… she always loved them, holding the kitten to her face for what seemed like 30 minutes, her eyes closed, while she petted the fur again and again, lost in bliss, Petunia quiet and enjoying the attention, rubbing her face against Mandy's cheek as they both shared the moment of solitude…

He went into the foyer and saw the painting of Lincoln by Rea Redifer above the Civil War table, the sepia watercolor lines streaked down from his right cheek, as if to show a tear. Passing the Southwest corner, he put the two mugs down on the leather coasters on each side of the table.

"What do we have lined up for today?" he asked as he sat down, the fireplace kicking in to give the room some warmth.

"We got that letter from Red Clay saying the appraisals were completed."

"Sounds good. I'll make breakfast before we go."

He looked out the window and noticed a large bird sitting on one of the tree branches. "I'm not sure, but I think that's the owl!! Might be the same guy we saw not too long ago."

"How do you know it's a guy?"

"He's got a woodpecker between his legs."

"Let me see." Natalie stood up in her pink pajamas and slippers, going quickly over to the window. "It's a big bird, for sure, but I can't tell if it's an owl or not. Whatever it is, it's getting a bit more adventurous, coming near the house. Get the binocs."

He went to the bookcase and took out the mustard-colored heavy leather case which held the JANA 7 X 35 Field binoculars, the ones he'd paid just $25 for years before in Denver, leftover items from the hundreds of possessions a widow's husband had left her. He took them out of the case, removing the grey plastic lens guards before walking back. He looked to the right as he entered the Conservatory and saw her standing up against the windows.

"Is it still there?"

"It is. Do you have the binocs?" she asked without turning around.

"Here you go." He handed them to her and waited for the appraisal.

"That's the owl, definitely. Just sitting on the branch. Too bad his head is turned away from us."

"Let me have a look." He adjusted the focus. "Oh, yes, he's a big guy. Never saw him up this close before. Waiting for some tasty field mice or baby bunnies."

"No!! Don't say that. I like bunnies."

"Sorry, so do I. Field mice it is for breakfast." He put the binocs down and sat on the couch. "So, we'll eat, drive up to Red Clay and then decide on lunch. Anything else?"

"There's always something. We can fix those tree guards that the deer have pulled off, do a clean-up of the fish tank, do two loads of laundry, unload the dishes from the dishwasher, clean up the kitty litter boxes, take out the trash and call my mother to make sure she's O.K.."

"Yeah, but that's easy. Then what?"

She laughed and almost spilled her coffee. "Isn't it peaceful just sitting here by the fire, enjoying the scenery around us?"

He looked out the window again at the owl, motionless, gazing to the West. "It is. That guy's probably doing a little recon work. Maybe checking out the local critters. Mice must be a nice change from seeds and berries. Our cats seem to like them." He put his mug down. "It is beautiful, just sitting here with you."

"Let's finish soon and get started on our day."

"I want to take this in for a few minutes." He closed his eyes... His mother was standing in the kitchen, her back to him as she faced the stove, making the spaghetti and meatballs which was just a side dish to the feast they would serve to their 25-30 guests on Christmas. Homemade ravioli, the Italian "seven fishes" platter, sautéed broccoli with onions and mushrooms, Italian sausage in red sauce, broggiole simmered in meat sauce, held together with tooth picks, homemade broccoli and cheese pizza… His childhood feasts were magnificent, not to be seen again...

"Would you mind if I just stayed here and got some things done? Plus, I don't really like that Broom guy, he bugs me."

"Sure, no problem. I should be back in an hour. Hopefully Robert's there instead."

The roads in most areas around the Christmas holidays are a poker game. It could be a losing hand, bumper-to-bumper traffic all the way North through Media…or a lucky one, fairly empty due to people putting off their errands for another day. Today was lucky. Almost no one on the road. Lights timed the way people love it, cruising through five of them without slowing down.

He pulled in and parked next to several other cars … a few of them SUV's, one on the corner with a canoe. "People don't like getting the lower mileage, but in cold weather, these come in handy" he thought as he got out.

"Can I help you?" came the shrill voice. Broom walked out from behind the counter.

"Is Robert here?"

"No, sorry. Mr. Peterson?"

"Yes."

"He's not here now. Should be back sometime soon. It's Jim, right?" Broom commented, reaching his hand out.

"Is everything done?"

"We have the evaluations. Let me get them for you." He dashed into the back room and came back out 30 seconds later, as Jim was admiring the Revolutionary War flag.

"Here you are. The artifacts you gave us... the button, the buckle and the five coins." He laid them out on the glass counter, along with the thin black binder. "There it is."

Jim thought "There what is? Am I supposed to know exactly what you're showing me, with no description?" He picked up the buckle, then the button. He put the button down slowly as he looked at the coins, then picked up the first of the five and stared at it for several seconds. "So, what are all these worth?"

"As you can see from the written evaluation, less than what I thought. The buckle is a common one from the period, worth only about $250. They're nothing special. Same with the button... about $250- $300. The coins are very poor quality, low count on gold, according to our assay. Many coins of the period had strong variations in their purity, some close to the 99% stated, others much lower, like these which are around 20%-25% pure. Based on that, we estimate they're worth only about $400 a piece." He looked away as he spoke the last words.

"I'm trying to like this guy, but it's hard when he doesn't even look me in the eye" Jim thought, putting down the first coin, then picking up the second one. "Wait a minute, the button and the buckle are worth $250- $300, but you're only offering $400 for each coin? That doesn't make sense to me."

"Well, they are very poor quality. We're willing to go as high as, let's say... $500."

He glanced at Jim for a fraction of a second before staring at the coins on the countertop.

Jim observed Broom, then felt the third coin and he

noticed something slightly different. "Do you have that magnifying glass? I want to take a closer look."

"We do, here it is."

"This is the big one. I want the smaller one to see detail."

"What is it you're looking for? Perhaps I can help you." Broom stood straight up and took a step back.

"I'd like the smaller lens, please. Do you have it?"

"Of course. Here you go." Broom's eyes wandered around the shop.

Jim inspected the third coin and sensed… something different. "The face seems a bit blurred… indistinct. The crown on the flip-side is also less sharp from what I remember" he thought. He picked up the fourth coin and saw similar features. "As I recall.… weren't these sharper?" He held it in the light, momentarily confused, but said nothing further, waiting for his response.

"Those are exactly the way you gave them to me, they haven't changed!" He frowned as he glanced down at the counter. "I'm firm on this… $500 per coin. That's my best offer."

"I think we'll pass."

"It's a very good offer. You won't get anything higher from the other dealers in the area. We pay top dollar." He tried to avoid Jim's stare, hoping he'd change his mind. "I'll offer as much as $550 per coin… that's the very best I can do."

Jim took the coins, button and buckle, dropping them in his pocket.

"I hope you'll come back soon. We have specials in January." Broom strolled past the counter as Jim walked out the front door.

"When hell freezes over" Jim thought as he got in the car and drove home.

"You were right. I don't like him, but at least we got our things back. Too bad Robert wasn't there. I really enjoyed speaking with him. Maybe he would have made us a better offer."

"He made you an offer? How much? Did you sell him the coins?!" Natalie asked anxiously.

"No, I didn't sell them. He only offered $550 each... said they were poor quality... but something wasn't right. I thought they looked... peculiar. Maybe not. I don't know."

"What do you mean?"

"It seemed there was something different about the coins from what I remembered when you and I first looked at them. The face, the crown... but I'm really not sure. I can't say because I never took a really close look when we first got them."

"I can't believe I'm asking this, but do you think he switched them on us?"

"I can't imagine he would do that!!"

"So what do we do now? Do you think it's worth getting a second opinion?"

"Here's an idea that could help resolve things. We'd been planning to do a trip downtown for quite a while. We could take these to the Living History Exhibit, across from the new Constitution Center. Maybe they'll have someone there who can examine them."

"If you want to go now, we could get there before Noon, have them take a look, then maybe have lunch at the Old City Tavern."

GENE PISASALE

"Excellent plan. Let's do it. I fly, you buy" Jim said.

"O.K., I'll pick up lunch if you promise not to buy any T-shirts or coffee mugs with Thomas Jefferson on them."

"How about one with George Washington? We don't have any Washington mugs."

"We don't NEED any Washington mugs. We have enough coffee mugs to serve the 101st Airborne."

"O.K., no mugs. Maybe just a Lafayette T-shirt."

"Forget it."

As they drove up I-95 toward Philly, she looked at the road ahead and only saw a few cars. "Not too bad today. We're almost to the airport." Natalie looked to the right and saw the 747's taking off thousands of feet over the Delaware River. "Do we bear left there, onto 476? I'm prepared for heavy stop and go- just in case. We're never this lucky."

"We turn right up there into town." He looked at the sky-line as they approached the city. "You want a helmet?"

"Only if you start driving backwards."

"There's the exit." The car weaved into the light traffic on 8th Street , finding a spot quickly.

"This is a certifiable miracle, less than 35 minutes. Hold on, I'm calling the Vatican." Natalie unhooked her seat belt as the car came to a complete stop.

"I believe you need three miracles for the Pope to consider it. Back in 1969, the third one was the Mets winning the World Series."

She laughed as they both got out. The cobblestone streets were still slightly icy, despite it being near mid-day with the sun shining brightly.

"Here we are... the Independence Living Archeology Center. The Constitution Center is up there, across Market Street, a few blocks away. Every American should stop by there when visiting Philadelphia. They'd learn a lot about their own heritage."

They entered the building and he approached the front desk. "Two please. Do you take triple-A?"

"Actually, we don't. Sorry. Did you still want two admissions?"

"Yes, two adults." Next to them, behind a large glass window, a young man stood looking over a long wooden table covered with dozens of artifacts, many of them only fragments, pieces of pottery, glass shards, broken pieces of metal.

"Is that your research room?" Natalie asked.

"Yes. We do evaluations and display many of our better artifacts right here. Feel free to take a look." The woman was in her mid-50's, with graying dark brown hair and a light blue top, attractive, tight jeans highlighting her slim figure, sitting on a swivel chair.

"Thanks very much. We will." He stepped over to the glass-enclosed room and stood watching the young man placing two brown ceramic bowls on the table, obviously centuries old. Jim knocked on the glass. "Hey, can we come in?"

"Yes, but just stay behind the railing. You can observe, but please don't touch anything." He was wearing a white Oxford-collar button down shirt and dark charcoal pants. "I'll let you in."

Jim stopped by the door, letting Natalie in first. "Do you conduct all your analyses here?"

"We do, in the back. Everything from pottery and silverware to guns, coins. These are all from recent excavations... right around the edge of this building... and next to the former Liberty Bell Plaza."

He felt reassured as he touched the coins in his right pocket. "Interesting. Are these all Colonial era?"

"Just about everything here is dated from around 1725 to 1855." His voice had the certainty of a young Ph.D. candidate ready to defend his dissertation.

Jim took the coins out of his pocket. "Perhaps you can tell me something about these." He placed the five coins, along with the belt buckle and the button on the table. Then he took the sixth coin from his other pocket and set it aside.

"Well, you've got a few things there." He took out his detail magnifying glass and squinted as he looked at the first coin. Then he put it down on the table and examined the second, third and fourth. "These are all reproductions... good quality copies of 18th century coins."

"What do you mean? These aren't genuine?" Natalie went right up to him and stared at his face.

"No ma'am. They're not. They look real enough to the untrained eye... very sophisticated work... but not originals."

"Somebody offered us over $500 a piece for these!! How can they be fake?"

"I'm not sure how much they're worth, but these are definitely not real. Let me look at this other one." He picked up the fifth coin. "Reproduction." Then he looked at the last coin, which Jim had deliberately placed to the side of the others. He stared at it for almost 30 seconds under the glass. "This… appears genuine. An 18th century Louis D'Or gold piece... dated... markings are clear. I can't give an exact value, but its worth quite a bit. Perhaps $8,000- $10,000. A museum piece." He looked up and sensed they were confused. "The others are Louis D'Or reproductions- good ones, though. I've seen dozens of them over the years. Some disreputable dealers sell them in the lower-end stores."

"I don't understand. Five of the six are fake? How can that be?" Jim asked.

Natalie grabbed his right hand so firmly that he flinched.

"Well, good reproductions can fool even relatively experienced antique collectors. The first five are very good quality repros. This one is clearly authentic. I don't have an explanation. I'm just telling you that I've seen hundreds of these and I know." Natalie was frowning and about to speak.

"Are you sure?" Jim said, leaning on the table next to him. His heart was pounding as he thought about Broom… and his 'offer'.

"Jim, he's an expert. He looks at these things every day. What about the buckle and the button?"

He put the button under the glass for a few seconds. "Reproduction." Then he picked up the buckle and examined it under the glass. "Unfortunately, another fake. I'm very sorry. There are a lot of fake antiquities going around. We had some guy in here about a month ago with several items he'd just bought from a dealer in New Jersey. He paid over $30,000 for about ten items. All fakes. I felt terrible giving him the news."

Jim cursed under his breath. "Well, now we have an evaluation from an independent, qualified third party." He picked up the coins and the other items, putting them back in his pocket, keeping the sixth one separate. "What do you think we should do? "

"We don't give appraisals for a fee. We just give our opinion. I won't comment on any particular dealer. There are thousands of reputable dealers around this area and around the country. They're honest, but some are not. If I were you, I'd go back to the guy and get an explanation… but that's my opinion."

"I appreciate your help." He felt the deep sinking feeling in his gut, knowing he'd made a serious mistake.

"You're quite welcome. Stop back anytime. We're always looking for volunteers to help in excavating."

"Do you allow volunteers to help in the digs?" Natalie said, her voice rising, excited to hear the response.

"We sure do. We can use all the help we can get. We've got mostly archeology students from the local universities. If you want to volunteer, just give me a call." He handed her his card.

"That's great. We'll be in touch."

"Well, that was interesting."

"Part interesting, mostly bad." She stared at him with her piercing blue eyes, now burning with anger.

"O.K., you were right. It's highly unlikely that five of the six coins we collected would be fakes. Broom was pretty slick, making me believe he was giving us a valid offer. I've seen some smooth operators before, but he's Teflon."

"We should have taken close-up photos of everything we collected. This would never have happened!!" She looked up at Jim. "Shall I say it now?"

They spoke in unison. "I TOLD YOU SO!!" Jim laughed for just a second, then looked at her. "I didn't mean to spoil our adventure." He curled his lower lip down like a scolded child, being forced to stand in the corner.

"Jim, this isn't funny!! That guy has five of our gold coins... not to mention the button and the buckle... which all could be worth well over $50,000!! How are we going to prove he swapped them for counterfeits... and get our originals back?"

He thought for almost a minute while observing the outside of the building across the street, the 18th century structure now abandoned, but still in good shape. "I was too trusting. My instincts told me not to give them to him, but my sense of practicality nudged me into doing business because it was convenient."

"Well, convenience may have just cost us over $50,000. What do you propose we do?"

He stared at the sky, the pink-grey clouds dotting the horizon. "There's a few options, want to discuss them over a beer at the Old City Tavern?" His tone rose as he hoped she would accept his mistake.

"I'm still waiting..."

"I'm so sorry, I really screwed up."

"Beers at the City Tavern!! Lunch is on you!!"

"Sounds fair. I'm having five Jefferson ales."

"To celebrate what... your stupidity?"

"No. It may take me five ales to figure out a new strategy."

They walked over to Old City and turned right on 2nd. "There's the Tavern up ahead."

They climbed the steps and opened the heavy wooden door. "Welcome to the City Tavern. Would you like to eat in the dining room or the bar?" asked the young man with a white wig under his three-cornered Colonial hat.

"The bar, please. Can we get a booth?"

"Absolutely, sir. Follow me."

They walked towards the back past the display case filled with pewter items and cookbooks and sat down. He looked around for their server. "Should I just go up and get us some drinks at the bar?"

"We can wait, the waitress should be here soon." She noticed the woman in period dress coming towards them.

"Welcome to the Olde City Tavern, the place where George Washington, Thomas Jefferson and Benjamin Franklin planned the future of our country. Anything to drink?"

"Yes, two Jefferson Ales, please. How about you, honey?"

"Jim!!"

"Just joking. Two ales... one for each of us." The waitress smiled and headed back to the bar.

"Do you think it's possible that Thomas Jefferson sat here... right where we're sitting?" Jim pondered out loud.

"I guess, although I think the tavern was rebuilt after a fire, so if you were looking for Jefferson's DNA, it didn't survive."

He laughed, putting down the menu for a moment. "OK, this place is known for its period food, specialties that Martha Washington would serve up. Lots of beef, potatoes and molasses biscuits. We certainly won't leave hungry." He took a long sip of Jefferson ale, the fizz going slowly down his throat, giving him a momentary rush, the one you need after making a big mistake.

"Well, I'm starving. Want to take a historic walking tour of downtown after lunch?" Natalie suggested.

"Sure. Another Jefferson please." Jim signaled to the bartender, even though his glass was still about half full.

Their meals came quickly and they both ate heartily. Jim gulped the last of his beer. "Do you think I'm sitting in the same spot where Washington sat?" he asked with a grin.

"We just went through this. Alright, cowboy, I think you've had enough ale. Let's move on."

"To the next... adventure!"

They walked the four blocks to the Independence Center and Jim stood at the front desk, waiting for the attendant to notice them. "Two, please."

The girl looked a bit distracted while she punched his order into the computer. "That'll be $22."

"Do you take Triple-A?" Jim inquired, knowing he might get a kick, but instead Natalie stood there, staring blankly at the ceiling.

"Yes, actually we do. Can I see your card?" Jim grinned back at Natalie while he handed the card to the girl.

"Thank you, that'll be $20 instead."

"See, we just saved $2" he noted to Natalie.

"Superb. I'll start a trust fund for the cats."

"The tour will start shortly out in front of the building" the girl indicated, pointing towards the entrance.

Jim and Natalie walked out just as the tour guide arrived. "OK, people, listen up! We'll be starting the tour right here in about two minutes. Gather 'round."

Jim stood up straight and moved closer to the guide, excited to get going.

"Alright now… follow me. Make sure your cell phones are turned off- and no smoking, please." They stepped onto the sidewalk and headed down the street.

"We'll be covering parts of Olde City, areas made famous by our Founding Fathers- Washington, Jefferson, Adams and of course, our own Ben Franklin."

"This is going to be great!" Jim exclaimed as he zipped up his jacket against the breeze. "Can't get enough." Natalie nodded and leaned against him to keep warm.

"To your right is the First Bank of the United States and just up the road is where Benjamin Franklin lived."

"I understand people liked to drink a lot back then. Did they have any favorite haunts that are still around today?" came a question from a young man in the group.

"Well, many of them drank and dined at the Olde City Tavern. That was where they often met to discuss the issues facing the colonies and they even planned the Revolution against the British there. In fact, it's known that General

George Washington first met Lafayette there. If you recall your 8ᵗʰ grade history, Lafayette was the Frenchman who helped our cause by offering both his services in the field and more importantly- his money. The story goes that they liked each other instantly. Both were members of the Free Masons, the ancient secret group which pledged allegiance to a code and shared the same values. Washington often invited Lafayette to dine at his table during the war, discussing current affairs and battle strategies. Clearly their friendship and the discussions they had throughout the course of the campaign had a significant impact on the outcome of the Revolution."

Jim moved in closer, making sure not to miss a word.

"Lafayette returned to Philadelphia after the war around 1824 and asked to be shown 'that house of independence', at the time known as the Pennsylvania State House. Lafayette's remark caught on in the vernacular, leading people to refer to it as "Independence Hall" thereafter. Let's walk down the street to this great hall of freedom. There you will see the original room where our Founding Fathers signed the Declaration of Independence."

The guide proceeded up the steps in front of Independence Hall and entered the foyer separating two main rooms. He signaled the group toward the left. "This is it folks – this is the room where it all happened. Where the Continental Congress debated independence. Where Thomas Jefferson, Benjamin Franklin, John Hancock and many others put their lives and fortunes on the line to defend liberty."

A woman in the group asked "Are the furnishings original?"

"They are mostly period reproductions, with the exception of that chair at the head of the main table." The guide stopped and pointed to the dark brown chair in the center at the rear of the room. "You'll notice, if you look closely, the back of that chair is intricately carved, with a sun in the center. That is known as 'Washington's chair'- the original one used when he presided over the group approving the Constitution in 1787. In our country's most perilous days- times of great uncertainty following the Revolutionary War when there was no real 'nation'- he gave great comfort to a concerned populace. When viewing the chair, Benjamin Franklin was asked by one of the delegates whether he thought it was a rising or a setting sun. Despite the uncertainty, Franklin replied with a firm, confident voice 'Surely it is a rising sun.' " The guide waited a few minutes to allow everyone time to look at the room and its contents.

Jim leaned towards Natalie. "Without those men, we wouldn't be living in the country we know today. There have been decades of debate about Jefferson, Washington and the others. Yet, what they achieved, in the end, charted a new course for mankind."

She smiled and raised her hand to his cheek. "You're my favorite historian."

"Want to head back? That antique dealer may still be open. I want to confront Broom with these 'coins' and tell him what that guy at the Living History Center said."

"What if he refuses to do anything?"

"Never show your cards until the hand is over. Play it smooth and don't let your opponent have the slightest idea what your next move will be."

"What is your next move?"

"I have no idea."

They made it through the congestion of I-95 and arrived back at Red Clay Antiques. He tensed up for a few seconds, knowing a confrontation was likely in store. Before getting out of the car, he made sure he'd separated the five fake coins from the original one they'd kept. He glanced at Natalie, who was ready for battle.

"I'll do the talking, but feel free to hit him with a large crowbar if tries anything funny."

"Fine. Where's the crowbar?"

Jim walked into the building first and saw Broom sitting at the counter. "Good, there's nobody else here if it turns into an argument and gets nasty" he thought. Broom saw him and instantly stood up, somewhat suspicious of his quick return.

"Hello. Change your mind and decide to take my offer?"

Jim walked right up to him. "I've discovered a problem and I need it resolved. We found these coins all together, the five we gave you for evaluation and the one we kept." He laid the five coins on the counter, along with the button and the belt buckle, pushing them towards Broom. Then he took out the sixth coin, putting it about a foot away on the glass, his hand resting nearby. "We got a second opinion on the coins from a Colonial history expert at the Living Archeology Center downtown. They've examined hundreds of artifacts from the 1700's and 1800's. Their staff archeologist looked at these five for us."

"Did you have a problem with our evaluation?" Broom leaned very close to Jim, his face less than two feet away, challenging him with his stare.

"You're darn right we have a problem" Natalie thought as she looked on.

"Yes, we do. The archeologist said these five... the ones you gave back to us... are fakes. This one... the one we kept... he identified as genuine, worth a considerable sum of money. The belt buckle and the button- he said they're fake, too. Seems like way too much of a coincidence. Everything we found along the Brandywine... that we gave to you... was fake... except for the one coin we kept ourselves." He glared at Broom, waiting for a response.

Broom stepped back. "Well, sir, what are you trying to say?" His forehead furrowed with a stern expression.

"These coins were all found together, in the exact same spot. It's inconceivable that five of the six would be fakes, the last one authentic. They'd be all one or the other."

"Yes and..."

"I don't know what happened to our coins. All I know is the ones you gave back to me weren't the ones I originally gave you. Perhaps your lab service switched them by mistake with someone else's order. I noticed when you gave them back that they looked somewhat different. I want my original coins back... now!"

"Are you accusing me of stealing your coins? How dare you!! I returned the coins you submitted to me for evaluation... YOUR coins." He stood his ground... staring directly at Jim.

"Look… you took my five authentic coins and kept them, giving me fakes in return, offering me a small amount of money to make the transaction look legitimate. I'll say this just one more time… give me my five coins back!!"

"I GAVE you your coins back… plus an accurate evaluation from our lab."

"You gave me fakes!! I want to talk with your partner. Where is Robert? He's much easier to deal with. I'd rather discuss this with him."

"Mr. Smithson is not available!! I don't expect him back for several weeks."

"I insist on seeing him!! How can he be reached?"

Broom took a deep breath, trying to gather his composure, but couldn't… and then exploded. "I made you a fair and valid offer and you attack me like this?? You wouldn't get anywhere near as good an offer from the other dealers. Get OUT!! Get out of my shop!!" He moved toward Jim, pushing him slightly, but Jim stood his ground, ready to hit him.

"Back off!! I'm saying the coins you returned to me were not the ones I originally gave you. Look, I'm willing to assume an honest mistake by someone, the lab, some other party. All I want is my coins back!!"

"I made you an offer and you rejected it! Our lab work is of the highest caliber. I gave you back your coins, do with them what you will." His eyes were on fire.

Jim glared at him, breathing heavily, tempted to jump at his throat, but said nothing for several moments. "You'll be hearing from the authorities about this." He took the items off the counter and put them back in his pockets. Natalie looked at him, wondering if it was over. "Let's go." They both walked out without saying a word.

"Where to now?" She buckled her seat belt and stared out the window as he started the car.

"Home. I should have done this to begin with. I'll do a Google search on this place and the owner. See if there are any complaints or lawsuits."

"Sounds fine, but that won't get us our coins back."

"Oh, trust me. We'll get them back." He sped out of the parking lot, gravel flying up almost to window level as he headed down Route 1.

"Hey, slow down, Mario. This isn't the final lap of the Indy 500."

"Sorry. I'm pretty steamed about this. We're going to get our coins back. He switched them… and that's fraud. A felony. Five to ten years in jail. I intend to make him pay for this."

He pulled into their garage and turned off the engine.

She went into the kitchen. "Ready for a glass of wine?"

"Maybe three. Bring mine in here. I'll be working at your computer." He sat down and logged onto the Internet. "Red Clay, lawsuits". Five hits. He read through them, but the stories mentioned the shop as one of many reputable places in the region which occasionally experience disgruntled customers who brought them to court. "Martin Broom, fraud, lawsuits"- 170 hits, over 12 pages. "I don't believe this… or, maybe I do. Let's see, first one: 'Broom charged with selling bogus antiques'. He scanned a few paragraphs, a story from a regional newspaper, dated 1997. It was a customer complaint regarding alleged fake Civil War artifacts.

The next story: 'Broom suspected of fraud ring', dated 2009. "Now this is interesting. 'Martin Broom, co-owner of the much respected Red Clay Antiques shop in Chadds Ford, Pa. is suspected of having sold hundreds of fraudulent artifacts to wealthy collectors in Chester County. Plaintiffs have sued Broom for what they claim were fake antiques purchased at the store and also ones submitted for appraisal, then swapped with reproductions. Broom is one of several antique dealers in the Mid-Atlantic region suspected of trafficking in bogus antiques. These establishments are also under Federal investigation as money-laundering outlets for the Mafia. Broom has been under investigation by the FBI since 2005. The case remains open'. Jim looked up from the screen. "Natalie!! You've got to see this!!"

His voice carried into the foyer and outer hallway. She came into the room and stood beside the chair, putting down her wine and leaning closer to the screen. "Oh my God! Should we contact an attorney… or the police?"

"Both, but I want to see more of what you mentioned earlier." He took a large sip of the cabernet and looked over at her.

"What's that?" She stood back from the desk.

"You… in my favorite clingy dress and high heels."

"You bonehead. Get serious!!

"Thought it was worth a try." He picked up the phone and called the Kennett Police. "Hello, I want to report a possible theft…"

"A POSSIBLE theft, sir? You're not sure? Could you please explain?" The dull monotone from the clerk at the police station was discouraging.

"Well, we found these coins…" He went through the series of events, the interaction at Red Clay and the two evaluations. "We think we've been robbed of our five gold coins."

"I see, sir. We'll need you to come down to the station to make a full report in writing. Bring the coins and anything else related to the case for photographs."

"I'll try to stop by in the next day or two. Thanks for your help." He put down the phone and looked at Natalie. "Well, that's done. I'll go by there tomorrow and complete the report."

"Remember what that guy at the Chadds Ford Historical Society said… something about a spice tin? There could more coins that we didn't find. We should checkout that Springhouse again" Natalie suggested. "I think we need to reevaluate those clues first… it could help pin point the exact location… or at least tell us where we went wrong. He made it sound like there were hundreds of gold coins, not just a few, like we found."

"I say we retrace the battle… stop by each place and compare them to Pyle's cryptic clues. I have the Brandywine Battlefield guide… and a copy of Sanderson's hand written map. There may be some pieces of the puzzle still to be solved. Recall… 'Hid while the waters lapped nearby, see what warms the old Blacky'. O.K., we know that's likely the old abandoned shed we visited in Dilworthtown, near where the last stages of the battle raged. There was that carving on the mantle, of a

river and a house. Clue number one... the blacksmith's shop...
Next, 'House where the rainbow ends'- that's key- that's got to
be where it's buried, or somewhere close by... there's always a
pot of gold at the end of a rainbow... maybe the Springhouse
by the Brandywine where we found the coins! I'm sure that
covers the first two clues. "Out of place at the steps to nowhere'. That's intriguing... what we should be looking for...
the last clue which should complete the message."

"Right, but what does it mean?"

"With a little luck, some poking around, we may just find
out. I'll drive."

"O.K., but no land world speed records" Natalie warned.

"I wouldn't think of it. Besides, the speedometer in my car
only goes to 160, well off the record." He clicked the garage
door opener as they pulled away. "Let's drive down Route 100
again, check out any possible battle sites, then head up Route
926 to the Birmingham Meeting House."

"Why there?"

"Because that was the decisive point in the battle. The
Colonials last stand before the Brits triumphed, driving
Washington back to Philadelphia. Most British soldiers who
participated in the fighting would have been there feeling
pretty cocky and confident after the battle. The British soldier
who hid the coins may have used some of the surroundings
in his cryptic note." He glanced at her to see any signs of
agreement.

"Interesting theory, worth a check."

They drove up Route 100, slowing as they passed the John

Chad house and the crumbled remains of an old stone barn across the street from the Wyeth homestead. Seeing nothing that matched the clue, Jim turned right onto Street Road and right again at Birmingham Road. "The Meetinghouse is less than a mile ahead." He turned at the Lafayette Cemetery entrance, then pulled ahead 20 yards and stopped. "Let's take a look around."

"I hate this breeze!" She put both hands in her pockets as she stepped out, glancing up at the setting sun. "It's gonna be dark soon, we need to make it quick."

"O.K., but check out all those monuments! That one has to be 30 feet high." They approached the three large granite carvings along the edge of the driveway and gazed up. "This one's to Lafayette. Pretty impressive, ornately carved. Also mentions Pulaski." They walked up and around the yard to the Birmingham Meeting House and he unhinged the gate. "After you, my dear lady. Place looks deserted... our luck." He walked ahead as she peered into the building.

"You know, this building was used as a hospital during the battle." She gazed up at the stones on the wall of the structure.

"Look back here... a monument and burial ground for the Colonial soldiers who died in the battle." He leaned over slightly to read the stone. 'In memory of those who fell in the Battle of Brandywine, Sept. 11, 1777. Back of this in a common grave lay those who fell in this vicinity. Marked by the Brandywine Valley Farmer's Club 1920'. He stood up and looked over the shrubs, nicely displayed, fringing the memorial.

"They are to this day... heroes."

"What's over there?" Natalie's voice came from the edge of the parking area.

He walked back through the gate and saw her standing in front of what appeared to be stone blocks. "Back there was a monument to the fallen soldiers." He moved forward and looked at the structure. "That is pure granite... blocks stacked upon blocks."

"Fine, mister petroleum geologist... but what is it?"

"I've seen these in old photographs from the late 1800's and early 1900's. Sometimes they built steps so that people could more easily get onto their horses. Probably more for the ladies."

She frowned for a second, then shrugged with a smile. "Actually, that makes sense. It's much easier for a man to mount a horse than it is for a woman, especially if she was wearing a long dress, which of course, they did back then."

His mind was working as he stared at the stone blocks, the light now fading to dusk. "Steps... steps... steps to nowhere!! Natalie, this is one of the clues! 'Out of place at the steps to nowhere'. These steps appear to lead nowhere... see?"

"You're right! Now... what's out of place?"

"Next task. Figure out what the hell that means."

She looked at the sky and noticed the sun was almost down. "It's getting dark. I say we head home and come back tomorrow."

"I guess you're right. We'll come back then... finish the clue." His heart sank as she said the words. He wanted to explore every square inch of the house and gardens. He could make out some very old gravestones in the fading light, fallen and chipped, barely visible below the grass about 30 feet away. "I'd like to check those out, too" he thought.

"I'm hungry. Want to grab a bite somewhere near home?"

"What about The Gables? It's on the way back. They have a nice menu, plus we have that gift certificate you got on your birthday from my sister."

"Good idea. Next stop… The Gables." After she got in the car, he lingered outside for a few seconds, staring at the steps, then at the Meeting House. "Are you getting in?"

"Just a second." He looked at the structure, then got into the car and headed for the restaurant. "The final clue" he thought.

"This is a nice place. We should come here more often, it's right up the road from us" she mentioned, eyeing the menu.

"They have an outdoor terrace where you can have cocktails. Some nice Spring or Summer night, we're sipping champagne out there."

"To celebrate what?"

"Us" he said as he peered into her eyes.

"Hello. Welcome to The Gables. We have a few specials, but can I get you anything from the bar to start?"

"Two glasses of the Talbott Chardonnay, Sleepy Hollow Vineyard 2006, please and we're ready to order." They watched as the restaurant started to fill up, each absorbed in their own thoughts until their food arrived.

"How is yours?" He looked at her as she put the last forkful in her mouth.

"Wonderful. I love fresh salmon."

"Mine was great, too. The lobster ravioli in light Alfredo sauce is superb. Check?"

He paid, then stood up, taking Natalie's coat and holding it for her...

———•((•))•———

"Nick, its Vinny. You guys on Peterson?" He was standing outside the house in the fog, the cell phone close to his ear as he zipped up the jacket with his other hand.

"We've got him. They just left The Gables. They won't be driving too far. They're done."

"Good. Let's get rid of this guy. Eddy says if they testify, we're all toast... plus Broom called, said this guy Peterson was trying to make trouble. Remember, this'll save your AND my ass."

"Vinny... don't worry. He's done." He closed the cell phone and started driving down the highway...

"Nice night. A bit of fog... actually, a LOT of fog, but not much traffic" Jim commented. He brought his speed up to 45, then looked in the rear-view mirror. His eyes widened. "There's some guy in an SUV about a quarter mile back, flying down the road. He's got to be doing 70." He looked at the road ahead briefly and noticed there was no one in front as they passed Route 52 heading south. He checked the rear-view mirror again and felt his chest almost explode. "Ohhh my God!! That guy is right on our TAIL!!"

"What?" Natalie turned to her left to see what was behind them. "Jim! What's he doing?!"

They felt a jolt and flew forward. Then another strong bump, throwing Natalie against the dashboard. Jim steadied himself and banged on the horn, swerving to the right onto the gravel shoulder and into a ditch, the car nearly tipping over. He turned the wheels sharply to the right to avoid the roll, then steered back out of the ditch as he regained control. The SUV rushed past them, almost sideswiping the car, then disappeared into the fog.

"My God!! That guy almost killed us!!" She stared at the red taillights as they faded in the mist. "They must have seen us... even with the fog!"

Jim regained composure and steered back over into the left lane. "That could have been VERY bad. Did you see that huge oak tree? That's what we would have hit... head-on." He peered in the side-view mirror and breathed out slowly as he observed the tree in the distance behind them.

"That was close... you saved us!!" Natalie sat back in her seat, putting her hand on Jim's thigh.

"One rises to meet a challenge." He was quiet for the rest of drive back. He knew he had seen the car before.

Chapter 13

"Nick?" He looked down at the floor as he held the phone.

"Yeah, it's me."

"Vinny."

He knew what was coming and held the phone away from his face.

"What the HELL happened??!! I hear Peterson's still alive!"

"I know! I know! Look, it was really foggy, I could barely see anything. I tried to run him off the road into the trees, but he managed to swerve and stay in control. Put a big dent in the front of my car, too!"

"Who gives a shit about your car?! You screwed UP!"

"Vinny, I'll get it done… I promise. I've been tailing him ever since. Don't worry."

"Well I am worried… and you better be, too! Big Tony says Eddy is feeling the heat from the Feds to spill his guts… basically rat on everyone. It could be me, you and the whole gang in the slammer for a long time. So get your shit together!! Take this guy out… NOW!!"

"You have my word. I'm watching his house every second. He can't go 50 feet without me knowing. I'll get it done this time. Trust me."

"You better… or else it'll be YOUR ass I'm looking for next!!"

Nick heard the dial tone and looked out the car window at the house…

———

Jim looked at the clock and realized they'd slept in. "Six-thirty, I'm a bum. Should've been up by five." He walked in the family room to turn on the morning music. "IPODS, our new addiction. Let's see… Selection… Morning… Shuffle… Play." He noticed her coming down the stairs as the sounds came through the speaker system throughout the house.

"We slept in."

"Sure did. You should have gotten me up." She rubbed her eyes and went into the kitchen. "Tea?"

"Done. I'll bring it into the Conservatory, you call up the kitties." He took both cups and strode past the Southwest wing.

"Frankie!! Francis!! Come up, kitties!!" She stood at the top of the basement stairs, then it hit her… the night Eddy had come down the same stairs and tried to kill them. She turned and shook her head to try to lose the memory, joining him on the couch. "Thank you… Hot!!"

"Well, we have a few things. First- these six coins were worth close to $60,000, although now we have five fakes and just one genuine Louis D'Or. We know more about some of the clues in the note. I'm doing more analysis." He took a sip, then looked out at the frost across the back lawn.

"I'm still puzzled by the 'steps to nowhere'. What could that have to do with the treasure? We need to go back there."

"I agree. Next stop... the steps to nowhere."

"Where will that take us?"

"Perhaps... nowhere. If we're lucky, to a very large prize."

"I need to clean the bird cage and feed the fish first."

"Exactly what Eisenhower said before D-Day. I'm going to fill up the car at Wawa, then stop by the store to pick up a few things for dinner tonight. I should be back in about 30 minutes. O.K.?"

"Fine. I'll be here." She could hear the garage door close as she pulled out the tray under the bird cage. The doorbell rang. She pushed the tray back in and thought "Who would be here this early?"

"Mrs. Peterson, I'm Agent Clark, from the FBI office. We met briefly when Agent Rawlins interviewed you."

"Yes. I remember. He said you might have some more questions. Come on in."

She proceeded to the parlor near the front door, not wanting him to come all the way into the house. He was a handsome man, in his mid-late 30's, thick, wavy, black hair, piercing blue-green eyes, the kind of eyes that drove all her friends crazy when she was in college, her wilder days. "That was a long time ago…" she thought as they sat down.

"Did you have some more things you needed to know from us? I'm the only one here. Jim is running some errands."

"Yes, just a few." He couldn't avoid looking at her clingy, low-cut pink top, which showed more than a little cleavage above her push-up bra. Then he noticed her tight fitting jeans as she crossed her legs. "You didn't have to wear that, but… I'm not complaining" he thought. "Well, ummm…", raising his head back up to look at her face, "We wanted to know if you had heard anything further from Mr. Caniletto or any of his crew. Any threatening phone calls? E-mails?"

She thought about the incident with the other car in the fog, but decided it was just a reckless driver. "Thank God, no." She noticed his face was so… young looking. "He can't be over 35. I didn't think you could be a Special Agent that young. He is kind of handsome."

"I hope you don't mind me saying, but you're in wonderful shape!! You must work out every day" he said, looking at her legs, then at her chest again. "She must be a swimmer. Nice floatation devices" he thought.

"Oh, well thank you. Jim and I like to get regular exercise." She sat closer to the edge of the couch, just two feet from him in the other chair. "This guy is flirting with me, but he's kind of sexy. I don't mind, really. This hasn't happened in quite a while. Why not enjoy it for a few minutes? It's harmless."

"Have you seen any signs of Eddy in the area? Any suspicious people walking around? Cruising cars?" He was trying to avoid looking, but somehow kept coming back to that sliver in the middle of her top, staring right at him. "I love it when women wear those low-cut tops… boobs pushed up tight… They know it drives men crazy. Especially when they walk, watching that bounce… up and down."

"Not that I've noticed." She liked the way his chin stuck out just slightly, the hint of a cleft at its end, then she looked at him closer. "He must work out two hours a day. Nice arms!! Could have been a Chippendale part-time, putting himself through college" she thought as she uncrossed her legs. "College… I'm old enough to be his mother!! Stop!!"

"Well, that's good news. We're continuing to monitor the area." He was jotting down notes into his Franklin Day-Planner, then he looked at her chest again and thought "I'd love to see you in one of those skimpy black bikinis. The ones those 'cougars' wear in Miami, hoping to do some… trawling for younger catch. They lay by the pool, sipping their daiquiris, leaning over to show off their… assets… when the younger men walk by. I wouldn't walk by. I'd get you a fresh drink, then take you back to your room and… God, she's gorgeous!! I love it when older women aren't afraid to show some cleavage! Makes a guy think nasty thoughts." He finished writing. "Did you or Jim take anything out of the satchel, any notes, slivers of paper? We found a few pages missing from the account statements."

"No, we gave you everything we had."

"I'd like to give you something!!" he thought, then looked down at his notes. "I bet she's great in bed… Wait!! Calm down, Clark… you're going way overboard here." He glanced up at her eyes. "Well, thank you. If you have any questions, feel free to call me personally. That's my direct number. I'm generally free most afternoons. In fact, I love this area. There's a great coffee shop right up the street. If you have anything you'd... like to share, maybe we could meet... say, later this week?" He stood up to leave.

"Was that a proposition?!" she thought. "This hasn't happened since me and the Killer Bees were at that bar in D.C. That was what? Eight or nine years ago? It's a little exciting!! He is very attractive..." She shook the thoughts out of her head as she got up to walk him out. "We'll let you know..."

"Hey, there's something on your face" he said, reaching out to wipe it off. Natalie stepped back, but not before the top of his fingers lightly brushed her cheek, then passed within an inch of her breasts. "I got it- just a piece of lint." Their eyes met and a slight smile crossed his face. They stood there for what seemed liked eons, but was really just a few seconds. He licked his lips slowly and Natalie blushed, snapping out of the trance. She headed for the door, opening it for him.

"Well, I...uhhh... If there's anything to share, I'm sure Jim will get back with your boss." She looked into his eyes and stopped. "There. That should give him a clear message. A little flirt is fine, any more than that is... not good." She stood by the door waiting to hear what he would say next.

"Uh-oh... boss... not me. O.K., back off." He couldn't help looking down at the curve of her breasts one last time, hoping she wouldn't notice the bulge in his pants as he turned away. "Well, I'm pleased to help." He put out his hand to shake hers and when she did, he wrapped his other hand around it. "I'm always available… if you have questions." He pressed his hands firmly around hers. "Give me a call." He nodded and walked out the door.

She liked what she saw from the rear as he got into his car. "Nice ass…" she sighed. "If I were single and 25, I'd jump you right here!! We'd do it all… day… long… sipping champagne in front of the fireplace. Stop it, Natalie! You're happy now. Very happy… but… the attention was nice" she thought to herself, then walked back to the kitchen and heard the car coming into the garage.

Jim's voice came through the back door. "I'm home! Ready for the day?" he said as he opened the door into the kitchen.

"I'm ready for you anytime, sweetie."

"Ready?! Hey, you look really… nice… super sexy!! I LOVE the way you look in that top!! You KNOW that push-up bra is my favorite… Mmmmm." He walked up to her and put both hands on her breasts, pushing them up and almost out of her bra, spilling over the edge of the clingy pullover. Then he grabbed her with both arms and brought her onto the couch in the Family Room. "Why don't you take those jeans off." He put her down on the couch, then took off both shoes and started unzipping his pants…

"Oh, I like what I see!! I have a really nice place for that."

"Oh, YEAH!!! Ohhh… YES!!"

They laid there for a few minutes, then he pulled his pants back on, put on the Nantucket jersey and tied the laces of his ankle-high topsiders. "Great way to start an adventure!"

The car turned onto Route 52. "Are you ready for the rest of the puzzle?" He glanced at the side of her face and felt happy.

"As long as it gets us our $50,000 worth of coins back." She looked out at all the dead grass, flattened along the side of the road, victims of the recent heavy rains and ice. "Is it Spring yet?" She felt the longing again to be out in the garden, the sunshine on her face, light breeze blowing the hair from her shoulders.

"Almost. I want to drive out to Punxsutawney and meet Phil. Doctor Phil, I mean." He looked at the road and saw several cars in front of him, all doing well over the speed limit.

"The Prognosticator of prognosticators?" she grinned as she glanced over.

"One and the same. I'll introduce you. Nice guy. A bit furry, though."

"Cute!!"

"He IS cute. First things first- you can't be flirting with a groundhog! I simply will not allow it!! Second- whatever we find, it may be a very small piece of the puzzle, but small things can lead to big answers."

They headed directly toward the Lafayette Cemetery. 'Out of place at the steps to nowhere.' It stuck in his head as he pulled into the parking lot. "A fresh pair of eyes and plenty of light."

"There are the steps, but where do they take us?" she said, pointing to the stone slabs. She walked up to the Meeting House and stared at the wall. "A lot of grayish-green stones.

Did you say these were all serpentine?"

He passed the steps and stood beside her. "Yes, serpentine is abundant around this area. Also some schist rocks." He walked out to the gravestones he'd seen the night before and tried to read the markings. Most were illegible from decades of wear. He went back to the house and looked up at the roof of the structure, then at all the stones down to the base. Natalie had gone around to the edge of the building.

"Hon, I'm back here… Come over when you can."

Jim kept studying the stones, then headed to the back and stood next to her examining the wall. "Look at that. The huge piece of yellow quartzite, about two feet wide, right there in the middle of the wall. All the other stones are serpentine and schist" he said, staring at the rocks.

"A bit out of place, don't you think?"

He examined the stone. "Interesting…"

"Well, there's quartzite in the area, too… right?" She looked at the yellow stone amidst all the sage-colored ones in the wall, then over at the garden.

The memory stuck in his mind and he thought about it slowly, trying to recall what he'd seen before. 'Out of place… at the steps to nowhere.' What's out of place? Out of place… The quartzite is out of place!!" he thought as he stared at the stone and the vision became clearer. "As I walked up to that springhouse, there was a huge piece of yellow quartzite in that wall… but only one. ONE!! Out of place…" He thought for over a minute and looked up at the sky. "That's it!!" he yelled.

"What?" She looked at the side of his face, then back at the wall. "Is the treasure behind the wall?"

"No. The piece of quartzite- it's out of place here in the wall! Look, it's the only piece of quartzite in all this green serpentine and schist. Do you remember that springhouse? There was a huge piece of quartzite in the side wall, but only one!!"

"I'll take your word for it. So, what about it?"

"That's the third part of the clue. We found what looks like a blacksmith's shop in the area where the battle raged. British soldiers were swarming all around there and even took some prisoners at the Inn down the street. The second clue is the end of the rainbow, which legend says holds a pot of gold, or some kind of treasure. We did find gold- the coins. Now this. 'Out of place at the steps to nowhere' is the link which takes us full circle, back to the treasure!! The soldier who wrote that note must have fought here after staying at the Gilpin House, stealing the coins Lafayette had left. He couldn't carry them with him, so he hid them and left a cryptic note afterwards which would be very difficult to decipher. We have to go back to that springhouse!"

"How can you can be sure the treasure's there? It might be- but the metal detector didn't indicate anything else." She glanced at the wall and started walking with him toward the car.

"Right, but we had it pointed at the ground… not at the wall!"

They got into the car and before turning the ignition, he thought 'Hid while the waters lapped nearby'. "Back in Colonial times, the Brandywine was much higher and wider than it is now. Plus they'd had several days of heavy rain before the battle. You know how easily the Brandywine floods. It must have been flooded then… which is why the soldier wrote 'waters lapped nearby'. Normally the bank's a hundred yards back from the springhouse, which is why no one ever made the connection over the last 200 years."

"Makes sense, but how can we be sure we're not wasting our time going back there? The place is nearly buried in mud. It took me three wash cycles to get my pants cleaned."

"Look- I'll buy you a new wardrobe if I'm right. The coins are enough of a clue. We already found six… There's got to be more… somewhere!" He put the car in gear. "We better get going, it's starting to rain again." He hit 55 on Route 100 as the rain turned into an icy downpour, cars ahead skidding on the turns. "It's really coming down." He looked in the rear-view mirror as ice pellets bounced off the windshield. "That's odd. The same car has been behind us for the last ten minutes. He's staying about 150 yards back. I can't believe they have a canoe!! You'd have to be insane to go canoeing in this weather."

"Are you sure you want to be climbing around that springhouse? We're going to be totally drenched!!"

"Treasures don't come easy… and if this guy doesn't stop following us, I'll be even more uneasy." He looked in the mirror. Same car, two guys in the front seat.

"Are they really following us?" She turned around and saw the vehicle, now less than 100 yards back. "I do remember seeing a car parked at the back of the cemetery. Don't recall seeing a canoe on top" she thought. She turned back around and looked at him. "I hope not."

He pulled off to the side of the road near where they had parked before and stopped, the wheels sinking slightly in the muddy gravel. "I'd like to walk around with the metal detector first. See if there's anything interesting before we go back in the springhouse. We really didn't explore the area by the river last time. I can start there and walk back."

"Why? What could be along the river?"

"Who knows? Maybe more gold coins washed downstream. We didn't check the area. We still have an hour of light."

"It's raining really hard now! Looks like an ice storm to me. I really don't want to go out in this."

Jim jumped out and grabbed the metal detector and shovel from the trunk. Natalie shrugged and opened the door as he headed into the field. "Alright... I'm coming!" she said, pulling the attached cap from her insulated windbreaker onto her head. "It's freezing out here!! Let's make this quick! I don't want to catch pneumonia."

He held the metal detector and proceeded slowly around the edge of the springhouse, his shoes sinking in the mud and icy puddles with each step, the rain pelting his coat and face.

"There's the river. Looks high... and it's probably getting a lot higher if this keeps up." He stepped gingerly, trying to put his feet on the spots where clumps of dying grass held the soil more firmly. It took him almost 15 minutes to go the 130 yards to the river's edge.

"Looks like a torrent. I haven't seen it this high in years." Natalie stood next to him taking the shovel, then started walking along the bank. "At least no one will let loose any dogs on us in this weather."

"I hope that dude is at home in front of the T.V., downing a few beers. Actually, I'd prefer to see him in jail." He stepped down about a foot over the edge of the bank to where a large rock jutted out, the water swirling around it. He looked upstream and saw the canoe. "You won't believe this. There's two guys canoeing."

"No way!" She had to turn slowly in the mud to avoid falling over. "My God, you're right. Are they crazy?" Then she heard the pops.

"What was that?"

"I don't know. Sounded like a firecracker."

Two more pops, the impact ricocheting off the rock where he was standing. He looked at the canoe. "That guy's got a gun!! Get down!!"

"I can't, it's all mud."

"GET DOWN!!" He tried to crawl off the rock, but his left leg slipped as he stepped onto the bank. "Oww!! Ugh!! Damn! I think I just twisted... my ankle" he exclaimed as he fell into the shallow pool a few feet from the bank.

"Oh, my God!! Jim!! Jim!! Are you all right??"

He grabbed the end of a dead tree branch that hung low into the water and pulled himself slowly toward the rock. "I'm... O.K, but my ankle isn't." Three more shots rang out, whizzing by his head, tearing the few brown dead leaves off the branch above him. He ducked and his head went a few inches into the water. "What the hell!! Owww!! I can't get a grip on this branch!"

"I'll help you!" Natalie got up on her hands and knees and started crawling toward Jim, dragging the shovel with her.

He saw Natalie as she was crawling through the mud and leaves along the water's edge. "Stay down!!" He glanced over to the river and noticed the man trying to stand up in the canoe with his rifle. He pointed the gun straight at Jim. Then the shot rang out and Jim winced, fearing this might be his last memory, the noise echoing through the woods.

"Jim?!! Are you all right?!!"

He opened his eyes as he heard Natalie crying. Then he looked back at the river and saw the canoe upside down in the water, the current pulling it quickly downstream and the two men flailing frantically as they tried to hold on. The river in that location was normally just eight feet deep, but with this rainstorm, it had risen to at least 12 feet, raging as it approached flood stage. He watched as both men went under, banging up against a large boulder, then were pulled further downstream. "They're gone" he thought. "Thank God."

"Are you O.K.?" Natalie looked at him in the water. "Let me help." She held out the shovel, but it wouldn't reach. "What now?" she thought, then saw the branch he was reaching for. "Here, I'll hold this branch down and steady it… you grab on!" she exclaimed, pushing it towards Jim. Her face and jacket were covered with mud as she knelt down closer to the edge of the current, the water swirling dozens of leaves quickly past her face.

"Ugh!! I'm… fine… but my ankle doesn't feel too good."

He pulled himself up onto the edge of the rock and put his good leg onto the surface. "Just need to get out of this freezing water." He put his other foot onto the rock and stood up slowly, favoring his right leg. "I'm in one piece. Did a job on my ankle. Those guys aren't doing too good." He looked out to the spot where they both hit the rock and went into the current. "I'm sure they drowned." He saw the canoe floating downstream in the distance, 75 yards away, upside down, being buffeted by the current, smashing into large tree trunks sticking into the edge of the water. The canoe disappeared into the icy fog.

"It's fine with me if they're dead. They tried to kill you!!"

"They tried to kill both of us."

"Let's get out of here... now!"

"O.K. No... Not O.K. We came all the way here, fought the weather and survived this. I'm going into that springhouse. You can go back to the car. I won't be long."

"Jim!! It's an ice storm!! Are you out of your MIND??!! You almost got killed!! What are you doing??"

"I'm going to find whatever was left in there."

He put each foot slowly onto the clumps of grass, his shoes slipping on almost every one, plunging into the mud which was now almost four inches deep. Every step took him deeper into the muck, but he kept walking, leaning on the metal detector for support. "You going back to the car?"

"Well... no, I'll come with you, but I'm turning into a popsicle. I can't believe you want to continue!! This better be worth it. I'm totally soaked!! We also need to report what happened to the police."

"We will, after we check this place out." He managed to stay on the firmer spots all the way to the springhouse, then ducked down as he started to go in. "You coming with me?"

"You first… You hit your head last time… which is probably why you need to have your head examined."

He went in and looked over at the wall where he'd seen the large quartzite boulder. "There it is, right near the top" he thought. The wall was crudely built, with several loose stones just waiting for the next big flood to knock them free. He knelt in front of the wall and could feel his legs starting to go numb from the cold, his knees settling several inches into the mud and leaves. He reached up and grabbed the edge of the boulder, about 12 inches across, four inches thick and managed to move it slightly.

"What are you doing?!! Are you trying to take apart that wall? This place could fall down on us any second!!" Natalie knelt against him, providing support to his back. With each pull on the stone, she could see nearby rocks coming loose. "Jim, this is dangerous!! This place could collapse and in this ice storm, it could come down on top of our heads!!"

"Look, this stone doesn't support the wall, it's at the top, so nothing's coming down." He pulled at the stone again and it fell down onto his right knee. "Oww!!! I didn't need that."

"Are you hurt?"

"Well, after twisting my ankle and now dropping a boulder on my good knee, I'm batting a 1,000 on my legs so far.

Hopefully no major damage. We should be able to get out of here before gangrene sets in."

"What??!!"

"I'm kidding, my leg's O.K." His knee throbbed for a few seconds. He felt the edges of the rock in the mud and noticed there were a few round objects lying on the ground in the dim light nearby. "Turn on that metal detector- and your flashlight, please. It's hard to see in here." He dragged his fingers at the top of the mud as she shined the small flashlight toward the wall. "No, over here." He looked down as he felt a few more of the discs. "What is this?" The shape had a familiar feel and he brought the items close to his face. The metal detector sent off a steady round of clicks as she pointed it toward where he was kneeling.

"What is it? Even with the flashlight, it's not that easy to see in here." She leaned over his shoulder.

"A coin, I think!!" He tried to scrape the thick layer of mud off the surface. "Feels just like the others we found before." He felt along the ground, picking up two more. "Coins!! Point the flashlight over here!"

She could barely manage to keep her knees in place as the metal detector continued to click incessantly. "I'm shifting a bit. My knees are locked and I was losing circulation." She stood up halfway and glanced at the spot in the wall where the quartzite boulder had been, shining the flashlight there briefly. "My god! Look at that!!" She saw a pile of the coins, spilling out from what appeared to be a metal box. She raised the metal detector and it erupted, the screaming pings echoing inside the small room. "This thing is going NUTS!!"

He looked up and had a feeling of elation as he leaned closer to the wall, putting his right hand on the stones for balance while using his left hand to grab some of the discs. There were dozens of them. "There's got to be over 50, maybe 100 or more!! What is that?" He tried to pull the box forward and got it to the edge of the stone. "It's filled with them." He grabbed it and saw the metal top against the wall, its back at a 90 degree angle to the base of the container. "It's got a few compartments. Bring the flashlight over here."

The metal detector was still beeping loudly, ringing in her ears. She leaned against his shoulder. "I can barely hear you... This noise is driving me crazy!!"

"Turn that thing off!! We don't need it anymore." The blare ended and peaceful silence filled the room... then he heard the dull pings of sleet bouncing off the roof. He pulled the metal box to the edge of the wall and took it in both of his hands, spilling more of the discs onto the floor. "This thing is heavy-must weight at least 15 pounds. Look at all these coins!!" A few dozen spilled onto the floor as he tried to steady it in the light.

"You get the box. I'll try to pick these up."

"Can you see O.K.?"

"I can see much better if I hold the flashlight over toward here." She pointed the beam into the mud and saw the discs scattered all around his feet. Then she picked one up and scraped the mud off slowly, positioning the flashlight for a closer view. The light illuminated the surface, revealing a yellow glitter. "I'm betting those are Louis D'Or's... I just know it!!" She grabbed each one from the floor and put them in her pockets.

"Let me have that, please." She handed him the flashlight and he took it in his right hand, trying to balance in the mud. Then he flashed it onto the serpentine rocks in the wall. "Look, there's something carved into that stone. Can you read it? My eyes don't focus that well up close. Here, you get closer." He moved to his left and Natalie crawled a few feet forward, leaning onto the wall.

"Looks like... ep...11... I can't really make it out." She focused the light right up against the rocks. "I read... ep...11... maybe...177. I can't understand what it says."

"Let me see." He took the flashlight and leaned right onto the stones, his eyes inches from the jagged edge of the wall. "Yes... ep. There's something in front of the e. Looks like... an S. S... ep...11...and yeah... 177. Wait!! I think I can see it!! It reads... Sept. 11, 1777!" His entire body shivered and his mouth hung open. He stared at the carving on the wall for several seconds.

"Yes!! That's the final clue!! This is IT!!!! This is the spot where the British soldier buried the coins he stole from Gilpin... dozens of coins... hidden in the spice box like the guy said at the Society... and he dated his entry the day of the Battle of the Brandywine!! We found it!!" She flashed the light at the wall and then down at the box, the coins overflowing onto the floor. She put her hand on his shoulder and could feel him shaking.

He looked up at her face. "Well done! Now we just need

to collect all this and get out of here before the river floods."
Just as he said the words, a strong gusty wind whipped by the
structure and two of the stones near the gap slipped slightly
toward them. He looked up at the roof. "We need to get out of
here right now! This thing could come down any minute." He
looked at his hands and his clothes. "I'm more mud than man
at the moment."

"Yeah, but if these are all real, we'll be golden soon."

They crouched down and put their hands along the ground
as she shined the light, picking up the stray coins and putting
them in their pockets. He grabbed the metal box and started to
duck down to get out of the structure, but stopped. "You go
first. If this things collapses, I don't want you hurt." Just then
one of the stones from the center of the wall fell down to his
feet, missing his shoe by less than an inch. He looked up. Even
in the dim light, he could see the roof was showing signs of
movement. "Go!! Now!!"

"Ouch!! I can barely get through in all this mud... holding
this stupid thing."

"GO!! We need to get out of here!!"

She crawled forward and stood up slightly as she cleared
the doorway, holding the metal detector as she was pelted with
icy rain, the wind whipping her wet hair in her face. Then she
heard the rocks shift. "Jim!! Watch out!! Jim!!" She heard a loud
groan as several of the stones started to collapse inward into
the center of the structure.

His head came out first, tucked into his arms as he held the
box, slipping as he exited the doorway. "Oww!! Ughh... my

ankle." He was kneeling in the muck and looked up at her face, her mouth and eyes wide open. He turned around and saw the stones from the walls collapse, taking the roof crashing down as the ice storm raged, stinging his face. He saw the scene in slow motion as the last stone fell and hit the very edge of his shoe. "Ouch!! Damn! Like I really needed to hurt my leg some more…" He pulled his leg forward, then got up out of the mud slowly in the icy torrent.

"Jim!! Are you hurt?" She let the metal detector fall to the ground as she moved quickly toward him.

"Oh, I think I'll survive. Luckily that last stone missed most of my foot. If it had hit me, I'd have a broken ankle for sure." Just then the storm raged harder, the rain falling like daggers on their faces, the wind plastering their wet clothes against them. "Let's get out of here before we're both under water… or a glacier." They stood up, trying to move with their pants and coats drenched. "Well at least some of this mud is coming off. Might only need two wash cycles this time."

She laughed, then caught several icy pellets on her nose. "Ouch!! Let's go. I can't take this much longer." They struggled across the marshy floodplain, a quagmire with the grasses mostly gone, now completely covered in deep puddles and a coating of ice. "I can't tell where to step… this place is starting to fill with water!" She walked slowly and with each step, her feet went deeper into the mud. "So much for this pair of shoes." She went straight to the car without stopping- the brown muck coming up to her calves. Jim walked favoring his right leg, slowly putting each foot down into the mud, taking him almost ten seconds for each step. He managed to grip some low-lying shrubs, pulling himself along the hillside toward the car.

"We did it!! Soaked, muddy, a bit frozen... but in one piece." He glanced down at his pants and jacket, wiping leaves from both.

"Jim... your ear!! It's bleeding badly!!" She moved toward him. "Did a bullet hit you?"

He felt his ear with his index finger and then looked at his hand. "Blood? Doesn't look like blood. Doesn't hurt any." He put his finger up to his ear again just as Natalie came up to touch the side of his face.

"Oh, Jim!! Your ear is all bloody!! Wait... no. Looks... like... red berries?" She put her fingers on the edge of his ear and upper neck and examined what was in her hand. "You must have rubbed up against some wild red berries when you fell along the river. Thank goodness!"

"So you're saying I'm not getting a medal for this? No Purple Heart?"

"No, but how about a hug?" She put her arms around his waist and kissed him. "Now, let's get out of here."

He opened the trunk door and laid the metal detector, shovel and the box on the grey rubber mat lining the floor, making sure the box was closed and up against the side wall of the car so it wouldn't fall over. "O.K., let's go." As the car cruised around 20 miles per hour in the icy rain, he knew he needed to call the police, but focused on the quickly disappearing road in front of him. The front had developed into a raging ice storm, with visibility less than 50 feet.

"Take your time. We were almost killed once- we don't need to try it again." They turned into their complex and the car went into "TRACTION' mode as it climbed up the hill.

"Home at last… and still alive! Let's get all this stuff inside and take a closer look." She followed him in after he took the box out of the trunk. "Wait, I should call the police and report what happened." He went to the counter and dialed the phone.

"Kennett Police, how can I help you?" The female clerk was holding the phone on her shoulder while trying to file her nails.

"Hi, this is Jim Peterson. My wife Natalie and I were hiking along the Brandywine about an hour ago, just off of Brinton's Bridge Road."

"You were hiking in this weather? What were you doing out there?"

"Just exploring… checking an old springhouse, not far from the river."

"Go on" she said as she raised her eyebrows and knew she was talking with a nutcase… but only a 2 on a scale of 1 to 10 covering all the ridiculous things she'd heard over the years.

"We were right at the river and I noticed two guys canoeing down the Brandywine. They shot at us!!"

"You say they were canoeing down the Brandywine?" That reached an 8 on her scale. "Exactly what time did this happen, sir?"

"Oh, it was about 3:30, almost 4:00 p.m. today. At any rate, they kept shooting at us several times, almost hitting me."

"Could they have been hunting? Maybe mistook you for a groundhog?" She chuckled to herself, not sure what to believe.

"What?! NO…. They could see me… plus, I think I'm a bit bigger than a groundhog. I think they were following us earlier. At any rate, the guy in the front of the canoe started to stand up… in this raging rainstorm… and took another shot at us, but he lost his balance and the canoe tipped over."

"Was this about the same time, almost an hour ago?"

"Yes, right about then."

"Why didn't you report it immediately?"

"Look, I was shot at, sprained my ankle and fell into the river!! It took us awhile to walk back to the car. I'm calling you now, aren't I?"

"Were either you or your wife injured by the shots?" The clerk was writing brief points on the small pad in front of her.

He felt his ear again and saw the red stain on his hand. "Actually, yes, he shot a hole straight through my head, but I'm fine." He heard silence on the other end. "No sense of humor" he thought and continued. "Luckily, we're both fine, but their canoe flipped over and they both went under. They floated with the current, which is pretty strong right there, then they both hit a huge boulder and went down. I didn't see either of them after that, just the canoe, washed downstream."

"Anything else, sir?"

"Well, I had noticed a car following us as we drove up to the springhouse and it caught my attention. It had a canoe on top, which I thought was crazy in this weather. It was a late model Honda SUV, black or very dark blue, two passengers, both men. When I saw the men on the river, I didn't think about who they were, just that they were lunatics. The guy in the front of the canoe appeared to be in his late 40's. They guy in back was younger, maybe mid 30's. They both had dark heavy jackets on and ski caps, so I can't be sure."

"What is your full name again? I'll need that, your address and the best number to reach you at so our officers can follow-up later."

"O.K., its James Peterson and I live at..." He gave her all the information and was eager to get off the phone.

"Thank you, Mr. Peterson. I'll have a patrol car out there along the Brandywine shortly. We'll be in touch."

He hung up and approached the sink where Natalie had already scrubbed the coins and metal box with a small nylon brush and had laid them on paper towels to dry.

"What a collection. Have you counted them?" he said, standing next to her.

"One hundred and twelve. Adding in the six that we found before makes 118. Well, now 113, due to that jerk."

"I may make a follow-up call to the police after I collect more data on Broom." He leaned over toward the granite counter and picked up two of the coins. "These are in pretty good condition and they do look like the same ones we found before."

"They are. While you were on the phone, I used the magnifying glass. All roughly the same, different dates, from around 1725-1767... and all gold."

He did some quick math in his head. "If one is worth over $8,000... maybe close to $10,000... and we have over 100 of them, that's roughly a million dollars" he thought while glancing at all the coins in front of him. His cheek twinged as he looked at Natalie. "We're $1,000,000 richer!" He wrapped his arms around her. "Good job, hon!! Thanks for braving all that mud and rain... it really paid off this time. We make a great team- and I owe you a new wardrobe!"

"This is amazing!!" She picked up the metal box. "I took a closer look at this. It does appear to be a spice box. See the small metal compartments inside? Looks pretty old, too."

"That would make sense... that's got to be the box Lafayette found in Gilpin's pantry, where they kept the spices. Little did Gilpin realize he'd open his pantry and find a fortune. When Lafayette went to see Gilpin during his return visit to America in 1824, Gilpin was an old man... bed-ridden and dying. Lafayette had wanted to thank him again for his warm hospitality those nights just before the battle. I wonder if Lafayette ever mentioned anything about the spice box and coins?" He picked up the box and turned it completely around to see if there were any markings.

"What do you think?" she said as she picked up a few of the coins.

"That's what I call Gold Medal Flour."

"Very funny!" She put the coins down and walked over to the refrigerator. "Ah... choo!!. Ahhhh... CHOO!" Natalie grabbed a tissue and put it to her nose. "Damn... I'm getting a cold… just like I feared. Hon… could you get me some of that Nyquil upstairs?"

"Sure… be right back."

"Ahhhh… Choo!" She blew her nose again. Jim came stomping down the stairs.

"Natalie, I couldn't find any- and you've been sneezing for the last ten minutes. I'm going to run over to the CVS and pick up some more."

"Jim… it's late. I'll be fine until tomorrow."

"It's no problem… they're open 24 hours. I'll be right back." He grabbed his coat from the closet and headed towards the garage door.

"Jim… really!! I'm O.K… plus the weather is still pretty crummy. I don't want you to go."

"I want you to get better. I'll be right back…" He got in the car, the garage door opening as he turned the ignition and headed out, pulling into the CVS lot a few minutes later.

"Wow, everybody must have a cold tonight. The place is packed. I don't believe this!" He pulled all the way to the back of the building, the next to the last spot in the lot. "They could use some lighting back here- I can hardly see the end of my car." He looked in the rear view mirror and noticed the headlights of another car as it pulled up in back of him, stopping. Jim opened his door and got out, then saw the man exiting the passenger side of the other car. He was well over six-feet tall, large build, the size of a grizzly bear, wearing dark pants, a heavy jacket and…a ski mask. The man ran up to Jim as his car door closed.

"Hey- you're blocking me, buddy!! Move your car" Jim said as he stared right at him. Then his blood rushed through his veins as he saw him come right up to him.

"You're the one outta' line, pal!!" He pushed Jim up against his car, then pinned him with his huge arms. "Look!! People who talk to cops- get HURT!!" He punched him hard in the stomach.

"Ughh!!" Jim almost fell forward, but his shoulders were still pinned against the door. "What...what do you want??" He tried to see his face, but the black ski-mask covered all of it.

"I'm gonna' SHUT YOU UP!!" He hit him in the groin, then put his large hand around Jim's neck. Jim watched as he reached into his jacket, taking out a knife, holding it up. "You've talked too much already!! You're dead!!"

Just then, two other cars pulled up behind them in the lot. He let go of Jim's neck and sprinted back over to his car, jumping in as it started to speed away.

Jim stood up, watching the red taillights as the car exited the lot. "I can't tell Natalie..." He shook his head and regained his composure as he went through the automatic doors into the light.

Natalie heard the garage door open.

Jim stepped in and handed her the bag. "Here you go, sweetie... hope you feel better soon."

"Thank you." She grabbed another tissue. "Actually, I'm feeling a bit better already... My sneezing stopped while you were out. Know what time it is?"

"Uh, my watch says..." He had to slowly pull up his sleeve, still soaked and difficult to move. He started to say the words, but she spoke first.

"It's party time."

Chapter 14

The waterfront loading docks were barely visible in the early morning mist, the sky just showing signs of light as dock workers lined up to unload the next freighter. The loading ramp dropped onto the edge of the platform and the men walked into the ship while others rode on forklifts, following them to each spot for pick-up. Vinny stood at the upper level of the docks, looking down at his men below. He glanced over at the man wearing the grey suit and a Brooks Brothers overcoat. "Hey, you always get this dressed up? You're gonna need a lot of dry cleaning if you keep comin' down here like that."

"I have to... the Senator insists on everyone being in business attire. I have to get back soon. Everything O.K. on your end?"

"Fine, buddy boy, as long as you keep the heat off. Here's this month's take." He handed him the envelope, glancing around to make sure no one saw him.

"Oh, that's not a problem. We're keeping it very cool. No one suspects... and nobody will ever know. By the way, the Senator wanted to give you a little token of his appreciation.

He knows you like a good steak. Here's two $500 gift certifi-
cates... one for Morton's, one for Ruth Chris."

Vinny took the certificates. "Hey, nice. Not enough good
meat and potatoes joints around here, but with what they
charge at those places, this should just about cover the bill." He
walked right up to him. "So, things are cool? No problems?"

"No problems. Everything's fine."

"Good. Keep it that way. See you next month... and tell
the Senator thanks." He walked down the ramp to the loading dock and didn't look back. "Hey, you guys... get goin'!! We
don't have all day!!..."

———⟫⟪⟫⟪———

The sun was already up and the pale blue sky didn't give
any hint of the frigid weather outside. He walked to the side
door and looked up at the circular thermometer. "Twenty-four
degrees." He noticed the hanging Santa Claus ornaments on
each side of the door were blowing almost sideways in the
wind. "With the wind chill, must be 15 degrees. Good day to
stay inside and do some detective work." He stood there in the
silence, thinking about him.

The microwave buzzed and he took the two cups out and
placed the Plantation mint tea bag in one, two Earl Greys in
the other. He took them both into the Conservatory, placing
them down on the table before he flipped on the switch for
the lights. He stared at the red service berry strand and the
ornaments, a Technicolor show of light, the fireplace below

warming his feet. "I wish he were here." He glanced down at the framed photo of his father, beaming with a wide smile in his blue and maroon shirt. "The best photo of him ever. I'm glad I still have it. At least I have that to remember…" His eyes started to tear up as he looked at him smile. The void had started around 35, as he got established in his career and started thinking about what it would have been like to have a chat with his dad, talking about current events.

"God, has it been over two months since I even THOUGHT much about him?" He remembered back a few months to the past Fall. His favorite time… Was it his father's, too? The colors in the countryside were startling… crimson, gold and amber, a canopy of joy. The katsoura tree in the yard was in its full majesty, the peach and apricot-colored leaves doing their seasonal ritual, their best effort to hold on through an early dose of what felt like Winter. Late October in the Brandywine Valley this year was a time of unusually cold weather, a "blue Norther" as his old grad school advisor used to say. Most of the sugar maples had started to peak, yet the near non-stop rain over the preceding two weeks had given all the trees, shrubs and flowers an extra dose of water to support their late Summer colors for a few more precious days. Red maples had been leading the pack, as if to say "This is the color you're looking for, isn't it? The color of Fall…"

He thought back to when he was around 6 years old, driving with his older brother and father up to the Poconos in Pennsylvania, the preferred mountain recreation area for the middle class in the Eastern half of the state. Jim was wondering whether they would all go on a hike, or just make camp and sit around the fire, toasting marshmallows as the sun went below the mountains in the distance…

———

"Did you get out all the utensils for dinner?" his dad asked, standing in front of him with a serious look of authority.

"Uh, well… I will. Are they in the car?"

"Of course they're in the car. That's where everything is."

He felt a few inches shorter as he started to walk away. "Oh, yeah… I know. I'll get them now." He knew his father would be thinking he'd lapsed in one of his chores and that gave him a moment of sadness, as if he'd let him down… and he wanted no part of it. His father looked at him disapprovingly, then turned to his brother and said "Well, nice ride up here today, huh?"

"Yeah, dad, really great!!"

"You want to try and catch some fish tomorrow? We have two poles. You and I can each see what we can get for lunch."

"YEAHH!! That'll be great, dad" his brother said, walking up to his father, welcoming the big arms around him.

Jim was sorting through the items in the car and didn't know exactly which ones they'd be using for dinner, but he'd overheard their conversation and felt empty, left out of the bond that was clearly there, which he rarely experienced. "Are these the pots and pans we need?"

"Of course. We use those every time we come up here, you

should know that" his father asserted, still with his arm around Jim's brother.

He sank lower, the sadness wrapping around him, a thick fog enshrouding his vision. He couldn't see for a few seconds, then almost cried, but stopped. "Is it me... or is it him? Does he love me, or does he just want me to be... better? I... don't know. I... just want to be... want him... to... to... be closer" Jim thought as he grabbed the aluminum pot, pan, coffee pot and utensils from the back of their 1963 Buick station wagon. "This is what we need, right?" he said as the lights from the car lit the way back toward his father.

"Yes, that's it" his father said, sitting down in front of the fire pit, waiting for Jim to come over. "Come on, we don't have much light. The sun's almost down. Did you bring the packaged dinners?"

Jim froze. He stopped walking toward them and turned around quickly, running back to the car.

"He forgot!! He doesn't even know what we have for dinner" his brother exclaimed, laughing quietly, but he knew Jim could hear him.

"I didn't!! I knew!! I'm bringing them now." Jim reached the back of the open car and took out the two medium-sized brown paper bags which held their dinners. "I have them!! I'm bringing them over." He looked at his father to see if he would give any sign of approval, but none came back, the sadness sinking deeper into Jim's chest. He almost didn't make it to the fire pit, stopping for a fraction of a second, gazing down at the leaves and pebbles scattered around the campsite, unable to look back at his father again, but then he heard something and looked up. His brother had thrown a large stick into some bushes and was heading toward the forest. Jim went right up to his father, looking into his eyes.

"Good job. We'll have dinner on in a little while." He wrapped his arms around Jim's shoulders.

Jim's heart leapt into the sky, his feet leaving the ground below, with him peering down at the scene with glazed eyes… thrilled… surprised. "Yeah!! I wanted to help."

"You did, peanut. Good work. Now you can help me start the fire." His father kissed his forehead before releasing him from his embrace. Jim didn't want to let go.

"I can!! I know how to start the fire!!" Jim yelled a bit too loudly and he stopped, looking at his face, hoping he didn't bother him with his loud voice. He was at home, the rare, fleeting feeling he craved all his life, in his father's arms, an angel, gifted to be there, treated to rare praise, uplifted in spirit.

"Good job, peanut!! Joe will help you with that, won't you Joe?"

"Yes, dad- I can help him, but he's smart enough to do it himself."

"We'll have dinner soon… a good meal."

His father stepped closer to him and bent down, touching his face against Jim's cheek as he gave him another hug, his heavy beard rough, but he liked the feeling, the one he felt so rarely. Jim wrapped his arms around his father's neck for a few seconds, then let go as the sounds of nightfall rustled all around him… the fire beginning to blaze in front of his eyes…

———— ‹‹O›› ————

"How long have you been up? I was so sleepy." Natalie walked up to him and kissed his cheek as he stood looking at the fireplace, the gold and orange flames bouncing among the flecks of blue.

"Oh, a little while. I have tea for us."

"I see, very nice." She grabbed the cup and took a long sip. "Any more worlds to conquer today?"

He was momentarily without a response. She normally was the one with the list of things to do, ready to start checking them off early in the day. "I'm going to do more searching on Broom. With all the hits I found the first time, there's got to be a lot more to discover. I'd also like to go back over to Brandywine View. Joni was the one who recommended him. I'm still confused by that. She seems honest, a decent person and businesswoman."

"We don't know why she recommended him. She may have just heard that Red Clay was a reputable place to take antiquities for evaluation. She probably had no idea Broom was a crook."

"Fair enough. I'm sure she recommended them because of Smithson, but I'd still like to talk with her after I get off the computer. We're the latest on a long list of people dissatisfied with Broom's service. Maybe their 'analytical lab' is a bunch of his buddies in a garage somewhere."

"You don't know that. Don't speculate."

"Why not? Speculating is legal and can lead to some interesting answers. Follow the money. The first search I did said the FBI was watching the guy for possible links to a multistate fraud ring. I'd say that's serious enough to ask some more questions." He took a long sip, gazed at the gold and white angel and thought of his sister that day with the kitten, her eyes closed...

"Will you remember me?" Mandy stood at the edge of the forest, younger, pretty as she was when she was 16, her huge brown eyes gazing up at him.

"Yes!! Of course I will!! I love you... I'll never forget you..." He recalled all the mornings he'd gone out onto the terrace, good weather or bad, praying... for health. Then afterwards... praying for peace.

"You seem far away." Natalie took a sip from her cup and sat on the edge of the couch. "Here Frankie kitty. Frank... come over here." She grinned as Frank walked between her legs at the edge of the sofa and then crawled under to hide.

"Just thinking about my sister. You know, it's interesting. She got straight A's in school, which by definition implies she got them in history. I wonder what she would think of our discovery, Lafayette, the battle." He looked at Francis, his largely black patches a contrast to the gold and silver angels and other ornaments. Francis rubbed up against his leg, then jumped up on his lap, staring right at his face as Jim tried to hold his cup. "Whoa, boy!! Almost caused a laundry job that time... Francis, you're my best buddy." He held him in his arms, then let him lie down and turn his head in his lap, craving a neck rub.

"She'd like it, I'm sure. Was she much of an adventurer?"

"In her mind. She loved to read. Read dozens of books every year. That's one area she was way ahead of me. She read all the time. I'd love to be able to do that. Where do you get the time?" He stopped and thought "Life's precious, you have to make the time for the people and things important to you." He looked down at the end of the couch. Frankie was swiping her paws at Natalie's feet. "I'm glad we spend time with these furry guys. They love it so much."

"I bet your sister would have loved to come with us exploring, going to the Sanderson House, the museum, the springhouse." Natalie petted Frank's head as she came back out from under the couch.

"I think so. She loved romance novels... enjoyed a good story."

"I'd say we're investigating a good story... or two. What do you want to do for breakfast?"

"Let's pass on breakfast. I'll do the computer search, then maybe lunch at The Four Dogs? We haven't been there in a while. Right next to the Marshallton Inn. That place has seen a few Presidents come and go... around since the early 1800's. We'll have lunch at the Dogs and then, if time permits, walk across the parking lot and see if there's anything worth noting at the Inn."

As he left the room, she thought back to when her mother was younger, her beautiful face and nice figure making men do double takes on the street, in stores and at restaurants. She was a beautiful woman, a cross between Ingrid Bergman and

Grace Kelly, always wearing high heels and close-fitting skirts with no stockings. Her legs were so nicely shaped, she didn't need nylons… laying out on the patio all times of the year… getting a tan…

——— »«⦿»« ———

Natalie was sitting on the couch. The oldest of four, she was close to her mother and liked hanging around with her. Her dad was at work in Downingtown.

"Let's go to the Mansion House and have some coffee. I need to get out of here. We'll just stay a little while."

"Sure, mom! I'm ready."

They drove into West Chester and walked into the old hotel. Natalie noticed the red carpet and dark wooden staircase curving up from the foyer… It was a place for older people. There were no kids anywhere. Then sitting at the table, her mother putting her coffee cup down to take a long drag on her cigarette, a man walked up to them.

"Having a nice afternoon, ma'am?"

"We are… and you?"

"Very nice, thank you. My, I must say, you are a very beautiful woman. Are you alone?"

"Yes… well, no. As you can see, my daughter is with me."

Natalie looked at the man as he walked away and noticed another man sitting at the counter, staring at them, about to do the same thing.

"Mom, those men like you! Do you know them?"

"Well, one is a judge from the courthouse across the street. The man over there is a bounty hunter."

"What's a bounty hunter?" Natalie asked.

"Someone who hunts down bad men... for money."

"Oh... like a sheriff... or something?"

"Sure honey... finish your ice tea and rice pudding."

"Do you like talking to them?"

"Not really. I just want to get a little peace. I'm done my coffee... want to go?"

"Do we have to? I like it here!!"

"Oh, well, maybe another cup. Waiter?" She signaled to him and he gave her a wide smile...

————))(()((————

"Are you awake?" he said as he looked at her face, bringing the cups into the room.

"Oh, yes... just remembering my mother when I was younger. I miss those days."

"Mind if I spend some time on your computer?"

"No... go ahead. I have some chores to finish."

He walked into her office and sat down. "O.K., time for more information. Google. 'Martin Broom, fraud'. The long list appeared and he scrolled down to see if any of the other headlines caught his attention. 'Broom under investigation for fraud, mob ties'. He read the first few paragraphs. "Mr. Broom is suspected of having direct ties to several New York Mafia families, his store being under investigation for money laundering, along with his two previous shops, one in lower Manhattan and one in Northern New Jersey. He clicked on the next story. 'First owner of Red Clay not implicated in Broom investigation'. He read the first few paragraphs. 'The original owner of Red Clay Antiques, Robert Smithson, has run the shop for 37 years, enjoying a solid reputation as a highly respected and knowledgeable dealer in antiquities before experiencing financial difficulties last year.'

The phone rang as he sat there reading the screen. He barely heard Natalie's voice from upstairs.

"I'll get it!!"

"O.K.!!" He looked back at each sentence and read them slowly again.

Upstairs, Natalie held the receiver to her ear. "Hello?"

"Natalie?"

"Yes…??" She recognized the voice, but couldn't quite place it.

"This is Carla, remember? The Beach Plum?"

Natalie was stunned, but tried to talk. "Uh, yes. I remember you very well. Your boyfriend tried to kill us!! At least you were honest about that."

"Look, I am so sorry about what happened, well – what almost happened - but I did try to warn you!! Are you both O.K.?" She looked down at the ground around the phone booth, knowing she'd come close to being an accomplice in a double murder. She glanced around the parking lot to make sure no one was nearby.

"Yes… we're both… O.K. Why are you calling now?"

Carla broke down and started to cry, but regained her composure. "Look, Natalie, I don't have anything to do with Eddy's business. In fact, I don't want to have anything to do with Eddy. He gives me money, buys me lots of things. He tried to be Mr. Nice Guy, but now I really know who he hangs out with. They're all thugs- and he could get ME into a lot of trouble, just for being with him."

"So when did you come to this remarkable realization, after deep therapy?" She shook her head and cursed under her breath.

"I had my doubts about Eddy from the start. I knew he was playing with some mean characters- but nothing like this."

"So why DO you still hang out with him? The police are going to put him away for life, you know."

"I know. He's still in the hospital. They took him out of intensive care last week. He can speak, he can sit up in his bed and he even takes phone calls when someone holds the phone for him. He can't do much more... he's paralyzed."

"He got what he deserves."

"Anyway, I was standing outside his room yesterday and I heard him talking with one of his buddies... He mentioned your names again... and I got really worried."

"Are you telling me he's still trying to have us killed?? So, what should we do?" Natalie looked at the painting on the wall, a field of flowers blowing in the breeze, a gentle reminder of a quiet, more peaceful time in her life.

"I don't know for sure... Look, Natalie. I DON'T love Eddy... far from it. He can do some things, say some things that are pretty mean… and cause me trouble… trouble I don't need at this point in my life." She thought about her daughter, who had gotten into drugs… and her son, who was in jail. "I'm going to see him at the hospital in a day or so. Don't worry, I have some connections. I'll take care of it… one way or the other. You take care, too." She hung up.

Natalie stared at the phone, then put it back on the desk. "Hmmm… this isn't good. I have to let Jim know, though he won't be surprised." She walked downstairs to the garage to bring out some trash.

Jim was reading the story again, slowly. "I was right about both guys. Smithson is decent, Broom's a total snake." Then he saw it. 'Broom is also suspected of having money laundering ties to Edward Caniletto, the owner of a New Jersey cement company, now in police custody, alleged to have participated in two murders aboard a luxury yacht in Edgartown, Massachusetts last year. Speaking on condition of anonymity, officials familiar with the investigation disclosed that the New York money management firm Leventhal and Company was using deposits from unsuspecting investors to fund shops where Broom and others sold bogus antiques for huge profits running into the hundreds of millions of dollars.' He stared at the screen and read it again. "My God!! Natalie!!" He got up from the chair, still yelling, but realized she might not hear him on the second floor at the other end of the house. "Natalie!!"

She ran from the hallway near the garage and almost slipped on the smooth wooden floor in the kitchen. "What happened? Is everything O.K.?"

"I'm fine. Everything comes full circle."

"What do you mean?"

"Broom may be in a multi-state fraud ring, with direct ties to several well known New York Mafia families."

"You'd mentioned something about that from your first search. That guy is a total slimeball. I sensed it the first time I saw him."

"It gets better... or worse. You know who laundered money through him? Eddy Caniletto."

"NO!!" Then she thought for a few minutes and looked into Jim's eyes. "That phone call was from Carla, remember-his sleazy girlfriend? She's not exactly thrilled with Eddy and apologized again for what happened. She called to say she overheard him mentioning our names while talking with one of his mob buddies on the phone in the hospital. Seems she's had a change of heart and is going to take care of things on her end..."

"What's that mean?"

"No idea."

"I need to get hold of that FBI agent. I assume they know all of this, including all the latest on Broom's bogus stuff here at Red Clay, but it's never good to use that word."

"What word?"

"An old professor of mine in grad school used to always say it. 'You know that word ASSUME. It'll make an ass out of you and me.' He got Rawlin's card out of the desk drawer and dialed the phone, hearing the receiver pick up on the other end.

The gravelly sound of a heavy smoker came on the line. "Agent Rawlins here."

"Agent Rawlins, the is Jim Peterson. We spoke and met recently."

"I know you, Mr. Peterson. The file is active. What can I do for you?"

"Start by keeping us safe and mobsters out of our back yard!!" he thought. "Well, I wanted to let you know we recently did some exploring along the Brandywine and found some coins. Old coins. Revolutionary War era."

"Lucky you."

"We took the coins to a local antique dealer here in Chadds Ford and dropped them off for evaluation. When they came back, the ones they gave us looked, well, slightly different, to my eyes. The guy offered us some money for them, but it wasn't what I thought they were worth. So we took them down to the archeology lab at the Living History Center downtown. The guy there is an expert on 18th and 19th century artifacts and he confirmed my suspicions. He said five out of the six coins we showed him were fakes, the same five I had given to the local dealer to evaluate. Only one was real... a 1724 Louis D'Or gold coin."

"Is that it? Is that why you're calling me... to tell me about your archeological excavations?" He took a long drag of the Marlboro.

"No, there's something else. The antique dealer's name... Martin Broom."

He exhaled quickly and the smoke enveloped him as he sat

up straight at the desk. "Broom. I know the name. He's on our watch list. Suspected fraud ring."

"Exactly. Did you also know that he's suspected of having money laundering ties to Edward Caniletto?"

He crunched out the smoldering cigarette and cleared his throat as he grabbed the black pen and made some notes on the small pad in front of him. "Of course, we're on top of that, Mr. Peterson. We're aware of the fraud ring." He recalled the page at the back of the dossier he'd briefly read a few weeks ago, but had almost completely forgotten amidst all the other events.

"It gets more interesting. We went back and confronted Broom with the other evaluation and he practically threw us out of his shop. He exploded."

"Did he threaten you?"

"No, but something else is strange. He has a partner... a Mr. Smithson."

"I know that."

"Smithson is the opposite. Nice guy. Cordial. Easy to talk to. We met him when we first went to the shop weeks ago, but haven't seen him since. When we asked about him as we were confronting Broom with the fake coins, he said he didn't expect to see him for several weeks. That's when he threw us out of his shop."

"Interesting. I know they're co-owners. Smithson had money problems; Broom came in and took a piece of the business. So you haven't had any contact with Smithson since you first went into the store? Haven't heard anything?"

"Nothing. To me it's a bit strange that the founder of a well-known and respected antique store, doing business in the area for almost 40 years, disappears for several weeks, with no word on where he is."

He was taking notes quickly as he exhaled toward the phone, a perfect smoke ring floating away, putting the pad in front of him in a haze. "Nice observation. We're on it. I'll be in touch, Mr. Peterson. You still at the same number?"

"Hope to be for a long time. Just have your guys keep a watch on us... and around our neighborhood. We don't want any doors kicked in at 2:00 a.m..."

"We're watching. Don't worry. I have a unit monitoring your area daily. We may still need your help on the case." He took another long drag. "Is that it?"

"Wonderful... the only reason you're in touch with us is because you need more information... not to protect us. Our tax dollars at work" he thought. "That's everything. Please keep in touch." He hung up the phone.

"What's he going to do?" She leaned on the back of the swivel chair as he turned toward her.

"He needs more information, so for that reason, he'll be in touch. Reassuring, isn't it? Makes you wonder if they really do have a guy watching the neighborhood." He looked down at the floor, knowing what was coming.

"This guy's with the FBI and he can't even give you anything more substantial than 'I'll be in touch??!!'"

"I know. It's hard to get good help these days. We can try Kelly Girl."

"Jim!! This is serious!! Some guy who stole our gold coins has ties to the same person who tried to kill us!! That's outrageous!! We have to talk to someone higher up who can help us, NOW!! This guy Broom is probably having us followed. There was that car that almost drove us off the road, then the dudes in the canoe. It's got to be him, or people working for him."

Jim thought of the incident in the parking lot at CVS, but didn't say anything. "I didn't mention that to him, as I'd already reported it to the local cops and I assume they all share information. ASSUME!!" He looked at her and almost laughed.

"This is NOT funny!! You need to call him back and tell him that. You know one of the reasons 9/11 happened was because agencies didn't share information. It's our duty to get information to people who can protect us."

He thought for a few seconds. He didn't like his attitude... close to condescending, borderline arrogant, but she was right. "Good point." He dialed the number again. "Agent Rawlins, Jim Peterson again. I didn't mention something to you just now because I'd already reported it to the local police. When we went back to the Brandywine to look for more coins, two guys in a canoe took shots at us. They could have killed us, but they ended up capsizing. We lost sight of them as their canoe got pulled downstream."

"Did you get any identification for the police? A facial or body description? A license plate?"

"We gave them what we knew. It was two men. Both taking shots at us. Seemed like they had been following us, but I can't be totally sure."

"Was this before or after you confronted Broom with the fake coins?" He took a very long drag while looking at the dull wall that had no windows, just the Most Wanted photos and Bureau updates on a tan corkboard hung off to one side.

"After. That's why it looks even more suspicious. Too much of a coincidence. First this guy steals our coins, then we confront him with evidence that says he's a fraud. He explodes and throws us out. Little while later, we get followed by some guys in an SUV with a canoe and then while we're looking for more of the same coins, we get shot at. They've got to be linked to him."

He was taking notes quickly and put out the cigarette. "Pretty clever way to try to kill someone. By going in the canoe, they knew they wouldn't leave any footprints nearby… no signs at all that they were at the crime scene. I'll be contacting the Kennett Square police for a full accounting of the event. Meanwhile, I think we'll want to put Mr. Broom under direct surveillance, but we may need your help."

"Incredible" he thought. "Can this guy do anything without me providing a blueprint?" He hesitated for a few seconds before responding. "What, are you guys going to do… a sting on Broom?"

"You've been watching too many old Paul Newman movies. It's called a DS. Domestic surveillance."

"Thank you, Professor. Now if you can just be more concerned with keeping us alive than the latest FBI acronyms, I'll be happy" he thought. "Fine, domestic surveillance. You think you'll need us?"

"It would be good to make it look like a regular visit to the antique shop. You had a change of heart. You need the money and you bring the coins back to him, agreeing to whatever he offers."

"It was $550 per coin... for the fakes."

"Sure, he was trying to make it appear legitimate. You go in, apologize for any misunderstanding and agree to his offer. You gain his trust. You walk around the shop and check out several of the other artifacts. That'll give our agents time to surround the place."

"What are you going to do? Break in and arrest him? What information could you have that would be enough to do that?"

"I already checked our files after we spoke the first time. We have enough right here to do a D.S. and we may be able to collect more during the raid to arrest him for fraud. With your statement and the coins as evidence- which our lab will check out and confirm- we can move forward. We just need to get more information from inside the shop, with him making statements guaranteeing authenticity. We haven't been able to do that up until now, but with you, we can."

"How are you going to do that?"

"If you'll agree to it, you'll wear a micro-camera and wire while you're in there, recording both audio and video. You'll need to ask about specific items and get his direct statements of authenticity. Our guys will be watching and recording everything. We have some antiquities experts on staff who know their stuff. They know fakes when they see them, but you have to go close up... very close. Hold the items in your hands, so we can get it on film. If he makes the guarantee and our guys know they're fakes, we get more evidence... and we can proceed with an indictment... or an immediate arrest."

"What if he gets suspicious and throws me out... or pulls a gun on me?" He peered up at Natalie who was clearly worried as she listened to the one-sided dialogue.

"Don't worry, our guys will be nearby. We can be inside that shop in a matter of seconds."

"So, what exactly are you trying to prove here? Are you going to arrest him... or just gather more information?"

"Hopefully both. Information is a precious commodity. We need more. We can get this guy and all his mob partners- we just need you to help us. That would be a tremendous accomplishment against organized crime in this region."

He gazed down, then closed his eyes, trying to think. "O.K., I'll do it. Hopefully, I don't screw up."

"You're an intelligent man, Mr. Peterson. You'll do fine. You handled the situation with the briefcase very professionally. I'll be back in touch to let you know the timing. Thanks for your help." Rawlins hung up the phone and took the last cigarette from the pack. "We'll get this guy... one way or another" he said as he looked up at the clock.

Jim turned toward Natalie. He knew she was thinking that he'd made a dangerous deal without consulting her.

"You'll do what?" She stared at him, putting her hand on his arm, gripping it firmly.

"They want to do a surveillance operation on Broom at the antique store. They feel we can regain his trust because he

GENE PISASALE

knows us and made us an offer on the coins. They want me to go in wearing a video cam and a wire so they can collect more evidence on his bogus merchandise and get him on the record guaranteeing their authenticity so they can nail him."

"Couldn't that be dangerous? He has ties to the mob... What if he gets suspicious?"

"Exactly what I said. Rawlins said they'll have their agents in there in seconds if anything starts to go wrong."

"I don't like it. It's too risky!! This is you... your life would be on the line."

"Would you like to convict this guy, put him out of business and get our $50,000 worth of coins back?"

"Well, that would be great, but this is a dangerous way to do it."

"Life is risk. If you don't take them, you cease to live- but before I do that, I have some questions."

"For whom?"

"First- my old buddy Erick who works for the Treasury Department in D.C. He's done dozens of these investigations over the years- checking out people involved in money laundering. He should be able to comment on this. I'm going to give him a quick call." He picked up the phone and dialed the 202 number.

"Hello?"

"Erick!! How are you??!!"

"Jim!! Haven't heard from you in a while – how the hell are you?"

"Hey, buddy – great!! How's Debbie and the little one?"

"Wonderful, thanks. Everyone's fine. What's new with you?"

"Well… interesting reason for the call… We found some 18th century artifacts – gold coins – up here along the Brandywine. Took the coins to a local dealer and we think he switched them for fakes after sending them out for 'evaluation'. Turns out the Feds have been watching him and several other antique dealers in the region for fraud and possible money laundering. I reported it to the local police and they connected me with the FBI, who are now watching the guy."

"I've actually done a few surveillances of dealers. What… do the Feds want you to get involved?"

"Yes – they want to do a 'sting' and have me wear a wire and a video camera. They claim its standard practice… routine… and they'll make sure I'm safe. Agent's name is Rawlins…"

"Frank Rawlins? I know him!! We worked a tough case together… about five… almost six years ago… great guy. He helped me out big time… got us out of a big jam."

"So… will I be safe… or a target for shooting practice?"

"With Rawlins, you'll be in good hands. Hey, keep me in the loop… I'm so sorry, but I've got to run. There's a concert my kid wants to see and I promised I'd stand in line overnight to get her tickets. Let's catch up again… real soon!!"

"Will do! Hey – thanks Erick. You're a great bud… I'll be in touch!"

He hung up the phone. "Now I want to talk with the woman who sent us there in the first place. Let's go back over to Brandywine View and talk with Joni." He got up and walked to the closet to get his jacket. "Want to go?"

"Not really, but if it gives us more information and gets us our coins back, O.K." She pulled the parka from the hanger and walked out to the garage. He closed the door behind her and got in, starting the ignition. "We'll make it quick. Hey, another gift... Look... no traffic."

"I want a gift... that guy in jail" she said.

"It'll work out. I can feel it." They pulled into Brandywine View and maneuvered quickly into a spot. "Let's go get some answers."

"You ask. I'll jump in if it gets interesting." They walked in the back door after passing the numerous metal sculptures and wooden carvings set up near the entrance.

"Hi there!! It's... Jim, right?" welcomed Joni.

"Yes, hi. How are you?"

"Fine. Out to do some more shopping?"

"Not exactly. I wanted to ask you about Red Clay Antiques. How well do you know that Broom guy?"

"Don't really know him. Smithson owns the shop. He's very active in the community... well respected" she answered, a bit surprised.

"We met Smithson... nice guy... but he hasn't been around lately. Broom's the one we've been dealing with... and he's a crook. We gave him five coins we found recently along the Brandywine, kept one and when we got them back from his lab, he switched them with fakes. He even made us an offer to make it look fair."

"How do you know he switched them? What if they

really were fakes?"

"We found them all together, gave him five, but kept the sixth one ourselves. We brought all six down to the Living Archeology Center downtown and had an expert evaluate them. He told us the five were fakes, the sixth one was genuine, worth almost $10,000. There's no way we would find five fakes and one genuine artifact all together along the river."

She thought for several moments, not knowing what to say. "I'm really sorry to hear that!! As I said, I don't really know him. I know the original owner, Robert Smithson. He's a straight up guy. Honest businessman. I've sent people there before and never heard about any problems." She appeared truly sincere and a bit concerned.

"When was the last time you referred someone to Red Clay?"

"Oh, it's been a while, maybe 18 months or more."

"Well, he got his partner about a year ago... he must have really needed the money. Broom's a con artist... under investigation for fraud."

"I'd heard something about that, but I didn't know it involved Red Clay directly. I'm so sorry you had that problem!! If I had known..."

"Hey- it's not your fault. I made the choice to trust the guy. I was just wondering, when was the last time you saw Robert Smithson?"

"You know, it's actually been a while, now that you mention it... and that's strange. I usually see him at Hank's for breakfast at least once, maybe twice a week. I haven't seen him in...

several weeks." She raised her eyebrows and thought for a few seconds. "Do you think there's anything wrong?"

"Maybe. I met Smithson the first time we went in there and we really liked the guy, but only talked with him for a few minutes- he had to leave. Broom was pretty evasive when I asked about Robert- said he wouldn't be back for a while. What do you know about Smithson?"

"He's a wonderful man. Comes from a well known family."

"Who in the family is well known?" Natalie asked.

"His great grandfather was a wealthy businessman... founded the Smithsonian."

It hit him as she said the words. The name had lingered in his mind after they first met, but then he figured it was nothing, just a coincidence.

"Quite a collector himself. His personal items are probably worth several million. Maybe well over that..."

"Really?"

"Oh- yes, definitely. Broom was smart linking up with him. Robert had 3,000 year-old busts from Egypt, hundreds of Roman coins, 16th- 18th century chests, ruby-studded swords, a huge collection."

Jim looked over at Natalie. "Now I know why Broom hooked up with him. Why didn't Robert just sell some of the collection if he needed the cash?"

"They were like his children... he couldn't part with anything. The collection defined him, I think. Once the economy slowed, he started to have money problems... and looked for an investor."

"Sounds like Broom saw an enormous opportunity. He came in as a legitimate partner, knowing he'd have Robert's trust. Then he probably stole some of the pieces from their inventory over time, substituting fakes and sold the real ones on the black market, all the money going into his pocket. He could have made millions. All the fakes sold at their store generated a bunch of lawsuits."

"Not exactly an ideal business partner." Joni's eyes were wide open as she listened.

"Broom's under Federal investigation for fraud, money laundering... and direct ties with the mob."

"I had no idea!! I'm really sorry... if only I'd known. Is there anything I can do?" Her face was tense, showing her deep regret.

"The police and the FBI are on the case now. In terms of your help... well... for us... we were wondering if you'd taken in any artifacts directly linked to the Battle of the Brandywine. We've been doing some research on the topic."

"Occasionally, we get a few Colonial period artifacts from the area. Not a lot. Actually, my grandfather told me a story once. When he was very young, back in the late 1890's, he was hiking along the Brandywine with some of his buddies. It had rained quite a bit, so the water was high and fast. They got on top of one of the boulders at the edge of the river and he swore that he saw most of a musket, bayonet and all, float right by him. He claimed it was exactly like the ones used by Washington and his troops."

"Did they ever get it?"

"No, the water was too high. After a really big rain you can easily drown in some spots. He never stopped talking about it. Called it 'Lafayette's Musket.'"

"Why Lafayette?"

"Gramps was part French… very proud of his heritage, so he had an affinity for Lafayette. Lots of places are named after Lafayette around here."

"She's right. I lived in the Lenape area when I was a kid. Our house address was 1710 West Lafayette Drive, not far from the Amusement Park. I'd always wondered why the name Lafayette was all around us" Natalie added.

"Did you ever find any artifacts yourself?" Jim asked.

"No, I preferred reading. Didn't like climbing in the mud along the water, but a few of the boys in our neighborhood did. They found cannon balls, part of a bayonet, a lot of musket balls- and one guy did find the back half of a musket one time."

"Pretty impressive. The area must be loaded with artifacts."

"It is, but it's also sacred ground. Many of the soldiers killed during the battle were buried where they died… so in one way, this whole area is sort of a giant cemetery. My grandfather's love of the region made me think about the battle, Washington and Lafayette. That's one of the reasons why I opened this store. The past is part of us, it's all around us. These artifacts, antiques… they're our heritage. We can't just throw them away. We need to do everything we can to preserve them because, in the end, they're the threads which bind us to our roots."

Jim felt a tingle up his neck as she spoke. "I'm with you. What's your favorite antique, or artifact, that you collected over the years?"

"Want to go in the back room? I keep some of the special stuff back there... it's not for sale. Follow me." She turned around and walked past the wooden carousel horse and Americana signs to a door with chipping white paint and stopped. "In here."

Natalie and Jim proceeded a few feet behind her. To Jim's right as he glanced about the warehouse were bronze busts, stone sculptures and oil paintings from the 1800's stacked all around the room. He stopped and noticed Joni standing right in front of him, pointing.

"There it is." She had her left arm outstretched, pointing to an old display case.

"What is that?"

"That is Lafayette's greatcoat. Mostly in one piece. The case next to it holds his pants. If you look close, you can even see a dark stained area. That's where he was wounded in the leg. That's my all-time favorite piece."

Jim stepped toward the two cases as if he were approaching the Pope. "These were really Lafayette's? He was wearing these on that day... at the Battle of the Brandywine?"

"Yes. A treasure, isn't it? Worth all the gold in Fort Knox to me."

Natalie walked up to the case containing his coat and leaned close to see through the dusty glass. "Very impressive. A wonderful part of your collection."

Jim stood there staring at the items in the two cases, his mind drifting... back along the Brandywine... that morning... His eyes went to a blur as he gazed at the coat, then the pants, his thoughts lost in the tattered fragments of cloth and the blood stain. He spoke low, under his breath.

"What? Did you say something?" Natalie was just a few feet away.

He didn't hear her.

"How did you get these?" Natalie asked as she turned toward Joni.

"My Grandfather admired Lafayette. He became a successful business man and over the years used some of his wealth to purchase anything he could find related to Lafayette... Made quite a few trips to Paris visiting the auction houses. I inherited it when he died. I really miss him..."

"Wow, that's interesting. You should consider displaying it at the Brandywine Battlefield visitor center or the Smithsonian."

"Maybe... someday. Right now it's my connection to my grandfather... couldn't part with it. Guess that's how Smithson felt, too."

"You're right... I understand completely. I'd do the same... We really appreciate your time" Natalie replied. "Ready to go, Jim? I'm sure she needs to get back to work" she said, turning toward him. "What do you think?"

He was thinking about the river, the troops crossing in the fog.

"What do you think of Lafayette's clothes?"

"Rare gems." His mind was fighting against letting go of

the scene, now fading as he focused on the items in the room around him.

"You folks are welcome back any time." She followed them to the door and waved as they got into the car.

"A nice treat. I never guessed I'd see that" he said.

"Fascinating experience. Not many people have seen that. We're probably among the lucky few" Natalie said as she glanced back at the sign, the car pulling away.

"We are lucky. All of us. We're here today partly because of what Lafayette did, what all those starving soldiers did that day- and throughout the Revolution." He gazed at the rolling hills nearby, once covered with dying patriots… and the blood that earned their freedom.

"Who would ever guess a rich nobleman would leave behind all the comforts of nobility- for what? What was he seeking?" She loved watching the horses with their Winter jackets on, grazing in the fields, steam coming from their nostrils as they probed the frozen soil.

"Something few at the time saw or truly understood. Liberty. Let's go to the Four Dogs and raise a toast... to him."

Chapter 15

The phone rang as Jim was flipping through the new issue of "Caribbean Travel and Life", viewing all the spots he wanted to visit with Natalie someday. He got up and went over to the counter. "This is Jim."

"Mr. Peterson?" He recognized the voice right away. "Hi, this is Agent Rawlins. I have some good news. First... Eddy Caniletto is dead."

Jim heard the words and felt the tension leaving his neck and shoulders. "That is great news!! What happened?"

"Cardiac arrest... in the middle of the night. He'd been out of intensive care for a few days. Looks like he'd been gone well over two hours before they knew he was dead, according to my sources. You should be happy."

"Definitely. Natalie was convinced he was going to follow us to the ends of the Earth."

"Well, you're much safer now that Eddy's gone. Seems he was still somehow getting instructions to his junior thugs, despite his condition. We're tailing them, too and will probably have at least three of his buddies arrested any time now."

"Good. What about the sting… sorry… the 'surveillance operation'?"

"We've got it all set up. We have the warrant… and we're ready to do the surveillance. Is there a day that's better for you to meet with Broom?"

He thought for a few seconds and knew he had a list of questions he needed answered first. "Tell me this, exactly how are you going to know what you're seeing through the camera is a fake?"

"I won't know, but our team will and they'll be the ones watching. They'll be receiving a digital high-definition video feed from you right to our office. We've done this before in other cases. The quality is amazing. It's like you're holding the item in your hands."

"So you can tell, without even seeing it yourself, that something is bogus?"

"We WILL be seeing it ourselves. Our cameras are far better than your eyes. They have special high resolution lenses which can magnify down toward the nanometer scale- along with light sensors that can indicate the composition of many types of materials. We'll be analyzing the images with our computers literally as they come through the video feed. They can tell us whether something is cloth from the 18th century- or nylon from the 1980's. Electronics have come a long way in the last 10 years."

"Fine, I'll accept that. What am I supposed to say… and do?"

"Look for anything special in the shop that attracts your attention. You know history, be creative. Go up to an item that looks really interesting and ask him about it. Ask about a few different things. That way, we can get him on several counts if he's lying. Misrepresenting the authenticity of items costing thousands of dollars is a felony."

He recalled the first time he went in the shop. The Revolutionary War flag had drawn his eyes away from everything else in the store. "I think I know what to look for. There's a Colonial-era flag, 13-stars and all, on display near some antique bookshelves and busts of Roman emperors. I'll ask him about that... and a few other things."

"Perfect. Make it low key, but when you start questioning him, make sure you're within 1-2 feet of each object and standing still, so we can get a good look. Then ask him 'Is this genuine?'"

"O.K.. Now the hard part. What if he gets angry or suspicious and tries to throw me out? What do I do then?"

"Look, you're going in there to say you've had a change of heart and want to make amends. Be sincere. You thought about his offer and you need the money, but DON'T take out the coins right away. Walk around the shop asking about all the other items of interest. You're not there to get paid. You're there to gather information so we can get this guy... and his mob cronies. That way they're gone... out of business... and hopefully you can get your coins back. If he gets out of line, we'll get you out of there."

"O.K.... I'm in. This week is fairly open. I've set aside a lot vacation days for this time of year. How about tomorrow, let's say 10:00 a.m.?"

"Done. That'll be a good time, too. They open then… probably nobody in the shop yet. Can you meet us at the Kennett Police Station to get wired beforehand? It'll only take about 30 minutes, so if you could be there by 9:00 a.m., we'll get you all set up and go over the plan."

"How am I going to know whether you guys are getting what you need, if the camera is working? How can I tell?"

"You'll have a micro-wire in your ear. Sound quality is crystal clear and reception is excellent. We've used it many times. If we need you to move closer to something, we'll tell you. We'll give you comments and suggestions the whole time and if there's anything to be aware of, possible problems, you'll know immediately. If it looks like you're in trouble, we'll tell you to get out of there… and just go." He took a look at the Seth Thomas clock, the second hand fixing his attention. "So it's a go for tomorrow… roughly 24 hours from now… right?"

Jim hesitated as his heart started to pound sharply, his temples feeling the heat of the blood flowing as his pulse raced before he could speak. "It's… a go. Should I bring Natalie with me?"

"Your call. We only need the wire on you. Fine with us. If she feels comfortable, bring her along. It'll give it an air of authenticity."

Jim glanced up as he heard her enter the room holding a cup of tea. "O.K., we're on. She'll be with me. We'll be at the station at 9:00 a.m. That'll give us plenty of time to wire up. We should be able to get over to Red Clay by 10:00 a.m. I'll see you then." He hung up the phone and stood next to the glass table, looking over at Natalie. "Good news. Eddy's dead."

"You're kidding??!! GOOD RIDDANCE!!" She hugged Jim for what seemed like an hour, then stepped back. "What happened?"

"Cardiac arrest... middle of the night. Our luck. Do you feel a bit safer now?"

"Yes... finally." She thought back to Carla's phone call. "Maybe now we can get on with our lives... What about the Red Clay deal?"

"Rawlins wants to move forward with the surveillance. We're going to get this guy. Are you O.K. coming with me tomorrow to talk with Broom?"

"We're doing this tomorrow? Why so soon?"

"Why wait? So he can defraud some other people or skip town? Do you want our coins back?"

"Of course, but... well, O.K... I'll go with you, but I'm not participating in the discussion. I may make a few comments on antiques that I like. You're bringing the fake coins to get payment for them?"

"Yes. I'll tell him I changed my mind, need the cash and you nod your approval, but before I take the coins out for payment, I start asking him about some of the artifacts in the shop. I get up close to a few and get him on audio and video-tape making fraudulent claims."

"Then what? What if he tries to sell us something... or gets suspicious? I want to go home in one piece."

"I'll be getting instructions the whole time through an ear piece. He won't have any idea what's going on."

"You hope."

"These guys are pros. Is it risky? Yes, but how else are we going to get this jerk?" He looked into her eyes to see if she was changing her mind.

"Alright... but on one condition. If we see or hear anything... ANYTHING... that looks threatening, we're out of there... immediately."

"That's the plan. We'll be safe. I promise."

"So what time is the show?"

"Tomorrow at 10:00 a.m., at Red Clay. We have to be at the Kennett Police station around 9:00 a.m. to get wired."

"I hope they don't want to turn ME into a circuit board."

"No, just me. I'll be a motherboard for the FBI. You'll be with me when we go in the shop, to give it legitimacy, but I'll be collecting all the data and getting instructions from the agents the whole time."

"If these guys are such pros, why haven't they caught Broom already? He's been under investigation for months!!" She sipped her tea and stared at his face.

"Who knows? Criminals are pretty sophisticated these days. The mere fact that the mob could have a multi-state fraud ring selling bogus antiques means they've come a long way from Al Capone and the St. Valentine's Day massacre. They probably tried to get a wire in there before, but it just wasn't the right opportunity until now. Look, it takes a long time- sometimes years of undercover work- to catch these guys. You know what? The FBI, police, all law enforcement personnel- they put their lives on the line every day for us.

They deserve some gratitude and respect."

"Oh, I'm thankful. I just don't want you to get hurt." She put her arms around him and hugged him tightly.

"We'll be fine. Don't get too tense on this. It'll all work out." He kissed her nose. "Besides, I always wanted to be in a movie."

She laughed. "You won't be IN the movie, you'll be directing it. Better call Spielberg for some tips."

"Maybe I'll get an Oscar. Should I start my acceptance speech? 'Ladies and gentlemen, it has been a long journey... but finally I'm here with you tonight... along with all the talented actors and actresses from years past...'"

Natalie rolled her eyes and punched him lightly on the shoulder. He walked to the closet and took out his leather jacket, then strode toward the garage door.

"Where are you going?" She put the empty cup down on the counter.

"Actually, I don't know. Something is... drawing me outside... I need some fresh air. Want to take a drive out to the Brandywine Creek State Park in Delaware? We haven't hiked there in a while and it's a sunny day."

"Good idea... maybe it'll take our minds off tomorrow. Afterwards we can drive up to Simon Pearce for lunch. That's right near where Lenape Park used to be. I loved the area when I was a kid."

"I'll get your coat. We'll take a stimulating ride in the country, my dear." He walked back to the closet and grabbed the violet parka.

Driving into Delaware, they passed expansive estates, bab-bling creeks and the rolling hills of du Pont country. The back road intersected Route 52 at Winterthur, where they turned left heading north.

"Wow, you can really feel the wind on the car outside. Hope it's not too breezy to walk around." She looked at the shrubs and reeds swaying along the side of the road.

"Weather says sunny and a high of 40 degrees, light breeze. Don't know where this wind came from." He saw the turnout and the maroon wooden park sign up on the right. "I love this park. You're right along the Brandywine, but slightly higher in elevation, so you can see the contours of the landscape below." He slowed and pulled up to the old log marking the edge of the lot. "Ready?"

"I am. Lucky I brought my earmuffs." She got out and noticed the lot was empty. "There's nobody here."

"Good. We'll have the place to ourselves. You take the low road, I'll take the high road…"

"… and I'll be… muddy before you!" She laughed. "Did you ever do any exploring in this area before we met?"

"A bit- belonged to a few hiking clubs… It was fun. Reminded me of my days out West, hiking and camping all around the Rockies. We're not that far from the old Mason-Dixon line. It should be straight ahead that way." He pointed to the southwest, away from the morning sun.

"I hope you brought your compass and surveying maps." She kicked a piece of serpentine along the path.

"Full gear. We'll have this country mapped in no time," He

leaned down to pick up a large, multi-colored stone, the size of a grapefruit. "Look at this... a very good piece of banded gneiss, with a granitic intrusion. See the way the layers are all bent at an angle?"

"That's interesting. Keep it for our garden."

"I was just thinking where it could go." He took her left hand as they walked on the dirt and gravel path strewn with leaves, broken twigs and footprints from the dozens of hikers over the past several weeks. "River looks nice today. Bet it's freezing. Can you imagine having to cross it just to get some food?"

"I can't even think about how hard life was back then. It's beyond anything we've ever come close to experiencing." She observed the water's edge and saw a beaver. "Oh, look!! Look at that furry little guy!!"

"Where?"

"Right over there... at the edge of that boulder in the water. See him?"

"Yes, I do now. He's a little dude. Dad probably sent him out on a recon mission to get more wood for the dam. Mom asked dad to go first... and you know what he said?"

"What?"

"Leave it to beaver!!"

"Cute!" She laughed, noticing the sound of her voice carried far enough so that their furry friend jumped back into the water. "Darn... I scared him away. I love animals... I could never hurt any of them... even bugs... as long as they stay outside. "

"Agree completely. I actually stop for bacteria at most intersections. Hard to see 'em, though."

"You're such a goofball!!"

"Kidding... I love animals- except for snakes, lizards, jellyfish, sharks, stingrays, octopus, spiders, scorpions and... basically all bugs. I HATE bugs. If you killed all the bugs in the world, I'd throw a party. Maybe pour some Chivas on the rocks and sit out on the terrace, watching the sun go down." He looked around at the forest, silent except for their voices and footsteps.

"If you killed all the bugs, life would slowly grind to a halt. Did you see that National Geographic special on bees? Honeybees are disappearing at an alarming rate and they don't know why. Bees are critical for plant pollination. Without bees, a large part of the flora on Earth would slowly die off. We need bees."

"Just keep them away. Bugs love me. Remember that time we were hiking and I had to run about 50 yards to get away from those yellowjackets?" He looked up at the sky and saw a few clouds moving in.

"I do. You were wearing cologne and a bright yellow shirt. Perfect combination to attract bugs. They thought you were a flower!!"

"I know- remind me if I ever think about wearing that combo again. I'll nix the aftershave and wear a dark blue T-shirt next hike. Every hike!!" He gazed up along the path, then peered over at the Brandywine. "Let's walk over there."

"What do you see?" She put her feet down carefully,

avoiding the small puddles and muddier spots.

"It's what I'm feeling." He stood at the river's edge. "Water. Vital for life. Clean water. The Colonials had little of it. Had to boil it to make it drinkable... and the soldiers, when their water skins were dry... what did they do? They had to find a stream, kneel down and take a chance, not knowing what animal or rotting debris lay upstream."

"It's a miracle many survived. Dysentery was a big problem back then. Every day must have been a struggle... I just know that I love being near the water..."

"The river re-charges me." He watched as several leaves floated downstream... right by two ducks paddling near a rock. He turned away and went slowly back to the path. "Want to saddle 'em up and ride 'em out? Simon Pearce should be open soon and we can get a good table overlooking the water."

They walked in through the double doors and saw the glass-blowing machinery, a young man in his late 20's at the forge holding a long metal beam with a bright orange glowing mass at its end. "That's how it used to be done in the 1800's."

"That's how Simon Pearce does it now. I'm glad they've preserved the tradition here. Not many places still do this. Their glasswork is really lovely." They walked up the two half-flights of stairs to the reception stand inside the entrance to the restaurant.

"Table for two?"

"Yes, along the river, please." Jim glanced around and saw that the place only had a few couples dining.

Sitting down next to the large plate glass window, they

looked out at the Brandywine flowing slowly in the distance. The Picnic Park was barely visible on the other side of the bridge. As the waitress approached, they turned to look back at her.

"I'll have the Vermont cheddar soup with a mixed green salad."

"Soup for me also- and the sesame chicken with an extra ginger sauce, please. We'd both like a glass of the Storrs chardonnay 2006."

"Great. I'll be right back with your drinks."

"Hey... there's two kayakers! I can't believe it" Jim pointed out.

"What hearty souls... in freezing weather... but if you get too wet, you're done."

"Oh, trust me- you can't kayak without getting wet. You have to enjoy the thrill of it all." He recalled the raft trips in southern Colorado with his grad school buddies... the thrill of going over the rapids... and the slight let down after the exhilaration ended...

"Here you are. Your lunch should be out in just a few minutes."

Natalie took her glass first. "You know, years ago when I was about 8 or 9, this was the Lenape Inn. We used to ride our bikes up the road to the amusement park. They had a merry-go-round and a roller coaster. I used to crawl underneath the roller coaster and lay on the ground, waiting for the cars to climb the steep hill, then rush down... WHOOOOSSHHH!!!! It would come straight at me, pulling away only three feet from my face as I looked up!! A free thrill..." She took a small sip of wine.

"That sounds like fun... but terrifying!! Pretty adventurous for a young girl." He raised his glass and took a long drink.

"We were always on the prowl. We'd ride our bikes all around the area, looking for abandoned buildings so we could sneak in. There were a lot of them. We did find a few places that could have been springhouses. I was always looking for the spring. A lot of old barns. This was a very rural area then. Still is, I guess..." Her eyes started to gaze into the distance, her mind going back.

"Little girls don't get into as much mischief as little boys."

"We did. I remember going up to John Chad's house when it was abandoned... falling apart. I climbed in a window and looked around. One time I found a phone book from the early 1940's and a copy of The Inquirer from 1951. We'd also bike up to the nearby prison farm and crawl through the fence. There was a broken spot with a big gap, so we'd go in and take some tomatoes. I ate one whole... right off the vine! It was a simpler time..." She took another sip and looked at the water. "This place is a part of me. I'm so glad I moved back after living away for so many years."

"So am I. Has it changed much since you were a kid?"

"Thankfully, not that much. Still mostly horse farms and rolling hills, woods. I'm glad they haven't gone overboard on development."

"My family used to go to that park, too, but I was so young, I just barely remember it. I thought I remembered them having a Ferris wheel… but…maybe not… It's good that they still have a park there… for the kids" Jim said. "Preserving our memories… that's all we'll have left someday…"

"Here you are… enjoy your meals."

They both started eating the soup, but then she put her spoon down. "I loved growing up here… in Brandywine Hills, on West Lafayette Drive. Those will always be special times. Now with our discovery, it's even more special." She raised her glass to his. "Cheers."

Chapter 16

"Ready to head over to the police station?" Jim asked after he took the last sip of French roast coffee.

"Almost... let me finish mine." She took a large gulp and put the cup in the sink. "Ready. Let's get this over with."

"If everything goes smoothly, the Feds will have this guy in cuffs today. Hopefully Smithson will be there to witness it. I can't wait to see him again. What a fascinating man."

"That would be nice. Let him run the shop on his own. If we'd only insisted on dealing with him first, maybe none of this would have happened."

The car went up the street, past the traffic light at the Old Kennett Inn and stopped about 20 feet short of the station lot. "I don't know if they let you park in there." The two-space police lot already had one car in it. "Don't want to get a cop ticked off. Better park here." He turned off the ignition and they walked up the cement ramp to the door.

"Hi, Jim Peterson. I think you have some people here waiting for us." He looked at the woman behind the small, glassed-in enclosure and noticed a few men standing behind her.

"Come on in folks. They're expecting you." She pressed a button and opened the side gait.

"Jim... Frank Rawlins. Good to see you both." He shook both their hands. "Back here, please." He led them about 30 feet down the hall and motioned for them to enter a room on the left. Rawlins walked toward a table covered with electronic gadgets, then gestured to the three men standing nearby. "This is Agent Gustafson, Agent Brownlee and Special Agent Markham. Special Agent Markham is our antiquities expert. Gustafson and Brownlee will wire you up. Don't worry, you won't get electrocuted. Have a seat."

Jim waited while they put the gear inside his shirt, taped onto his chest. "None of this will explode, right?"

"No, never. Completely safe. O.K., you're done. This goes in your ear. I know, it's tiny, but it won't get lost in there. It's specially designed to sit right inside. See?" He held it in front of Jim's face before he put it gently into his left ear.

"That's amazing. I can barely see it."

"That's the idea. Works very nicely. We used it a while back for some big time mobsters. Nailed John Gotti this way... along with a bunch of his buddies. Now, this here is the video camera." He pointed to a small silver square chip, less than the size of an orange seed.

"That's a camera?"

"Yep... wireless... hi-res, digital... indispensable in surveillance. It's helped nab a lot of thugs over the years. I'm putting it right here, in your lapel where nobody can see it. Just make sure you don't bounce around too much or make any awkward bending motions. If you do, it might get out of calibration and be useless." They did a quick test of the equipment. "You're done. Button up and we're ready to roll."

Jim rose slowly, glancing over at Natalie. "Do I look like the Unabomber?"

"You look fine. A bit stiff, though... like you hurt your back. Be more flexible in your motions. Don't worry... I can't see anything."

"Ready... let's go" he signaled to Rawlins. "We should be at Red Clay within 20 minutes. Will you guys be communicating with me the whole time?"

"Yes... continuous contact. Remember, you're on tape, so if you say anything personal to your wife, we'll hear it. Just be sure when you're in there to get close to each item, then ask him if they're genuine. Make sure he responds positively for at least one item or we'll have no case... it'll all be a waste."

"Hey- look!! My husband is volunteering for this. His life could be in danger, so don't call this a waste." She stared at Rawlins, giving him an icy glare.

"I'm sorry, Mrs. Peterson. You're right. Regardless, this will be a worthwhile exercise and we sincerely appreciate your help." Rawlins glanced at the other agents and realized he'd almost nixed the whole operation.

"Come on. Let's move out." Jim headed towards the station door, holding it for Natalie, walking with her to the car and opening the door for her. "Here you go."

"At least the weather's good" Natalie replied, gazing out her side window.

"Yeah, if it was raining, I'd be a major short-out."

She grinned, but only slightly. She couldn't bring herself to look at him as the car pulled into the lot at Red Clay.

"D-Day. I'll walk in first, you stay behind me. Be totally casual. You guys hear all this?"

"We hear you fine. We know you'll do an excellent job, Jim. Good luck" said Special Agent Markham, sitting back at the room in front of the computer screen.

He got out of the car and shut the door as he watched Natalie exit. He stared at the ground for a few seconds and took a deep breath. He glanced over at the Red Clay sign. "I'm going in now. You guys will be in touch, right?"

"We're with you all the way." Markham smiled at the other two, knowing they were about to get what they had waited many months for.

"O.K., hon- I'll go in first... Remember, you stay behind me." Jim opened the door and saw Broom standing at the far end of the shop. "Hello. Are you open?"

Broom stepped forward slowly, watching Jim's face. "Sure... we're open." His voice had a cold tone and he focused on Jim's hands as he entered the shop.

"Well, I've been thinking. We got off on the wrong foot last time. I didn't mean all the things I said. Look- you're an expert and you gave me a decent evaluation. I could really use the cash and I've decided to accept your offer... for the five coins I showed you."

Broom studied every line in his face. "Really...?"

"Yes... but I was wondering if you could help answer some

GENE PISASALE

questions about a few items I admired in your shop the last time I was here. I'm a huge history buff… See that bust over there? That's Napoleon, isn't it?" He walked up to the table and stood right in front of it.

"Good close-up… excellent, Jim. Great photo-op" Markham said in a low voice.

"That is Napoleon. Are you into European history?"

"A bit… but mostly American." He stood motionless for several seconds. "How old is it?"

"That bust is circa 1820."

"Is it real marble… genuine?"

"It is." Broom looked again at his face as he spoke. "Stood in a French palace for many years."

"Can't make it out with total clarity. Appears genuine. Very hard to say with stone. Move on to the next item" Markham whispered.

"Impressive." Jim looked across the room and saw the flag. "Now that's pretty incredible." He was getting warm and un-zipped his jacket as he walked up to the flag and examined it. "Is that a real Revolutionary War flag?" He positioned himself in front of the display.

"Good view. Perfect." Markham stared at the image on the screen in front of him and turned on the sensor, scanning the image.

"It is genuine… over 220 years old. Came from right around here… Battle of the Brandywine… from Sullivan's Brigade." Broom stood near him as he looked at the flag.

"It's bogus. I can tell right away. That fabric wasn't made

LAFAYETTE'S GOLD

more than 30 years ago. It's nylon, or some blend. Anyway, it's fake." Markham got a pat on his shoulder from his partner as the sensors confirmed his comments.

"Incredible. This is really from the Battle of the Brandywine? The real thing?" Jim queried Broom.

"It is 100% genuine. A real treasure."

"How much?"

"Well, due to its important historical significance, that flag is quite expensive… appraised at $145,000."

"You can get that at the Constitution Center for ten bucks!!" Markham tried to keep his voice down as he looked at the computer screen and the reading on the five digital sensors.

"Wow. Pretty pricey. How about this Lincoln bust… or is it a reverse face-mask?" He was wondering where Natalie was, but didn't turn around.

"Very good. You know your American history. That is one of only three casts made in the 1860's of Lincoln's face. They were created by a famous sculptor of the time. That is a rare item… a real collector's piece."

"No way. The only known casts of Lincoln are in the vault at the National Archives. Fake!! This guy is quite a scam artist." He glanced over at his partner, who was grinning and giving him the 'thumbs up'.

"How much is it?" Jim stared at the cast.

"We get a lot of questions about that one due to the popularity of the Civil War. It's $65,000."

"Interesting. If I had an extra $65,000, I'd put it in my collection." He walked over to a bust of what appeared to be a

Roman emperor. "How about this? Nero?"

"That is one of only three completely intact stone busts of Julius Caesar. Solid Italian marble, from the Appenines. Not a crack or chip in it- it's a world-class artifact. Beautiful piece. That is genuine."

"How much?" He stood right in front of it, touching the head gently.

"That is $40,000." Broom walked closer to Jim, watching his movements as he approached each item. He noticed something ajar in his shirt, but stayed silent. He started to think "What's with all the questions? This guy never showed this much interest before…"

"Hard to tell. Looks… real… Wait!! That's on our watch list of items stolen from the museum in Rome!! I know it!! I saw the brief and all the photos. That's it… the stolen bust of Caesar!! We can nail him right now on that one alone. I think we have enough, Jim. We'll be coming in soon…"

Jim tried not to move his head as he heard the words, then walked over to a weathered oak table where several books were situated between granite bookends. "What's this?" He pulled one book out of the mix, its binding slightly frayed and faded.

"That is a first edition of Huckleberry Finn. Very rare."

Jim flipped to the title page and let it lay open on the table as Broom walked right up beside him, looking just above his belt.

"That is so obviously bogus. It doesn't have the 'A' next to the date indicating a first edition!! I learned that in my first antiquities class. Fake!! This guy is more of a crook than I thought. Half the stuff in his shop is crap!! Let's go in. We're coming in now, Jim... stay calm." The agents at the rear of the building put their cell phones away. Two agents standing outside the front door waited for the signal. "Go!!"

Broom was deliberately standing right next to Jim as he turned around, knocking open his jacket. He could see wires underneath the white shirt. "Well, now... what is this? Are you taping me?" He put his hand on Jim's chest, then pulled a gun from inside his blazer and held it against him. "You're trying to set me up..."

Jim froze, his eyes bugging out as he stared at the gun, then at Broom's face. "Well..uhh..."

The rear door to the warehouse burst open and Broom turned around, startled. He grabbed Jim and held the gun tightly to his chest, pulling him toward the back room.

"FREEZE!! FBI!! Put your hands up and drop the gun!! Now!!" The agents raced into the room and pointed their pistols directly at Broom's head.

"YOU drop your guns or he's dead!! I mean it! Drop 'em!!" He pushed the gun deeper into Jim's side.

Natalie walked up slowly from the table behind them, grabbing a heavy bronze bust of Ulysses S. Grant, then stepped quietly towards Broom's back. She inhaled, closed her eyes, then flung the sculpture down on Broom's head.

"Ugh!!!" Broom fell to the ground and the gun dropped from his hand. Rawlins kicked it away, then bent over to pick it up. The two agents rushed up beside her.

"Where have YOU been? I was waiting for you the whole time!!" Jim stared at her, then at Broom to make sure he wasn't getting up.

"You told me to stay back, so I did." She smiled and put the bust down on the oak table. "Besides, you're a Civil War buff. You like Grant."

Jim grinned, then noticed Broom was starting to move. Broom managed to get to his knees, but the two agents grabbed him, pulling his arms behind his back, slapping on the cuffs.

"Martin Broom, you are under arrest for suspicion of fraud, interstate trafficking in stolen antiquities and money laundering. You have the right to remain silent..."

Rawlins stepped up to Broom, took out a cigarette and lit it, blowing out the match towards his face. "Nice to see you again, Mr. Broom."

"This is totally outrageous!! You men can't just barge in here with guns!! You're breaking the law..." He looked at Jim with an icy stare.

"The only person in this room breaking the law is YOU." Rawlins looked at Brownlee and Gustafson. "Guys, check out the back room. There was a funky odor in there when I came through... smelled like... something rotting."

Broom's eyes opened wider. "You CAN'T go in there!! You have no right. Where's your warrant??"

"We have every right- and here it is." Rawlins flashed the papers in front of Broom's face as the other agent held his arms more tightly behind his back.

"You can't go in there!! I demand to speak with my

attorney... NOW!!" He was yelling so loudly, two yellow parakeets at the far corner of the room started squawking, flying
around their cage.

"Relax, you'll have plenty of time to talk with him... in jail."
He looked over at Jim. "You O.K.?"

"Fine." He put his arms around Natalie. "Both fine." He
looked at her face and she attempted a half-grin. Jim walked
up to Rawlins and put out his hand. "Good work. Thanks very
much for all your help."

"It's our job."

"Hey, Frank!! Joe!! Back here... now!!" The voice came from
the rear room. They passed through the door, holding Broom
tightly and saw Brownlee staring down at the floor. "Blood.
Several drops. Looks like it's leading over... there." He turned
his head and saw a very large, old black wooden trunk in the far
corner of the room, its slats fractured and corners weathered
to a powdery pulp, the wood cracked in several spots around
the rusty metal lock. He pointed to the trunk. "Break it off."

Joe looked around the room and saw a small sledgeham-
mer near a work bench. "This should do it." He grabbed the
hammer and walked over to the trunk, slamming it onto the
edge of the lock as Broom turned his head away and looked at
the wall. "This thing reeks. I can barely stand it." He thrust the
sledge down again, but the lock was only cracked a bit. "They
made them good back then. My grandfather had one like this."
On the third try the lock broke open. He lifted the lid as he
held his breath and peered in. "Looks like we have at least
one more thing for the rap sheet, Frank." He stood above the

body, wrapped in heavy plastic sheets and duct tape. Blood was splattered across the side of the victims' head, dripping down through a small crack at the base of the plastic into the bottom of the trunk. The agent looked back at Jim and Natalie.

"Oh my God!! Is that... Robert? Robert Smithson?" She started to cry as she ran up to him.

"It is. I'm sure of it... I met him several months back when we were first starting the investigation. That's him. I'm so sorry we couldn't move in more quickly." He took the cell phone out of his jacket. "Chief, we have a homicide. We're at Red Clay. Robert Smithson's dead, but we'll wait for a positive I.D... Over."

Jim walked up to the trunk and saw the face... the same honest face he'd seen when he first visited the shop. "I'm really sorry this happened." He looked at Broom, who was glaring at him. Then he glanced over at Rawlins, as he was taking another drag of his cigarette.

"So are we. We have a lot of work to do here, Jim. You two can head home after Bob gets the wires off you. Then we'll be in touch."

Jim took one last look at Smithson. His eyes welled up, but he kept back the tears and turned to Natalie. Her eyes were deep red. "Let's go." He looked over at Rawlins. "Thanks again."

"No, thank you, Jim. You've been a huge help. You gave us a critical piece of the puzzle with that satchel. I can't tell you much, but I can share that it provided the missing link... pointing us to Levanthal... and a much wider web..." He scanned the room for an ashtray and found a small one on an antique table nearby. "Is there anything I can do for you?"

Jim thought for a moment as he saw Rawlins bringing his hand inside his coat for another Marlboro. "Well, no, not really for me. My sister smoked for many years. She passed away last April... lung cancer. I know you must hear this all the time, but I think you should try to quit." He focused on Rawlins' eyes, waiting for any reaction.

Rawlins already had the pack out, tapping it for a cigarette. He'd been craving another one, only his fifth that morning and held the Zippo in his other hand. Then he stopped. "Well, I've had a few today." He put the lighter back in his pocket. "We'll be in touch. Take care."

"Actually, one more thing. Do you ever give medals to animals?" Jim asked.

"Animals? Well... sometimes... to police dogs... who saved agents' lives. Why?"

He looked over at Natalie quickly, then back at Rawlins. "Our two cats, Frankie and Francis- they saved our lives. They ran up our basement stairs, stood there in the dark and caused Eddy to trip over them as he was coming down. We would have been killed, for sure." He glanced briefly back at Natalie before looking into his eyes, hoping for a reasonable response.

"Well... I don't know." He then sensed Jim was totally serious. "I'll see what we can do." He put the Marlboro back in the box. "We appreciate everything you've done. I'll call you soon."

Jim stood there while the agent took off all the wires, one

by one, pulling the tape off his chest, causing a sharp sting, taking a few hairs each time. He buttoned up his shirt and put his jacket back on. They all walked slowly into the front room, Natalie crying loudly. Jim held her hand as he peered over at Broom, who started screaming as the agent continued to hold back his arms.

"You'll pay for this!! I promise you. You WILL pay!"

Jim stepped right up to him and stared directly at his face. "Let me guess... about $500? That's a very good offer. I'll go as high as $550... That's the best I can do!!" He turned to look at Natalie and went toward the door. "That's my final offer!!" He could hear Broom yelling as they got in the car. "Well, we survived that one. Tough, but not as bad as the Colonials had it... freezing cold Winters, blazing hot Summers, torrential rains..." Then he thought about the day they met Smithson, the excitement on his face as he described each of his famous digs, the joy of his many discoveries... and he wiped a tear from his face. "God rest his soul...a very fine one." He started the ignition and pulled the car out onto the highway.

Chapter 17

He noted the last few clumps of snow at the edge of the pine trees, melting in the late morning sun. He held the steaming cup in his right hand while pulling the heavy glass door aside. The cool breeze magnified the mist rising up from the coffee as he stepped out onto the terrace. He glanced at the cardinals, eight of them in the tree at the edge of the forest. "A good sign." He went back inside.

Natalie stood at the table. "Look at all this!! Hard to believe. We'll get the official appraisal next week... but it's worth roughly $1.1 million." She gazed at all the coins spread in front of the rusted metal spice box.

"I've been thinking. God's been very kind to us. I say we sell a million dollars worth to a reputable dealer... and keep that. We can give something to the Smithsonian, in honor of Robert Smithson and make a donation to the Chadds Ford Historical Society. The story that guy told us is why we pursued the treasure in the first place."

"I'm fine with that. How much do you want to give to each place?" She glanced at the Louis D'Ors scattered across the table.

"Say, five coins to the Smithsonian and $25,000 to the Society. It's money we never would have gotten anyway. We already have more than enough to live on."

"Where do you think we should sell the coins? There's dozens of antique dealers around here."

"Brandywine View. Joni loves the history of the area as much as we do and she deserves it. She's an honest businesswoman."

"That's a great idea. I know she'll give us a good bid and she's entitled to a decent profit on the re-sale. What'll we do with the spice box?"

"I've thought about that, too. I want to take it up to Gettysburg… and bury it at Joshua Pyle's grave." He looked out at the snow melting on the limbs of the trees, icicles pointing toward the ground… then his eyes went upwards… and he saw the sun's rays on the edge of the forest.

"How will you know where it is? There are thousands of graves at Gettysburg."

"I was online this morning. Evergreen Cemetery is now into the 21st century. Their records of the burials are completely computerized, indicating where all the soldiers are interred. The no-name graves are also identified, with comments on the brigades which fell in the immediate area. I located Pyle's grave... Here's a print-out of his plot. They did all this for the upcoming 150th Anniversary of the Battle of Gettysburg."

"Nice job. So, does that mean we're driving back to Gettysburg some time today?"

"I'd like to- what do you think?"

"O.K."

The doorbell rang right after she spoke. Natalie opened the front door and saw Agent Rawlins.

"Hello, Mrs. Peterson. I hope I'm not disturbing you."

"Not at all. Here to give us an update on Broom?"

"Well, I have something for you... actually... for your cats." He noticed Frankie and Francis running up behind her.

"Really?! I'll look for them. They should be right around here." Just then, both cats rubbed up against her legs, waiting to be petted. "Here you are!!" She picked them both up in her arms as Jim took a step toward the door. He looked at Rawlins and waited.

"Here's to Frankie and Francis... Hero Cats in the War on Crime." He placed a bronze medal with a red ribbon on each of their necks.

"Oh, that is so nice!! What do you think, furry guys??" She looked at both of their faces as she held them in her arms. "Francis, you're a hero!!" Francis put his cold nose to her cheek, then struggled to get free. Frankie put her paw on Natalie's ear. "You guys got medals!!"

"That was above and beyond. Thanks!" Jim looked at Rawlins' eyes and sensed he was pleased.

"You know, Jim... you saved MY life."

"How's that?"

"Quit smoking. Threw the whole carton away. Even my trusty old Zippo."

"Great job." He shook his hand. "I'm sure that was tough- but it's the best thing you could ever do for your health."

Rawlins hesitated. "You know, we actually have something in common."

"What's that?"

"We both love the Southwest. I spent four years there while I was in college- University of Arizona. Really enjoyed it." He thought about her, his first love... she was his soul mate... driving around the mountain towns in Arizona and New Mexico... stopping in the dusty, seedy places all along old Route 80 which were so much fun... way back then... the No-Tel Motel... the Stumble Inn in Tucson... drinking ice cold Coors, dancing to all those country rock bands... "It was great... at least... I thought... but she didn't understand why... I wanted to go into law enforcement." He could still see her face...

———◦《◉》◦———

"Why are you doing this? I HATE cops!! They threw Sally in jail... and all she had in her car was half a joint!!"

"Honey, look... it's the law... I can't do anything about what happened to her... and it's what I really want to do... I respect the law... and I want to make it my career." He took her hands, but she pulled back.

"Well, I lost all my respect for you!! If you want to hang out with cops- forget US!! Goodbye!!" She turned and walked out, slamming the screen door without looking back. That was the day he'd started smoking- and the last time he'd seen her. Soon after, he applied for his first job in the Phoenix field office of the FBI.

He saw Jim's face and tried to get away from the pain. "You know the ashtray in my office- don't know if you noticed it on my desk... I almost threw it out. It's carved onyx, made by Indians on the Hopi reservation in New Mexico. Even though I quit, I'm keeping it. It'll always remind me of that area..." Rawlins grinned, despite the sadness inside.

"My first real trip to the southwest was in January 1977, a field trip with the geology department at Bucknell University... We hiked all around the Sangre de Christo Mountains, ate some great Mexican food at the Kachina de Taos... drove all the way down to Big Bend, collected minerals on the way at Crystal Cave. That was a great time... made me fall in love with the area. Drove back out West with a buddy in January 1978... stopped in at the University of Arizona... Red Rocks was a great place for concerts... having dinner beforehand at the Morrison Inn out on the terrace, drinking margueritas as the sun set... I used to ride on the back of my buddy's Honda 1150 Redwing up to the Little Bear in Evergreen... saw Jerry Jeff Walker there.... but I wanted to move back East to be closer to my family- so I came back to Philadelphia in 1998. Glad I did... I've gotten a chance to be much closer to my mother, who just turned 89... and I met Natalie." He looked up at her and winked. "We were in Sedona just last year- what a great trip!! Loved hiking around the Wupatki Indian ruins... then taking the train ride through Val Verde Canyon... I didn't know you spent time out there" Jim said as he looked back at Rawlins.

"I remember the Little Bear!! I was there back in the late '80's… caught a concert at Red Rocks, too!! Maybe we can talk about it over a beer sometime, huh?"

"Would love to… that'd be great." He saw Frank's eyes were wide open and bright… shining above the friendliest grin he'd given Jim since they'd first met.

Rawlins nodded, then smiled. "Good day, folks." He turned and headed back to his car.

Jim closed the door and looked at the two kitties standing at Natalie's feet. "Well guys, it's official. You're heroes!!" Frankie was already trying to take the medal from her neck, while Francis was nibbling at the silk sash. "I have two quick errands before we go to Gettysburg. First, I want stop at church. I won't be long. I also want to go over to Brandywine Battlefield Park. Just for a minute. Did you see the Kennett Paper? Attendance at the park is way up. They say they've had more visitors in the last week than in the last six months! I heard attendance at the Brandywine River Museum is also up. Here's the article."

She took the newspaper and scanned the first few sentences. "Well, that's good news. You going to church now?"

"Yes. I'll be right back." He drove up along the back roads of Kennett Square, the streets narrowed by the recent 18" snowfall, then turned right onto Meredith Street and parked. "Not a bad day- at least it's not snowing." He walked up, opened the heavy oak doors and saw the glow. Looking up at the crucifix, he knelt down on one knee, then approached the table covered in small candles, many of them lit in front of the Virgin Mary. The church was empty, his footsteps echoing as he went to the front.

He closed his eyes as he knelt on the small cushion, then looked at the candle holders. He put the coins in the slot and lit the first blue candle in front, staring at the flame. "I'll never forget." His eyes went up toward the statue of Mary. "Please, keep her in your grace." He stood up and glanced around at the altar. At least a dozen baskets of poinsettias were placed around the church, red, beautiful in their simplicity. "I'm glad they still have the decorations up." He saw the large Christmas tree with silver ornaments, a white star at the top, then he looked back at Mary.

"Can you give me a sign that... she's O.K.? Anything?" Her face angelic, he stared at her hands down at her sides. After well over a minute, his heart sank as he turned and walked to the back of the church.

He took one last look at the poinsettias around the altar- and he saw a flash. He gazed up toward the top of the Christmas tree. The metallic star had several lights all around the edge, all of equal brightness. "None of those lights are blinking. I know- I've watched over the past few weeks at Mass" he thought. "That can't have happened. Must've been my imagination." He knelt down on one knee and looked at Him, then over at Mary- and it happened again. The light at the top shined brightly for almost a full second. He felt intense warmth, like blankets being wrapped around his shoulders, although he knew they turned off the heat to conserve energy between masses. Then he went to open the door. "Thank you." The light shone down on his face as he stepped outside, smiling up at the sun.

"I'm home. Ready for a quick stop at the Brandywine Battlefield? I promise it won't take too long."

"I'm ready." She already had her coat zipped up. "I'll drive. I have a full tank."

As they headed out of the neighborhood, Jim commented "I've been thinking. We make a good team and enjoy so many things together. With all this money, I can retire. We can pursue all our hobbies that we've been talking about the last few years."

"Finally!! I'd love that! What should we do first?" She kept the SUV at an even 45 miles per hour, right at the speed limit heading up Route 1.

"I want to start a treasure hunting firm!! There's got to be hundreds, maybe thousands of artifacts around this area. I'm not aware of any companies like that around here. Even if we have to search on private land, we'll do what that guy in Britain did... offer the landowner 20% of whatever we find, plus maybe a small visitation charge for any digging. We keep roughly 80% of what we get... Who knows what we'll uncover out there?!"

"I like the way you think... I'm game!! I'll be your Chief Operations officer."

"Great!! I need your discipline and organizational skills. It could be fun!!" The car pulled into the lot at the battlefield.

He opened the door to the visitor's center and saw his face. It was the same young man he'd spoken with weeks before. This time he was smiling.

"Hello. I don't know if you remember us. We were here a while back. We talked with you about the future of the park."

"Sure, I remember you. Is it… Jim?"

He was amazed, with all the visitors they have every week.

"Yes, but I apologize. I've forgotten your name." He put out his hand.

"It's Rick. Glad you could stop back!" he replied, reaching out for the handshake.

"You seem to be in a very good mood" Natalie said, noticing a pile of historical gifts placed along the top of the counter.

"I am. We're staying open- or at least that's what I hear from my boss. Attendance is up 60% just in the last week!! Year over year it's up well over 40%. There's a rumor going around that some guy found gold up along the Brandywine. Heard it from two different people. Kennett Chamber of Commerce reports that most of the businesses around here are seeing the best revenues they've had in over three years."

Jim glanced over at Natalie, then back at Rick. "That's great. Lucky guy."

"He must be lucky. Heard the coins were from the 18th century… hidden in some old structure… and could be worth millions. It's great news. The area attracts more tourists, the businesses in the area thrive and we get more visitors. We all win."

"I'm really glad to hear that. You know, when we were here last, I thought I saw a children's book. It was kind of a play on the Battle of Brandywine, how Washington lost, but survived to fight again and won. I can't remember what it was called."

"Oh, yes. Lucky George!! It's right there on the bookshelf."

Jim went over and grabbed a copy. "You know, when things looked pretty bleak, Washington knelt down in front of his horse in the snow at Valley Forge and said a prayer. 'I consider it an indispensable duty to close this last solemn act of my official life by commending the interests of our dearest country to the protection of Almighty God and those who have the superintendence of them into His holy keeping...' He looked up at the young man and could tell he was familiar with the quote.

"Yes... that was a great one!! I've done a bit of research into the local battles and Washington's encampment at Valley Forge."

"Do you get many people here asking about Lafayette? Seems like he's the undiscovered hero..."

"Some, yes. When we give tours of the two houses, the guides mention both Washington and Lafayette- and their roles in the battle."

"I read in the newspaper a while back that a gold medal presented by Washington's family to Lafayette was auctioned off. It had been given to Lafayette in 1824, I believe, by Washington's adopted daughter... and had been in the Lafayette home in Paris for almost two centuries." Jim hoped to get more information as he watched his expression.

"To me, Lafayette is one of the unrecognized Founding Fathers. Without him, things could have turned out far differently."

Jim grinned and said "I'll take the book." He paid cash and noticed the room was filling up with people as the young man was completing the transaction.

"Here you go. Hope you visit Brandywine Battlefield Park again soon. It's a very underestimated and little known part of our nation's history." He smiled as he handed Jim the book.

"You bet... and good luck!"

Jim nodded and turned to leave. As he approached the exit, four more adults came in, each couple with two young children, Jim holding the door for all of them. Heading toward the parking lot, he saw three more cars pulling up. "Well, see what a little adventure can lead to?" He glanced over at Natalie as he started the car. "Mind if I drive from here?"

"Not at all. Next stop- Gettysburg. I project the Royal Horses will get us there swiftly."

"All 300 under the hood. Pretty hazy, though. It's still a little dark out and with the mist, it's like driving through Piccadilly Circus in London... in the early morning hours, as werewolves stalk the night." He pulled out of the parking lot. The area was enveloped in a deep fog, the lower valleys and stream beds completely covered, the embankments a blur as their car sped by.

Natalie gazed out at the open fields and farmland, thinking of her childhood... and her father, who she missed so much.

"I wish he was here with us. He loved to explore, do fun things like hiking, roaming around the region. He really loved the fog, too."

"Who's that?"

"My dad." She looked out at the mist and remembered the day, one of the rare days during a thunderstorm, when he piled them in the station wagon and drove into the country-side. They parked at the top of a big hill to watch the lightning flash all around… rain pelting the rooftop. "Dad taught us to love adventures!" she thought, as her mind drifted back, her father excited to see the storm raging around them. "A lot of fog, huh? I can't see 50 feet ahead of us. Surprised that traffic seems to be moving so well… isn't backed up at all."

"We should make decent time, despite the fog. I think we'll be there less than an hour from now." The car headed west on the Pennsylvania Turnpike and he eyed each of the billboards along the way, one of his favorite pastimes from long trips in the car as a child. "Look at that one… My sentiments exactly."

"Which one? I must have missed it." She sat up straighter in her seat.

"Up there. 'Preserve your local historic sites… cherish your heritage. Give to the National Trust for Historic Preservation.' They list the website and phone number. Do you have a pen?"

"Oh, I see it. I'll remember. It's nationalhistorictrust.com. I'm sure they have a phone number listed on the site. I'll check it out when we get back."

"I've been doing some more thinking." He glanced at

Natalie and could tell she was in a good mood.

"You've been working overtime. What's your latest idea?"

"Well, after we sell most of the coins and give some of them to the Smithsonian, I want to keep one."

"For old time's sake?"

"For us. For posterity. To keep the spirit… alive."

"Sounds good. We can keep a few of them if you want."

"No, I just want one. I was thinking about the battle… and the gold that helped support the cause. You know what I'm going to name it?" He glanced over at her, then back at the road ahead.

"What?"

"Lucky George." He saw the sign for the Gettysburg turn-off and signaled.

She looked at his face and noticed a slight smile. "I think that's a good choice." The car turned south on Route 15 toward Gettysburg.

He thought again about the battle, how a twist of fate caused him to lose, but he survived to find victory. "You know what? Washington had both on his side."

"Both of what?"

"Luck… and fate… but mostly he had character. Most men, even career soldiers, would have shunned the responsibility of leading a ragtag group of inexperienced misfits, almost certainly doomed to fail… "

"Yet they didn't- because of him… and Lafayette." She kept looking out the window as they entered the town limits.

The car pulled into the parking lot of the old Visitor's

Center in Gettysburg. "Here we are."

"Wow, that was quick. It's faster when you have good conversation and beautiful scenery." She unhooked her seat belt and opened the door.

"The cemetery is up there. Nothing left here but the parking lot… weird. There's the path… it's about 100 yards. Still really foggy, though."

They crossed the road to Evergreen Cemetery. He took the print-out from his coat. "This says it should be… right… up…. there… on the left." He kept the papers in his hands as they headed toward the plot of gravestones. "Did you bring the spice box and the trowel?"

"I have them both in this bag. Don't worry, I've got everything." She noticed the hundreds of gravestones, pearly white in the low-hanging fog. "You know, early in the morning 232 years ago- on Sept. 11- the Brandywine Valley was enveloped in heavy fog just like this." She looked around, but could barely see the inscriptions as they passed each marker.

"This area where we're walking was also blanketed by fog in the morning on July 3, 1863… the third day of the Battle of Gettysburg, right before Pickett's Charge. Pyle was defending this hill- right here- with the Union troops."

"I can barely see my feet on the ground. Where are we?"

"You tell me." He held her hand as they walked very slowly among the gravestones. "Well, you know what Yogi Berra said."

"What?"

"We're lost, but we're making good time." She laughed as

she held his hand tighter in the fog.

Then he stopped. "There it is!!" He knelt down and read the headstone- 'Joshua Pyle, 1770-1865, participant in three wars of the young Republic- the Revolutionary War, the War of 1812 and the Civil War'; defended Gettysburg July 3, 1863 at Pickett's Charge, the turning point of the battle; died in Gettysburg, a strong supporter of the Union.' "Do you have the spade?"

"Are you sure you want to do this? We might get in trouble." She peered over her shoulder, then handed him the spade and watched as he dug a rectangular imprint in the brown, dying grass in front of the headstone.

"Nobody can see us. I can barely see you, it's so foggy." He dug an eight inch hole, putting the clumps of grass aside. "Could you give me the spice box?"

She handed it to him and then stopped. "Oh, Jim!! I think I saw something over there. Maybe somebody's coming… I think we should get out of here, now!!" She looked up and saw the pine trees bowing slightly in the breeze, fog enveloping the entire grove.

"No way. There's nobody here. You'd have to be crazy… or a lost Confederate soldier… to be out here in this." He placed the spice box in the dirt and looked at the headstone. "Thank you. In the end, you were a patriot. You helped save the Union… and all of us." He carefully picked up each clump of grass with the soil beneath it and placed them back on top of the box, tamping each down with his fist. "Good. Done." He stood up slowly, glancing down at the ground, then at the writing on the stone. "Peace." Jim stared up at the sky and took Natalie's hand, holding it tightly. He felt her squeeze back as he gazed at the words on the tombstone. Then he peered upwards again, noticing a slight change in the sky... and he felt a warmth, despite the freezing mist all around him. He glanced across the landscape and could feel it growing. "Franklin was right."

"About what?" She looked all around, shivering as she tried to warm her hands... not seeing anything besides her shoes.

He saw a break in the fog, the mist parting as rays shone through from the sky in the East. Small patches of blue slowly appeared, radiated by a bright glow, building in intensity in the distance along the horizon.

"Look... over there!! It's a rising sun."

About the Author

Gene was born and raised in Wynnewood, PA on the Main Line outside Philadelphia. By the age of 30, he had visited most of the 50 states and several foreign countries, trips which fueled his desire to write and share the wonderful places through words and photographs. Gene has worked in the investment industry since 1986. His lifelong fascination with history – mankind's story about its many triumphs, tragedies, sorrows and accomplishments- propelled him to start his writing career. Gene enjoys hiking, visiting historic sites, museums, cooking and fine wines. He lives in Kennett Square, PA.

"Vineyard Days", Gene's first novel, is a 'hybrid'- a travelogue wrapped around a murder mystery describing the sights, sounds and tastes of Martha's Vineyard. Written in September 2008 while he vacationed on the Vineyard during the height of the financial market collapse, "Vineyard Days" sets the scene for this latest novel. "Lafayette's Gold – The Lost Brandywine Treasure" continues the adventure...

CPSIA information can be obtained at www.ICGtesting.com
Printed in the USA
BVOW08s2349111113

336056BV00001B/3/P